WHAT WAS HIDDEN AT ARDMHOR

Lea Booth

CONTENTS

Title Page

Copyright

Prologue   1

Chapter One   3

Chapter Two   11

Chapter Three   18

Chapter Four   25

Chapter Five   36

Chapter Six   45

Chapter Seven   58

Chapter Eight   66

Chapter Nine   75

Chapter Ten   82

Chapter Eleven   90

Chapter Twelve   96

Chapter Thirteen   104

Chapter Fourteen   115

Chapter Fifteen   125

Chapter Sixteen   133

Chapter Seventeen   144

Chapter Eighteen   156

Chapter Nineteen   165

Chapter Twenty   172

Chapter Twenty-One   183

Chapter Twenty-Two   195

Chapter Twenty-Three   202

Chapter Twenty-Four   211

Chapter Twenty-Five   217

Chapter Twenty-Six   228

Chapter Twenty-Seven   239

Chapter Twenty-Eight   246

Chapter Twenty-Nine   256

Chapter Thirty   265

Chapter Thirty-One   271

Chapter Thirty-Two   278

Chapter Thirty-Three   289

Chapter Thirty-Four   295

Chapter Thirty-Five   303

Chapter Thirty-Six   312

Chapter Thirty-Seven   324

Chapter Thirty-Eight   338

Chapter Thirty-Nine   346

Chapter Forty   351

From the author   365

Books By This Author   367

PROLOGUE

My life ended the day he died. Amidst the chaos of that last day, as women wailed and people fought and flames danced, his passing was the only moment when time stood still. As his body crumpled to the ground, the air was already thick with smoke and fear. At first, I thought the noises I could hear, cries like a wounded animal, were coming from him, but it was me. He would make no more sound. I fell to the ground alongside him, his blood seeping into my clothes as I turned him over and cradled him in my arms. I tried to ignore the destruction of his face as I felt for his heartbeat and willed him to live. But my will was not enough. That face, which had been more familiar to me than my own, was a mess of blood and bone. His piercing eyes would see nothing else. It had been a day full of fear and destruction, but it was as he took his final ragged breath that everything ended. In that moment, mere seconds that felt like centuries, the future I had expected dissolved before me. Gone were the heather-clad hills rolling down to the sea. Gone were the jagged peaks of the distant mountains and the dark shelter of the woodland. The soft rain, the billowing mists, and the sounds of the village, all of them were gone. Gone, along with the person I'd thought I would walk alongside for ever. Everything I had known, and everything I had expected to know, disappeared as quickly as he did.

CHAPTER ONE

The present

Eilidh McRae could think of nowhere she'd rather be that morning. She could think of ways to improve the moment: if she could remember where she'd packed the teaspoons it'd be great—but she wouldn't change where she was. After what seemed like weeks of mist and rain, the sun was shining. The light felt different. It seemed as if spring was finally on its way. The sunlight pooled across the slate tiles of the kitchen floor, and she wriggled her toes in contentment. It wasn't just the fact she'd spent the last few years living in the world's grottiest house that was making this place seem luxurious, it really was amazing. In fairness to the previous home she'd shared with her husband Rich, it had looked pretty good by the time they'd moved out, and they wouldn't have been able to afford it in the first place if it had been in a better state. The improvements they'd carried out, with the help of her dad, were what had made this huge leap up the property ladder possible. In her current good mood, she could forgive it for its sins. But this house, well, this was something else. At first, no one had understood why they wanted to buy it. They already had a two bedroomed house, why swap it for another? However, as soon as people saw it for themselves, they understood. It might only offer the same number of bedrooms as the house they'd left behind, but the scale of it was totally different. A couple from London had built it as a holiday retreat, but a change in circumstances meant they'd put it up for sale instead. It was high spec, spacious, and brand new, but best of all, it nestled on the shore just across the road from the Ardmhor Hotel. It was in the centre of everywhere Eilidh ever needed to be, but through its vast windows all she could see was the sparkle of the sea and the beauty of the Scottish coastline. There were boxes dotted all over and she hadn't got a clue where anything was, but she couldn't help performing a little dance of happiness as she looked around her.

The only problem was, although she didn't want to be anywhere else, she needed to be. In fact, she needed to be heading elsewhere five minutes ago, and today wasn't the day to be late. No one would have been particularly surprised if she was. Eilidh had many fine qualities, but timekeeping wasn't one of them. Despite her petite stature, one of the most commonly used descriptions of Eilidh was that she was a force of nature. Unfortunately, being your own personal whirlwind meant it was easy to get swept away and lose track of time. Not that anyone seemed to hold it against her. People were Eilidh's superpower. She loved them and they loved her in return. In any situation, she seemed to know the right thing to say and do. She could put people at ease with a single smile and change someone's mood with a few well-chosen words. So her tendency towards lateness was always forgiven, but despite that, she didn't want to be late today.

Today was a big deal. It felt like she'd been working towards this moment for years. In fact, that wasn't too far from the truth. It had been almost two years since the plans for the holiday village on the Ardmhor estate had first been put forward, and today was the day they would be breaking ground. 'Village' perhaps wasn't the right word for the twelve self-catering lodges that were being built in the fields to the side of Ardmhor House, but that was what everyone had got used to calling the project. Eilidh had been in charge of its organisation since early days, co-ordinating its passage through the planning process, putting the plans out to tender, choosing the construction team, and ordering supplies. Today was when everything was finally coming together.

Lady Angela MacAird, the owner of Ardmhor House along with her husband Jim, was never one to miss a chance to celebrate, so not only had Eilidh been busy making sure everything was ready for the workforce, she'd also been rushing around finalising plans for a breaking ground ceremony. Jim and Angela were going to say a few words, and then everyone was going to toast the holiday village as the big digger made its first ceremonial impact on the soil. Then, after a while of watching the progress, everyone was to make their way back down to Ardmhor House to continue celebrating, leaving the construction team to work without obstruction. Much as Eilidh knew no one would keel over in shock if she was cutting it fine arriving at the site, as project manager, she wanted to make sure everything was exactly as it should be before any guests arrived. Finally spying her chunky boots poking out of a box in the corner, she breathed a sigh of relief, shoved her feet into them, and headed out of the door.

Safety boots might not be everyone's first choice of footwear, but they were right up Eilidh's street, which was a good thing considering she'd be essentially living in them over the next few months. She'd been comfortable in her own personal style from an early age. Vintage finds, tight jeans, and heavy boots had been her look of choice since she'd been old enough to buy her own clothes. An ever-increasing rainbow of hair colours finished the image. It wasn't something Eilidh could ever see changing. She'd always known who she was, and she was totally happy with that person. Filling those work boots effectively didn't worry her too much either. She'd been around building sites all her life, helping her dad with his construction business, and she knew they'd picked an excellent company to complete the work. All she felt as the site came into view was a thrill of anticipation. Today had been a long time coming and she couldn't wait for it to get started.

She'd overseen the arrival of champagne bottles, checked the construction team had everything they needed, and ensured the area for guests was safely roped off, before she spotted Angela and Jim making their way up the field.

"Everything alright, Eilidh?" Angela shouted as soon as she was close enough to be heard.

"Yes, all sorted. We just need everyone else to arrive now," Eilidh replied.

As she spoke, she noticed a group of people making their way up the field. Ali, Angela's youngest son, was at the front struggling to keep up with his energetic little boy, Rory. In the middle of the group, she spotted her dad, Alan. Her mum was working, otherwise she'd have been there too. Alan and Claire loved any excuse to spend time together, and even after years of marriage they could usually be found with their arms around each other or their hands lovingly entwined. They were always the picture of togetherness, but never in a way that seemed to exclude others. There was more than enough love to go round in the McRae household. Eilidh put a hand above her eyes to counteract the glare of the sun and strained to see if Rich had made it as well. Eventually, her eyes found him bringing up the rear of the crowd, keeping Beth, Ali's wife, company as she made her way up the hill. Beth's new baby was strapped to her front, and her progress was slower than usual. Bless him, Eilidh thought to herself, Rich was always looking out for people. She was also thrilled that Beth had made it to the ceremony. Despite being opposites in almost every way, Eilidh and Beth had been best friends since Beth had moved to the area to run the museum at Ardmhor House, but it was only a month since baby Grace had been born, so Eilidh hadn't really expected her to bother coming. She smiled at the thought that Beth had dragged herself from the comfort of her home in order to support her. Where Eilidh was petite, Beth was tall and willowy, and where Eilidh had always had an inner confidence, Beth could find something to worry about in any situation. Eilidh couldn't really relate to uncertainty. She always knew exactly what she wanted, well, apart from the one time when she hadn't and had almost lost everything, but she didn't allow her mind to revisit that time often. She preferred to focus on the here and now and leave raking over the past to Beth. As a result, Beth's anxiousness could drive Eilidh to distraction, but she had to admit they were good for each other, each helped to balance the other out and they'd supported each other through a lot. After Rory was born, Eilidh had been worried Beth was drowning under the weight of her new responsibilities, but fortunately, it seemed she was finding Grace less of a challenge. Eilidh supposed that was the way of most things in life. Nothing was ever as hard, or as scary, the second time round. However, she had no intention of finding out for herself. Rich and her both agreed that children weren't on their agenda. It didn't stop people questioning them on when they were going to start a family though. Eilidh pondered on whether the new house, which was definitely not child friendly, might help to clear the matter up in people's minds once and for all, and then she pulled her thoughts back to the moment. The guests were all assembled. It was time to get this show on the road.

The little crowd cheered as Jim finished his speech. Eilidh had organised a couple of staff from the café to pass the champagne round, and everyone raised their glasses in a toast to the holiday village as the digger set to work.

"Job well done," Eilidh said to herself.

In a few minutes, the guests would make their way down to the party in the café, and she could tick off the first step of operation holiday village. The problem was, she had spoken too soon. The silence was almost as deafening as the chugging of the engine when the digger came to an abrupt halt. The guests, who'd been moving down the hill, stopped and turned in the direction the sound had disappeared from.

"What's up?" the digger driver and the site supervisor shouted in unison.

The reply from the worker who'd told the digger to halt might have been shaky, but the gasp from the crowd showed no one had missed it.

"There's a skeleton," he said. "We need to call the police."

CHAPTER TWO

The present

It was a good while before Eilidh was able to re-join the guests, who had eventually been shepherded away to the cafe. She'd waited at the site for the police to arrive and watched as they arranged for the relevant experts to travel out and deal with the remains. For now, all she knew was that they had cordoned off the skeleton, and that all work on site had to stop. *So much for thinking we were off to a good start,* she grumbled to herself as she headed to the cafe. Then she gave herself a telling off, remembering the remains weren't just an inconvenience: they had been a person, someone who'd had hopes and dreams just like her. The build really wasn't important in comparison.

People had always gravitated towards Eilidh, and she usually loved it, but that didn't mean the clamour for her attention when she finally reached the cafe was easy to deal with. There were questions from every direction, which she answered as well as she could.

"Yes, it seemed the skeleton was human and that it was real."

"Yes, the police would remove the remains and check missing persons records."

"No, they didn't know who it might be, and no one was currently under suspicion,"

"Yes, they might want to talk to people further."

"No, work can't continue at the moment."

But there were many more questions that she wasn't able to answer. People wanted to know whether the police would use DNA to identify the body, and whether they would be wanting DNA samples from everyone present. Eilidh had to explain that she knew little more than they did.

"Can you even get DNA from a skeleton?" Eilidh asked Beth once the questioning had died down.

"I think so," Beth started, momentarily stopping speaking as she checked baby Grace's position in her carrier. "I'm sure that when they found those remains in a carpark somewhere and thought they belonged to Richard III, they extracted DNA and matched it to living descendants."

"That's amazing," Eilidh replied with a shake

of her head. "You wouldn't think it'd be possible after all that time."

"I know. Ali got me one of those DNA testing kits from FamilyFinder for my birthday, and it can tell you all the places in the world you have a genetic connection to, just from a tiny sample. You can do loads with it."

"I didn't realise. I think all my relatives live around here though, so it probably wouldn't tell me anything I didn't already know."

At that point, Eilidh's father, Alan, appeared alongside them. After making a fuss over Grace, he tried to get more details about the skeleton out of Eilidh.

"I've already told everyone everything I know," she protested under the barrage of his questions.

"Och, I know, but it's just so intriguing," Alan persisted. "I can't believe there was a body hidden away out there. Did the police at least give a sign of how long it might have been buried for?"

"No, nothing at all. I don't think we'll hear anything else until they've taken the remains away and examined them properly."

"It could have been there years, I suppose," Alan mused. "My granny used to tell a story about a man, well, a boy really, who disappeared during the Clearances. Maybe it's him."

Eilidh noticed Beth's ears pricking up at this.

As the coordinator of the Ardmhor museum, Beth loved all aspects of local history, but the Clearances particularly fascinated her.

"What story is that, Alan?" Beth asked.

Eilidh rolled her eyes at the pair of them. She knew her dad liked to tell a story as much as Beth liked to hear them. This conversation wouldn't be over any time soon.

"Well," Alan began. "I don't know if you know this, Beth, but I was raised by my grandparents, and for a while my great-granny lived with us too. Anyway, she loved to tell a story, and one of her favourites was about her granny when she was a lass. So, the main part of the story was a sort of cautionary tale about her granny's big sister. Apparently, she was a bit full of herself, thought she was better than everyone else. Anyway, this sister, she'd been having a bit of a thing with the factor's son."

"The factor's son?" Beth interrupted. "Does that mean he'd have lived in my house?"

"Yes, I suppose he would have. It would have been practically brand new back then. So anyway, the factor and his bully boys turn up to clear the village and turf everyone out of their houses and there's chaos everywhere. Well, during the chaos, the sister gets separated from the family, deliberately, as my great-granny used to tell it. She said that the sister ran off with the factor's son, without so much as a goodbye to her family. Anyway, it didn't turn out well for her, as the pair of them died of some illness or other, on a boat to wherever they were running to. The moral, according to my great-granny, was that you should always stick with your own or woe betide you."

"So who was supposed to have disappeared then?" Beth queried. "There's no mystery if the sister and the factor's son both died on the boat."

"Ah, well, that's the other part of the story," Alan continued. "So also living in the village was this sort of golden boy. My great-granny said that everyone loved him, and he could do no wrong. The girls all swooned over him, the boys looked up to him, the fathers trusted him with their animals and their daughters, and the mothers hoped he'd become their son one day. Apparently, the only person who didn't really like him was the big-headed sister who ran away and died. But anyway, on the same day she sets off on her ill-fated journey with the factor's son, this golden boy just vanishes. He doesn't get on the boat with those who'd decided to set sail for Canada, and he doesn't head off for Glasgow with those who'd decided they wanted to stay in Scotland. It seems they were all devastated by losing him and their homes at the same time, but no one heard another word from him."

"But couldn't he have just gone somewhere else in Scotland?" Eilidh asked. "Just because they didn't see him again doesn't mean he died, does it? I mean, from what I've seen in the museum, the evictions weren't known for being calm and organised. Loads of people must have got split up in the confusion."

"Well, of course, that's possible," Alan conceded. "I think it was out of character for him not to have tracked his family down and got back in touch though. My great-granny said that after a while they heard stories he'd gone to Edinburgh, but they never actually heard from him again. He was greatly missed, apparently. I was just thinking maybe he never made it away that day, maybe he ended up dead in the woods instead?"

"Maybe, but it's not that likely, is it?" Eilidh concluded. Then another thought struck her. "So, did any of our relatives go on the boats to Canada?"

"Aye. My great-granny's granny's whole family went."

"Wow, so we could have loads of relations out there. Maybe I should do one of those DNA tests like you, Beth. I might find loads of Canadian cousins to visit."

"I think you'd be disappointed, Eilidh. My great-granny's granny married a lad who was desperate to return to Scotland. She was over there for less than twenty years before she ended up back here. Any relatives in Canada would be very distant ones."

"Oh well," Eilidh responded with a shrug. "I suppose I'll just have to be content with the mystery of the body in the field instead."

Actually, she didn't mind one bit. She'd always known who she was and where she belonged, and she was completely happy with that. Yes, she might want to do a little exploring one day, but she knew this was where she wanted to stay. She had her family, her friends, her gorgeous husband, her beautiful new home, and a job she loved. To be honest, she could live without the macabre mystery of the body in the field as well. She just hoped it would be solved quickly and not cause too many more delays.

CHAPTER THREE

The present

The weekend after the discovery of the remains saw Eilidh heading along the coast road to her parents' house. Alan and Claire's house in Strathglen was about forty minutes away from Eilidh's house at Ardmhor. She'd made the trip so many times, she could probably describe every twist of the road, but familiarity didn't spoil her enjoyment of the ride. The first stage of the journey, from Ardmhor to Inveravain, hugged the coast. The road followed the shape of the coves, and the sea was a constant companion, sometimes tropical blue and sparkling, sometimes dark and brooding, but never out of sight for long. After Inveravain, the road headed up and inland slightly, crossing the moors to avoid a long detour around another peninsula. Then gradually the gradient dropped, and the sea reappeared, before the village of Strathglen finally came into view. Strathglen stretched itself contentedly around a wide sheltered bay, as the smooth sloped hills flattened out to meet the sea. Eilidh had been in her teens when her parents had moved there. Before that, they'd lived in another village a little further along the coast, but even though she hadn't really grown up there, it still felt like home as soon as she saw the white chimneys of the house coming into view. As she pulled onto the drive, she pondered whether this was what she was trying to recreate with her new home next to the sea at Ardmhor. It made sense. She couldn't imagine anywhere nicer to live than a house where every window reflected the colours of the water back at you.

As her mum opened the door, the first thing that hit Eilidh was the delicious smell of baking and the second was the view. The fact that she was used to it made no difference. From the door, you could see right through the house and out of the floor-to-ceiling windows in the kitchen. It was a sight that never failed to impress. The vista of islands floating in the bay, with the high tide almost lapping at the garden wall, was hard to beat.

"What's cooking?" she asked, removing her shoes. "It smells amazing."

"It's shepherd's pie for lunch," Claire called over her shoulder as she made her way back into the kitchen. "But I think it's the cake you can smell. I've done us a lemon drizzle."

"My absolute favourite," Eilidh sighed contentedly, following Claire and taking a seat at the table.

"I know," Claire said with a smile. "It'll just be you and me though. Mrs Smith's roof sprang a leak in all that rain last night and your dad said he'd sort it out."

Alan disappearing to do a favour for someone else was a common occurrence. He was a big bear of a man, whose usual facial expression made him look nothing short of menacing. However, anyone that spoke to him for more than a minute was quickly reassured that under the gruff exterior there was a heart of gold.

"Has he told you about what happened at the site?" Eilidh questioned.

"You mean the body? He's told me lots of stories about it, and all of them at great length. I was going to ring you to find out what had actually gone on, rather than the 'Alan' version, but then I thought I'd save it to hear today."

They stayed in the kitchen to eat, watching as the clouds rolled over and the rain came and went. The clouds hid the islands and the distant hills one minute, then revealed them in all their glory the next. A heron perched on the shore was the only part of the view that didn't seem to change in the time it took them to devour the shepherd's pie. Eilidh filled Claire in on the events at the holiday village site as they ate.

"So there isn't actually anything to suggest it's this missing lad from your dad's stories?"

"No, Dad has just come to his own conclusions. The police really didn't say much at all."

Claire didn't respond for a while. She was busy cutting the lemon drizzle cake into slices. Once she'd refilled their drinks and placed two generous slabs of cake in front of them, she continued the conversation.

"Well, you know your dad, he's got a theory for everything. But I'd rather him be right than it be someone who went missing recently. I suppose they might not be able to find out who it is, with the remains only being a skeleton."

Eilidh shook her head. "Not necessarily. Apparently, they can get enough DNA from bones to identify people. Beth was telling me about it."

"Oh, well, maybe they will figure it out then. Have you heard anything from the police since they took the remains away?"

"Not about the identity of the body, no. But they had some officers searching all around the site, and it looks as if there used to be houses there."

"In the edge of the woods? I thought it'd always been nothing but trees."

"We all did. The plan for the holiday village has always been to build right up at the tree line because that's the flattest bit of land, and also the view is better. So, last year they cut back some of the woods to prepare the ground. Anyway, it looked like it had been covered in trees forever. Beth says all the records suggest the houses were just at the bottom of the fields, not that there's much left of them either, but there's no record of the village going all the way up there."

"I suppose it's getting on for two hundred years since the land there was cleared though. Things will have got forgotten or misremembered over time. I've just thought, does that mean you'll have to wait longer until you can start work again? Will they have to get archaeologists and such to come and look at it?"

"Well, we definitely can't start work until they've decided how long the body has been there and whether it's an active crime scene, but I don't think realising there were houses there is going to be a problem. They aren't ancient ruins, and as much as Beth finds the Clearances fascinating, abandoned villages are really two a penny round here."

"True," Claire agreed. "But Beth does love poking around in the past, bless her. She'll be excited about this, I bet. She hasn't had a mystery to investigate for a while."

When Beth had first arrived at Ardmhor,

she'd found out one of her ancestors had lived there for a time. Then, with the help of an old diary, she'd uncovered a relationship between her great-great-grandmother and the son of Lord MacAird. Hidden letters had then confirmed that Beth herself was distantly related to the MacAird family. More recently, she'd found another set of letters, unlocking secrets that had been hidden for over a century. Things had been quiet on the mystery front since then though.

"I think she was as freaked out as everyone else by the skeleton. But you're right. She's totally excited about the idea of unrecorded houses. The old office in Ardmhor House has so many papers in it, there's hardly anything that's gone on at Ardmhor since the house was built that hasn't been documented. So obviously she's intrigued as to why there is no mention of these houses."

"It's probably just that they've been mixed in with the lower houses," Claire suggested.

"Probably, but Beth will make sure she finds out. She must have been looking for something to investigate because she was telling me she's done this DNA test thing. Apparently, it can tell you where all your family comes from. It can even put you in touch with relatives you didn't know you had. It sounds quite interesting."

"There would be no point in you doing that," Claire responded sharply. "It'd be a total waste of time and money. You already know everyone you're related to. There are no surprises in our family tree."

"Yes, but Dad said about his great-great-great-granny, or whatever she was, and her family going off to Canada. We could find relatives over there."

"They'd be so far removed from us that I doubt they'd even count as related. You'd be better off spending your money on a train ticket to visit your uncles in Edinburgh than wasting your time on DNA. They're always complaining that they don't see much of you, and they only live a couple of hours away. Also, your dad's got so many relatives around here, you wouldn't have time for any new ones."

"Maybe," Eilidh mumbled in response, her mouth full of cake.

As she continued her demolition of the lemon drizzle, Eilidh was lost in thought. It wasn't like her mum to be so dismissive of ideas. Now that she came to think of it, her dad had been pretty quick to squash her enthusiasm about looking into the family tree as well. If there was one thing guaranteed to spark Eilidh's interest in something, it was being told it wasn't worth pursuing. Shovelling the last morsel of lemony heaven into her mouth, she resolved to look into what the FamilyFinder tests involved and how much they cost.

CHAPTER FOUR

The present

"Thanks for letting me know. Bye."

Eilidh sighed as she ended the call. The news from the police hadn't been terrible, but it wasn't as good as she had hoped either. Although they were fairly certain the bones were old, too old to need further criminal investigation, nothing had been confirmed yet, so work on the holiday village still couldn't continue. However, her dad was going to be happy. One of the forensic scientists the police worked with, Professor Blake, had a personal interest in DNA identification of unknown remains and was keen to investigate further if it turned out police involvement wasn't required. Eilidh had passed on Alan's details so that Professor Blake could speak to him directly about his stories of the village. All Eilidh wanted to hear was that the case was finally closed.

She took a detour up to the site on her way home from work. A week on from the breaking ground ceremony, there should have been real signs of progress up there, but the only evidence of change was where the remains had been discovered and removed. The police had already taken down their cordon, as they'd scrutinised the area thoroughly when they'd exhumed the remains. So although work couldn't yet continue, there was nothing to stop Eilidh wandering around the site. With more of the shrubbery cleared away, it was obvious there had once been houses up there. There were no remaining walls, unlike the houses lower down the fields, but enough stones remained to show the rectangular outlines of dwellings. Eilidh could make out the shape of three buildings in the space around where the skeleton had been removed. Perhaps they would uncover evidence of more ruins when work continued. Eilidh hoped that if the police confirmed they weren't interested, she wouldn't have to deal with Beth demanding a full investigation of the area instead.

Even Eilidh's practical nature had to concede that whoever had made their home here had lived in a truly beautiful spot. The wooded hills rose behind her and the fields in front rolled gently down to the sea. As she walked between the stones, she tried not to think about the fact it had also been a very lonely grave. She sat down on one of the larger stones and tried to visualise the finished holiday village around her. The twelve lodges would all have enormous picture windows to take in the views and private verandas to sit out on when the weather obliged. The plans had the lodges set out in an arrangement that at first seemed haphazard but was carefully designed to ensure each lodge enjoyed privacy from the others. Eilidh was finding it incredibly hard to deal with the delay in bringing the plans to fruition.

She was dwelling on the idea that maybe the project had been ill fated from the start, when the sound of footsteps pulled her from her thoughts. Rich was making his way towards her with a huge smile on his face. Ever since they'd met, well over a decade ago, that smile had never changed. It would always be her favourite of his features. She'd first set eyes on Rich in the cafeteria of Inveravain college. It was the first day of her business course, and Rich was in his final year of a course in IT. Eilidh had been sixteen and unusually nervous: it seemed a big step from high school, and her group of friends hadn't all started college with her. Rich had been over in the corner, at the centre of a huge, noisy crowd. Their laughter had drawn Eilidh's attention, and she desperately wanted to feel part of the group. Her nerves had quickly been overridden by her natural compulsion to be at the centre of things. She'd picked up her tray and sauntered straight over to their table. Rich had looked up and seen this tiny figure, with bright green hair and a huge smile, and they'd never looked back. Their eyes had locked, he'd returned her smile, and the rest was history. Rich hadn't been short of admirers. He was well built, well dressed, and his megawatt smile finished off an already very pleasing face. But despite his muscly appearance, he wasn't your typical, sport obsessed, popular boy. He'd been into film and drama as well, and because he was kind and good at listening, you could guarantee he'd know the full details of any college scandal. Eilidh had always thought that if he hadn't gone straight from college to an IT job with the local council, he'd have been an excellent journalist. He knew the ins and outs of every local event and he could tell a story almost as well as her dad. He pulled her to her feet, drawing her into a tight hug.

"Are you okay?" he queried, releasing her a little in order to hear her answer.

"Yeah, I'm fine. I'm just worried about keeping everything to schedule, now that we're behind before we've even got going."

"You'll get it all sorted, no bother." Rich smiled down at her. "I've got total faith in you."

"Thanks," she said, laughing, "but I'm not sure your opinion is totally unbiased."

They stood quietly for a while. Eilidh enjoying the feel of his arms around her.

"You don't think the whole thing is cursed, do you, Rich?" she asked after a few minutes.

"Cursed? What do you mean? You don't believe in stuff like that."

"It's just... I mean, I know it sounds silly, but things didn't exactly go well for us when the idea was first getting off the ground."

"You mean the thing with Jay?"

"Yes," Eilidh answered quietly. Grateful that Rich could make the fact she'd considered leaving him for someone else, while they were in the middle of planning their wedding, sound like no big deal at all.

"That's not a curse, Eilidh. That was just you panicking about getting lumbered with me for the rest of your life."

"Don't say that. I'm not lumbered with you. You're the best thing that ever happened to me."

"I know that, and I know you do too. Also, you should know none of that matters anymore. I like Jay. We go for a drink every time he's back up here and I enjoy it. You honestly don't have to feel bad about what happened."

"Nothing happened," she added defensively, unable to help herself. She didn't think she'd ever stop feeling guilty about the feelings she'd had for Jay, her boss at the time, and the man responsible for the whole holiday village idea.

"I know nothing happened, which is another reason you don't need to feel guilty, Eilidh. We were both in a rut, coasting along and taking each other for granted. If it hadn't been you getting your head turned, it'd have been me. We needed a wake-up call. Maybe we'd have drifted too far apart to come back if something hadn't shaken us up. And to be honest with you, Jay's that good looking that I'd have considered running off with him myself if it'd been me he'd taken a shine to."

Rich pulled her closer, leaning down to kiss her gently.

"I love you, Eilidh McRae, and everything will be fine. So no more worrying about curses."

"I love you too. But what about the skeleton? It's not exactly a good sign, is it? People won't want to come on holiday to a murder scene, will they?"

"But we don't know that's what it is yet, and it's not like you to worry over things that might not happen," he replied, lowering himself to sit on one of the old stones.

"You're right," she said as she positioned herself on his knee and wrapped her arms around him.

"I mean, look around you, Eilidh. This place is amazing. The view alone is enough to make anyone forget about skeletons, or whatever else might turn up. The lodges are going to be fabulous, and you are going to make sure everything runs smoothly. Yes, things were a bit rocky for us when all this was getting started, but that rough patch would have happened whatever. We are so much stronger because of it. Also, if Jay hadn't set this project in motion, you wouldn't have had this opportunity. Running this has shown everyone at the estate office that you're not just the admin girl anymore, and if you do ever want to get a job elsewhere, it'll look fantastic on your C.V. So I know for definite there's no curse. If anything, this place is lucky for us. Now could somebody swap this anxious imposter for my self-assured wife?" he said, looking around as if someone was going to emerge from the trees and complete the handover.

"Shut up," she whispered, planting a kiss on his lips.

"As long as you keep doing that," came the muffled reply.

Two seals were basking on the rocks in the bay in front of Rich and Eilidh's house, sleek as they dried off in the sun. Another bobbed about in the water. Eilidh was eagerly waiting to see where it would appear next as she ate her breakfast. Every few minutes the enquiring eyes, atop a shiny nose, would rise from the sea, looking for all the world as if they were checking she was still watching. She was just finishing her coffee when a loud thud from the hallway distracted her from the wildlife.

"What was that? Are you okay?" she called out, unfolding herself from the chair by the window and making her way into the hall.

"I'm fine," Rich replied, handing a slim but deceptively heavy box to her. "It was this coming through the letterbox. Looks like it's your DNA thing."

"Oh yeah, it's got their logo on. I didn't expect it to be so heavy. I wonder if I've got time to do it before work."

"Maybe. I can't imagine it takes too long. Are you going to tell your mum and dad that you're doing it?"

"I don't know," she replied, just as her phone buzzed in her pocket. "Oh, speak of the devil. It's my dad."

She swiped the screen to answer.

"Hi Dad, is everything alright?"

"Oh, everything's great, sweetheart. I've just had a scientist called Professor Blake on the phone. The police told her about me, and she was really interested in my stories about the cleared village, unlike some people I know!"

"I was interested, Dad!" Eilidh protested. "It's just sometimes your stories are particularly long. Anyway, it was me that passed on your number, so actually you should be being grateful."

"Oh, so you already know about this?" asked Alan, sounding a bit deflated.

"I only know she wanted to speak to you. You'll still need to fill me in on the rest."

"Well, if you're sure you don't mind listening to one of my really long stories," a much perkier sounding Alan replied.

Eilidh smiled to herself as she told him to get on with it. It wasn't like she'd have been able to stop him, anyway.

"So, Professor Blake has a special interest in identifying historical remains from the DNA of their descendants. She thinks that if the skeleton is old, then it probably belongs to someone connected to the village, so she wanted to know if I could put her in touch with relatives of people who lived there, so she can try to find a match to the skeleton."

"Does that mean she's pretty definite that the remains are old?"

"She certainly seems to be. She made it sound like the confirmation will just be a formality."

"Well, I wish they'd get on and confirm it then, so we can get back to work on the site."

"I'm sorry, sweetheart, I was being insensitive there. I forgot all this investigating is causing you problems."

"No, I'm sorry, Dad. I know you're really excited about this. I shouldn't have been so negative. So, do you know any other relatives of people who used to live there?"

"Yes, a few. Fergus was the name of the lad that went missing, and there was a lady descended from his sister that used to visit my granny. I'm still in touch with her daughter, and there are a couple of others that were connected that I call in on from time to time. I'm going to visit them with Professor Blake. I'm sure they'll all be happy to give samples once they hear what it's for."

"I'm sure they will," Eilidh replied. "But I thought you weren't keen on DNA research. You seemed dead against me doing one of those FamilyFinder tests."

"Well, that's different. That'd just be a complete waste of your money. Whereas this is about helping to solve a mystery and possibly even helping someone to rest in peace."

"Alright, point taken. Anyway, I'd better go. I've a couple of things I need to do before work."

Rich reappeared in his work clothes just as she was saying her goodbyes.

"So, did you tell him about your little DNA experiment?" he asked.

"No, he still thinks it's a waste of money. I thought I'd just wait and tell them when I'm on the plane to Canada, ready to meet all my newly discovered cousins."

"Sounds like a plan to me," Rich replied, depositing a kiss on the end of her nose. "I reckon you'll still have time to get the test done before work, then we can get those flights booked!"

As Rich headed out of the door to his car. Eilidh picked the FamilyFinder package up from the hall table and carried it back into the kitchen. Taking the scissors, which had finally been unpacked, out of the drawer, she carefully sliced open the edge. The instructions sounded fairly simple. All she had to do was take the swab out of its envelope, wipe it against the inside of her cheek and then seal it up in the return envelope. It suggested not eating or drinking for an hour before doing it. Only half an hour had passed since she'd had breakfast, but by the time she'd showered and finished getting ready, it'd easily be an hour since she'd eaten. That'd mean she'd be fine to take the test, and she'd still have time to post it on her way to the office. Apart from the amazing view, one of the other perks of their new house was that it only took her two minutes to walk to work, and a cancelled meeting meant she had a late start today, anyway. She picked up the test and carried it through to the bedroom, her head full of images of herself and Rich, stepping off planes in exotic destinations and running into the arms of excited, long-lost relatives.

CHAPTER FIVE

The past

Esther

There haven't been a great deal of surprises in the sixteen years I've spent in this world. My life follows a pattern: I help my parents, I look after my sisters, I eat, I sleep, and then I do it all again. The seasons change as the days get longer and warmer before shrinking and cooling again. The work varies between planting, harvesting, making, and storing. But nothing really changes, nothing new ever happens. My mother says my head is in the clouds rather than down where it belongs. She says that life is what it is. That it is what it has always been, people making a living from the land around them. She thinks I should stop dreaming and be more helpful. But I know that is not enough for me. I don't see how it can be enough for anyone. We are approaching the second half of the nineteenth century. There are railways that can speed people around the country in days. There are boats that can take people right round the world. In the lowlands, there are factories making every product man could ever conceive of. How can a life of animals and fields be enough for anyone?

I know my mother is lying, anyway. Everything is not the same as it has always been. I hear the stories that the old men tell, just as everyone else does. And I sometimes hear my mother complain to my father at night, when she speaks quietly, thinking we are all asleep. The old men talk about the history of our clan. They tell stories of chains travelling right back through time, joining each of us to the great men who set this family in motion. They say we are all linked to those men, that although some of our names have changed along the way, our bonds are just as strong, our rights just as important as those held by Lord MacAird. Our lands belong to us, according to them. I think they are talking nonsense.

If we are all the same, why is Lord MacAird building a house as big as a mountain, while my whole family live in one room? Why do we work all day barely making ends meet, while he spends time in London? Why do we have to struggle to pay him rent? It doesn't feel to me that we all have the same claim to the land. I don't say those things out loud though. I'm not a fool. It's one thing for the adults to grumble amongst themselves, but girls should respect their elders. I've heard my mother and father reminiscing though, speaking in low voices about the days when our livestock could roam the area, and when we could use whatever nature provided for us. They talk of when the salmon from the rivers were ours to take, along with the deer from the hills, and the birds from the air. When our food is scarce, Mother mutters under her breath about how easy it used to be to feed a family. Whereas now, all of nature's bounty is for Lord MacAird. When he returns from London with his guests, they like to hunt, collecting the food we used to eat as trophies. The Lord isn't present very often. The rumours are that he doesn't think his house grand enough to show his friends. Never mind that the whole of our village could live in it comfortably. That's why there's been building work going on there for the past year. It has almost doubled in size already. I wonder if it will reach our houses and swallow them up in the end. Mother says we are lucky to still have land, and in a way, she is right. In some places, the people have been sent away and their lands given to new farmers who just look after sheep.

I don't know whether I'd mind having to leave. I know the world is so much bigger than our cluster of houses. Even adding the low houses to ours up the hill, we barely number one hundred souls. Would it be so terrible to mix with some more? Every time I look out to sea, I wonder what else is out there. I'm determined to one day know. At the very least, I won't spend my days bringing in peats, lighting fires, milking cows, and churning butter. There are a couple of lads my age around here, which I suppose some people would be grateful for, but they aren't for me. I've already set my sights on something better. Hiram Stewart, to be precise. Yes, Hiram will be my husband, and I'll sleep every night on a bed with a metal frame and a feather mattress. I'll watch as someone else sweeps my floors and lights the fire each day, and the milk and butter will make their way to my table without me so much as lifting a finger.

I know everyone thinks I have an overly high opinion of myself. Maybe I do. I know I'm the prettiest girl for miles around, but I also know I'm not the kindest, or the best at making a stew from nothing. I can dance beautifully, but I lose patience with retelling the old tales, and my singing voice leaves a lot to be desired. Not like our Cait, every time she opens her mouth, people go glassy eyed over the sounds that come out of it. I'm not worried about that though. Hiram likes pretty things, and he's always made it clear he likes me. We've been friends since we were children, and I think he's loved me all that time. When we marry, we won't live far away, but it might as well be a million miles from the village. The factor's house is one of the loveliest buildings I've ever seen. I often go out of my way in order to walk past it, partly so that I might glimpse Hiram, but more so that I can admire the house itself. It is so clean and new. The stonework is neat and straight, not like our house with misshapen rocks piled up to make the walls. The walls of the factor's house don't stop at the height of your head. Oh no, they soar up a whole two levels. There is a staircase inside and an entire floor above it. The windows stick right out of the front of the house, with huge panes of glass, as big as some on the house of Lord MacAird himself. And the roof isn't grass like ours, instead it is covered in solid slate. I can only imagine how easy my life will be within it.

So to me, things seem simple. I will continue to smile at Hiram as he joins his father, the factor, on his business. He will continue to return my smiles, and eventually we will marry. We'll live with his parents: there will undoubtedly be room for us all. Then one day, Hiram will take over his father's position, and we'll want for nothing. Admittedly, I won't be on the same level as Lord and Lady MacAird, although Hiram will mix with them as he goes about his work. However, I certainly won't be toiling away like my mother.

Mother isn't too keen on Hiram. Although I

have known him for almost my entire life, she doesn't see him as one of us. Hiram's father was brought here from the south. He is not one of our kin. Before him, the land and the rents were managed by someone from within the clan, and many have found it difficult to adjust to Mr Stewart.

Mother makes it clear she would like me to marry Fergus. Everyone loves Fergus. In fact, from the way people talk, I'm constantly surprised the sun doesn't rise and fall on the say so of Fergus himself. I sometimes wonder which I detest the most: the monotonous toil of my life, or that Fergus must always be part of it. When my back is aching from a day in the fields, you can be assured Fergus will be there cheerfully smiling and making the task look easy. When the men take the boats out to fish, the successful days will always be the days they took Fergus with them. If someone is struggling with a heavy load, Fergus will appear to lighten it for them. It's as if there is not the smallest drop of badness within him. But no one can really be that good. Surely he doesn't actually want to listen to old Annie, as she tells the same tales again and again? He can't really want to help with every single task from sunrise to sunset. And there is no way he can find Isobel's chatter entertaining. She might be a year older than me, and she is lucky that her hair is flecked with gold, but I've known for years that she is as dull as a day with no gap in the clouds. Yet Fergus will be walking alongside her with his head thrown back in laughter. He really is quite insufferable, and the worst thing about him is that Hiram constantly seeks him out.

Earlier, when I was collecting water, I saw Hiram in the distance. As usual, he turned to head towards me when he saw me waving. I straightened out my clothes and held my head slightly to the side. I've been studying my reflection in the stream, and I think that angle gives the most pleasing effect. So I was waiting for him to reach me, already hearing in my mind the beautiful words he would say. If people think me full of my own importance, well, Hiram's words make me feel like a goddess to be worshipped. He speaks like no one else I've ever met: like a poet. However, there were to be no soft words and whispers. Instead, Fergus appeared as if from nowhere, and after the shortest of greetings, the pair of them disappeared off into the woods. Their conversation was as intense as if they'd been separated for months, and they didn't spare me a backwards glance as I struggled to carry the water home. It seems the only time I can avoid Fergus is when he'd actually be of some use.

I saw him again later on, Fergus, that is, not Hiram. It was in the time between the finishing of the work and the setting of the sun.

I must admit that when summer arrives, and the days became almost long enough to melt into the next, even I can appreciate some good in our home. In the winter, there is so much darkness and cold, everything feels small and confined. But on those summer evenings there is freedom. Mother says it's nothing compared to the summers when she was a girl. Then, they used to leave our land by the sea and travel to the summer pastures. She says there would be less work to do and singing and dancing every night. That's how she came to marry my father. Their eyes met as they danced on a night when the sun hardly left the sky. At least that's what they whisper to each other when they think no one is listening. It's hard to have secrets when you live in one room. Anyway, we don't do that anymore. We can't travel to the shieling, as that land is no longer ours. It is part of a sheep farm. A farm one hundred times the size of our lands and owned by just one man.

Our summers now might not compare to the ones my mother remembers, but in those special extra hours of daylight, I see a hint of the times she speaks of when her voice sounds young. In those hours, the old folk tell stories, and the boys show off. Sometimes a fiddle appears, or the singing starts. I think there is far too much singing in our lives. People sing when they are happy and they sing when they are sad; they sing when they cut the peats, and they sing as they milk the cows. They sing when a storm threatens the fishing, and they sing to steer the plough across the fields. I could live with a lot less song in my life. However, I love to dance, so I tolerate the singing because without it I would lose so many chances to twirl and to skip and to feel as if I am somewhere else.

When I saw Fergus, it was before any music started. He'd been running some races with the other lads and was catching his breath. I walked over to ask him what he'd been talking about with Hiram. And this is why I find him so hard to tolerate: everyone thinks he is as kind as the Good Shepherd himself, but he hardly gave me the time of day. In fact, he was plain rude. When I enquired what he had needed to discuss so urgently with Hiram, he simply told me it was none of my concern, turned his back on me, and stalked off. Stalked off to talk to dull Isobel with her gold flecked hair, I might add. Fortunately, a fiddle burst into life, and Hiram appeared to spin me back to happiness. Without that time in his arms, my appreciation of the summer evening would have been completely lost.

CHAPTER SIX

The present

Hailstones, big enough to sting as they hit the backs of your legs, were bouncing off the ground as Eilidh sprinted towards the house. The promise of spring, that had made everything seem so positive on the morning of the breaking ground ceremony, had long since disappeared. It seemed as if winter had settled back in and didn't want to loosen its grip. The miserable weather reflected Eilidh's mood. Despite many phone calls to the police, they still hadn't received permission to resume work at the holiday village site. Eilidh felt that control was slipping through her fingers. The construction workers they had engaged for the project were highly in demand, so they had easily been able to go off and work on some smaller jobs elsewhere, but if the police didn't give the go ahead for work to continue soon, the chances were they'd have to commit to bigger projects elsewhere instead. Then there'd be absolutely no chance of the holiday village being completed on schedule.

After hanging her sodden coat to dry, Eilidh flipped the switch on the kettle and began warming up with a nice cup of tea. She curled up in the armchair by the window, which was rapidly becoming her favourite spot in the new house, and opened her emails. She'd been hoping for a response from FamilyFinder about her DNA sample, but her inbox was empty, well, apart from special offers from companies she couldn't remember buying from in the first place. The clouds had stolen the distant hills from view, the seals seemed to have gone into hiding, and Rich would not be home for at least an hour. Eilidh knew she needed a distraction from her wallowing. She flicked through a few TV shows she'd been meaning to catch up on, but nothing held her attention. What she wanted was to chat to someone. The hail seemed to have died back to a light drizzle, and her coat had dried enough that it was no longer dripping, so she slipped it back on and made her way across the road to the Ardmhor Hotel. The name gave the impression of something much grander than the one and a half storey, whitewashed pub with rooms that the Ardmhor Hotel actually was. However, that was the name it had been given many years ago, and that was how it would always be known.

You could rely on there being someone to chat to behind the bar, and Eilidh hoped that with it being Friday, a few of the locals might already be in. Just as she made it into the shelter of the porch, she felt her phone vibrate in her pocket. A text popped up from Beth.

'Ali's home and I've just finished feeding Grace. No one will need me for an hour or so. Are you free for a quick drink? I'm going stir crazy!'

Perfect timing, Eilidh thought to herself. Beth's house was only a minute in the other direction from the pub, so she quickly replied, telling her she'd get the drinks in.

Beth had arrived and claimed a table in the corner, by the time Eilidh placed the drinks in front of them. A large wine for Eilidh and a tiny one for Beth. Although she'd just fed the baby, Grace was still so little that Beth never knew when it'd be time to feed her again, so she didn't want to risk too much alcohol in her bloodstream.

"So, Ali says you still haven't been able to restart work on the holiday village," began Beth. Her husband, Ali, worked alongside Eilidh in the Ardmhor Estate office. "You must be going mad, not being able to get on."

"Totally," Eilidh replied flatly. "In fact, I was already on my way over here, in search of someone to distract me from my woes, when you texted."

"Well, I'm glad I could be of service," Beth smiled. "I feel like all I've done is feed Grace and change nappies for days. At least when Rory was a baby I could watch whatever I wanted on telly while he was feeding, but now he makes a fuss if it's not 'his' programmes on. It's been back-to-back toddler TV today."

"Aww, I used to love watching telly after school. I wonder if any of the same programmes are still on."

"Probably, even I recognise some of it, and I've got a few years on you," Beth replied. "I've watched so much children's telly recently I even dream about it. And after Rory insisted on a nonstop marathon of his current favourite, it's left me genuinely worried about how easily fires can start! Do you want me to give you a rundown of the multiple ways the same two characters accidentally started fires today?"

"It's maybe not quite what I had in mind to distract me," Eilidh said, laughing. Then she groaned again. "I just thought we'd be able to see some progress at the site by now, but there's nothing."

"It's only a couple of weeks since the ceremony. I know you're behind where you wanted to be, but it wouldn't have looked much yet, anyway."

"You're right. I'm just frustrated. I can't help worrying that the longer the police take to come back to us, the more chance there is they'll decide they need to investigate after all."

"But it doesn't sound likely from what Ali's filled me in on. However, I wouldn't mind a bit of a chance to have a look around before work begins. I'd love to find out how many houses there were and see if I can work out why there aren't any records."

"I knew you'd say that!" replied Eilidh, taking a big gulp of wine. "The site isn't cordoned off or anything now. You can go up and have a look whenever you want. But I suppose if we're not allowed to work, you're probably not allowed to do any digging."

"Exactly," said Beth. "I wouldn't want to disturb anything while the police might still need to investigate further. But I'd love the chance to have a good poke around once we're allowed. There's a man who comes into the museum sometimes who makes detailed plans of cleared sites in the area. He got in touch with me as soon as he read about the discovery in the local paper."

"Oh great, more people that want to delay work. I already checked with the authorities that there doesn't need to be an archaeological dig or anything, so you'd better not try to organise one anyway! I'll tell you what. As soon as the police say we can start work again, you and this bloke can have as long as it takes for me to get the construction workers back on site to look around. But we can't delay things any longer than that."

"I reckon that'll probably do," replied Beth. She smiled reassuringly before adding, "and if not, I'll just have to get Angela to make you hold off a bit longer. She's as interested in what used to be there as I am."

"I'll bet she is. It's like she's your mum rather than your mother-in-law, you're as daft as each other when it comes to the past. I can't believe you'd use your family connection to my bosses to overrule me though!"

"Well, you know me—I probably wouldn't dare! But it was fun to see you panic."

"Wow, you really don't get out enough anymore, if that's what you find entertaining," Eilidh replied, gently nudging Beth with her elbow.

"What can I say?" Beth smiled sheepishly and shrugged her shoulders. "Three hours of toddler TV in one day is enough for anyone. So, please say yes to us getting another drink."

By the time Eilidh arrived back home, she was feeling much happier. Nothing had changed with the building site, but catching up with Beth had provided the distraction she needed. As she shut the door behind her, Rich appeared in the hallway, holding a pizza box in each hand.

"I was just about to come looking for you. I picked these up on the way home as a Friday night treat."

"From the café on the pier? I didn't think they were doing pizzas over the winter."

"They weren't, but they've just restarted the full menu today. I noticed they'd put a sign out by the road, and I thought it'd be a nice surprise for tonight."

Eilidh leaned in between the pizza boxes to plant a kiss on his lips. "You thought right. It'd better be a ham and pineapple in there though."

"I've known you too long to have risked anything else," replied Rich, leading the way into the kitchen.

Feeling much more relaxed and having eaten far too much pizza to contemplate moving, Eilidh got tempted into another trawl through her phone. She knew she shouldn't. She should chat to Rich, or read a book, or just do anything more stimulating than lose herself down the rabbit hole of the internet, but she was too full— so phone it was. That was when she noticed her email notification flashing. There had been two new messages since she'd last checked, and both were ones she actually wanted to see.

The first was from the police officer she'd been liaising with about the site. Her name had become very familiar to Eilidh as she made her twice daily enquiries about whether work could finally begin again. She opened the email eagerly, and, despite the weight of pizza in her stomach, almost jumped for joy when she saw its contents.

"We can start work at the site again!" she shouted to Rich. "It's all confirmed. The remains are definitely too old to need criminal investigation."

"That's fantastic," he replied, coming across and wrapping his arms around her as he read the email over her shoulder. "Does that mean I'll get my cheerful wife back? Instead of the misery guts I've been living with for the last couple of weeks?"

"Oi, I have not been miserable," Eilidh said, laughing as she wriggled out of his grip. "Well, maybe just a bit. Do you think it's too late to ring Donald now and see if he can get everyone back on site by Monday?"

Within an hour, Eilidh had confirmation that work would begin again first thing on Monday morning. She'd also spoken to Beth, to let her know she had the weekend to do whatever investigating she wanted. That was a conversation which had resulted in Eilidh being roped into bracken and bramble clearing the next day, but she didn't care, she'd do anything if it meant work could get going again on Monday. It was only as she was sinking into bed that she remembered she hadn't opened the second new email, the results she had been waiting for from FamilyFinder.

Saturday morning found the building site teeming with life. Beth had contacted Graham, her site enthusiast contact from the museum, and rounded up friends and family to help. Eilidh, Rich, Ali, and Jim were busy pulling up bracken and removing brambles so they could see what lay underneath. Andrew, from the local activity centre, and his girlfriend, Leonie, were dragging the waste out of the way to a bonfire, which was being enthusiastically overseen by Beth's dad, David. Beth's mum, Jean, was chasing Rory around the fields, while Lady Angela and Eilidh's mum were taking it in turns to cuddle baby Grace. Alan had taken it upon himself to follow Beth and Graham around, imparting every story he'd ever heard about Ardmhor before the Clearances as they walked. Although the sky was grey and the air was chilly, the rain had ceased, and the group was in high spirits when two staff from the cafe at Ardmhor House appeared. They were weighed down with food and drinks that Angela had requested to fortify the workers. It was quite a party atmosphere as people munched on sandwiches, squabbled over who got which cakes, and quenched the thirst their efforts had built up.

The morning's work had uncovered the outlines of a further six buildings and it looked as if they might find a few more over the course of the afternoon. Graham brought out a plan showing an aerial view of the lower houses, the ones everyone had thought made up the full extent of Ardmhor village before the Clearance. He explained that his plan recorded the ruins as they had been twenty years earlier, but they did not represent the entirety of the old Ardmhor village. Workers had cleared all traces of some houses in order to make way for the road.

Whereas many areas had been cleared to make way for lucrative sheep farms, Ardmhor village had been cleared for aesthetic reasons instead. The Lord MacAird in residence when the village was cleared was responsible for almost doubling the size of Ardmhor House. He had spent most of his life in England, only spending a few summers on the family lands at Ardmhor. However, on his father's death, he had decided to renovate Ardmhor House to make it somewhere suitable to entertain his guests. His wife had taken issue with the proximity of the village to the house. The rough stone houses with their thatched roofs, surrounded by goats and cows and barefooted children, did not fit with her impression of what the landscape around a grand house should be. She did not want her guests to be assailed by the sights and smells of the village as they travelled the rough path between Ardmhor

House and the picturesque natural harbour, so she petitioned her husband for its removal. She reasoned the tenants paid so little rent that the loss of income would be nothing against the improvement in the appearance of the area. Especially as they were already getting so much more rent from the other areas they'd cleared to create large sheep farms. Losing the village would allow them to build a new road down to the harbour, which would make it so much easier for their guests to enjoy the beauty of the area. Also, it would remove any obligation to help the tenants through difficult times.

So it came to be that Lord MacAird ordered the removal of the tenants. The records in the office of Ardmhor House stated he had approached this endeavour with generosity. In return for leaving the lands their families had occupied for generations, the people were to be offered passage on a ship that would take them to new lives in Canada. Lord MacAird would kindly meet their travel costs, after he had taken anything of value from their homes to offset this expense, of course. Those who did not want to take up the opportunity to travel to new lands overseas would be free to make their way to the lowlands, to find employment in the factories there, but there was to be no choice of remaining in the homes they had known all their lives. As time passed, things changed. A later Lord MacAird thought that a fishing village might be a good money spinner and oversaw the building of the pier. The new houses he built were closer to the pier than the old village had been, on the far side of the factor's house. It was this Lord that developed the Ardmhor Hotel as well. However, in one of fate's funny twists, he struggled to attract people back, and the fishing scheme stalled. The village failed to develop into the model town he'd envisioned. What had been the village of Ardmhor remained only as a few ruins, hidden behind trees at the side of the road, and the fields its occupants had so carefully tended were absorbed into the wider grounds of Ardmhor House.

Big Jim, no one ever referred to him as Lord MacAird, shuddered as Graham reached the end of his tale.

"I was brought up to be so proud of being a MacAird. As if it was an achievement of mine to be heir to all this. My parents taught me that becoming Lord MacAird meant I had a responsibility towards the people in this area, and I've always taken that very seriously. They led me to believe all the Lords had. But the more I learn, the more I feel ashamed of the title. I suppose it should have been obvious that the Lord MacAirds became rich by taking from their kin rather than looking after them, but that wasn't as comfortable to believe."

"You can't beat yourself up over what

your ancestors did, Jim," Alan interjected. "My relatives, as well as yours I suppose, were those being cleared from here, but I wouldn't hold that against you. None of us were here for that, and the changes you've made to the ownership of the estate have done so much for everyone around here."

"Aye, but it's Angela and me that are living in the big fancy house paid for by all this, isn't it?"

"True, but you share it with a museum, and a cafe, and hundreds of strangers walking round it each day, so I won't be volunteering to swap," Alan quipped, lightening the mood.

"The records don't mention anything about these buildings at the top of the fields," said Beth, changing the subject slightly. "There is a huge inventory in the archives, listing everything removed from the houses and sold to offset the costs of the passages to Canada, but it's all about the houses centred round the path down to the harbour. There's literally nothing about houses higher up the hill. It's as if they never existed. Except now we know they did."

"With the discovery of the body, I suppose we have to wonder if someone wanted the memory of those houses to disappear," said Jim. "Maybe they were trying to cover up the death by erasing the houses from history. Which makes me even more curious about who that body belongs to and who wanted them to disappear."

CHAPTER SEVEN

The past

Fergus

It was lucky the dancing started when it did, or I'd have been tempted to give Esther a piece of my mind. I could see her glaring at me. Giving out looks that could cut a man down as easily as a shot takes down a deer. All because I wouldn't tell her what I'd been talking about with Hiram this afternoon, as if she somehow has a right to his thoughts. She acts as if Hiram belongs to her, but I'm not sure she cares for him anymore than she cares for the other men she smiles at as she dances or the lads she leaves tongue tied when she teases them in the fields. She expects to be admired with her fine features and her pretty eyes, thinking herself above all the other village girls. But her high opinion of herself, and the way she expects Hiram to be at her beck and call, makes her quite ugly to me.

I don't think I am being too harsh in my assessment of Esther. We have known each other since our first moments on earth. There was only a week between our births and my mother delights in telling me that we followed each other everywhere. Maybe we did get on all that time ago. But I cannot recall it myself. I can only remember her being as demanding and self-centred as she is now. It's not as if it was ever just the two of us, anyway, there was always Isobel and her brothers, and later on, our own siblings as well. I do remember when Hiram arrived though. It was just before my fifth birthday. I remember there being some sort of problem amongst the adults. There were lots of angry discussions and a meeting was held. I know now that they were angry about increases in rents—increases that came even though the lands we could use were constantly being reduced and we could no longer hunt or let our animals roam. But I didn't understand any of that then. All I knew was the tension in the air. On the day of the meeting, the angry voices made me feel both scared and excited at once. Then suddenly all the voices stopped, and a man stepped into the centre of the crowd. However, he wasn't what drew my attention. My focus was entirely on the boy beside him. A boy who looked about the same age as me. A boy who was clinging onto the man's leg until the man pushed him roughly aside. The boy tipped his head forward so that his curls covered his eyes, and I knew he was trying not to cry. Even though I was only small myself, I felt as if I wanted to protect him, in the same way I would protect my brothers and sisters. I knew how embarrassing it would be to cry in front of a crowd of people, but I was too scared to approach him. The man beside him was obviously the man everyone was angry with, so I watched him from behind my mother's skirts instead. I didn't expect to see him again, but over the next few days, he kept appearing. He would watch from behind the trees as we practised jumping the stream, or hover a few paces behind as we walked down to the shore. Eventually, we got over our shyness and introduced ourselves. He said that his name was Hiram, and he lived in the big new house to the side of the bay. When my mother and father discovered we were playing together, they weren't pleased. They warned me that Hiram wasn't one of us. They said I needed to be careful, as his father could have us turned out of our home if I upset him. But I knew Hiram would never do that. He was gentle, and kind, and he thought for a long time before he did anything. Eventually, I think they got used to Hiram's presence, they didn't have much choice as he's appeared at our house every day since, but I don't know if they've ever stopped worrying. It's always that way round though. My parents have got used to Hiram, but Mr Stewart will never accept our friendship. He tells Hiram constantly that he can't mix with the people he will one day have to control. Our friendship is Hiram's act of defiance. Admittedly one he tries to keep hidden most of the time, but I can't blame him for that. Mr Stewart's temper is as fiery as the sun itself. He is a big man, with powerful fists, and he doesn't shy away from using them to make his point.

So I suppose I am a little protective of Hiram. He sees things that are almost invisible to me: the way the leaves change colour or how the bird song alters over the seasons. I don't notice things like that. One day the leaves are green and then I'll realise they have gone, but Hiram will take in every step of the change. He can see people too. I mean, he can see what they are thinking and feeling, and he takes those feelings to heart. He feels things much more than I do. For me, life is quite simple. The life I have is all I need. There is enough food to eat, and I have clothes to wear. My family loves me, and I have the sea and the hills to accompany my every move. I know our life was even better once and that my father rails against the injustice of our situation, but I feel we are lucky. Our land is good, and even without the right to hunt, or to fish the streams, we can still make a living. Lord MacAird might not do much to help us, but he likes to show off to others, so he has insisted on his tenant's children being educated. I don't know how much good it will do me, being able to read and write, but I know that not everyone has that opportunity. My father and grandfather only had the chance to learn the parts of the Bible that were read to them in church, but I can read every word of it, and I can read the words of the books Lord MacAird and his wife give to the children at Sunday School each year. And even if I wasn't able to read about the different worlds in those books, the village has its own songs and stories which have passed down through the years. I know that my life is good.

For Hiram, things are not so easy. He questions everything, right down to how the animals took their shapes and how the first men came to be. He sees the injustices that Lord MacAird orders, and he sees his father's role in carrying them out, and he finds it all hard to accept. His father does not understand his nature at all. He would prefer Hiram to be like his younger brother, George. George Stewart is just like his father, powerful and strong. He shares his father's quick temper and fixed views as well. Mr Stewart's fists have tried to remove Hiram's sensitivity time and time again, but no matter how much Hiram wants to please his father, he cannot become the man Mr Stewart wants any more than the tide can stop turning. So, although many years have passed since we met, I still find myself wanting to protect Hiram from the father who shoves him aside.

It is not all one sided though. I gain as much from my friendship with Hiram as he does from his friendship with me. That is why I can't stand to see him get hurt by Esther. Watching them dancing together tonight, I could see Hiram looking at her as if she was the only other person there. But Esther wasn't focused on him —she was too busy looking around, making sure everyone else had noticed Hiram was looking at her. Everyone in the area knows Hiram, all the girls know that marrying him would be the key to a different life, and Esther loves everyone knowing that she alone holds that key. I don't believe she actually cares about him at all, just the status he brings her. I wonder if she cares for anyone apart from herself. Hiram, however, believes her to be perfect. Considering he notices everything else, it amazes me that he cannot see her faults.

Even if I had wanted to tell Esther what Hiram and I had discussed today, I couldn't have because Hiram had sworn me to secrecy. He'd accompanied his father on his rounds and had questioned one of his actions. Mr Stewart had not reacted kindly. He'd belittled Hiram in front of the others present and beat him when they returned home. Mr Stewart told him he has to stop mixing with us in the village, that our uncivilised ways have damaged his ability to see what is right. He said Hiram needs to recognise that Lord MacAird knows what is best for the people. He wants Hiram to go to Edinburgh to complete his education. Mr Stewart believes that living purely in the company of young men will toughen Hiram up, that he'll have to learn to be a 'proper' man to fit in. Finally, Mr Stewart said that once Hiram's education is complete, they will find him a suitable wife to return to Ardmhor with. Hiram is used to these outbursts and beatings from his father. Sometimes they make him angry, sometimes they simply make him sad. But today seemed different. There was a coldness to him as he told me what had happened. A resignation to the fact that he cannot both please his father and live as he wants to. He knows he has to decide. Either he has to deny his father to be himself, or he can follow his father's wishes and lose who he wants to be. I could not bring myself to say to him that if he chooses to be himself, his dreams of marriage to Esther will be over, anyway. Esther would no more marry Hiram if he was just another village boy than she would choose to marry me. But maybe he knows that, maybe that's why he seemed so cold and withdrawn. Perhaps I'm wrong to think Hiram can see no fault in Esther. If the real reason for her interest in him is clear enough for me to see, there is no way Hiram, with his much greater insight, can have missed it. Perhaps it's not that he doesn't know, it's just that he loves her enough to ignore it.

CHAPTER EIGHT

The present

With all the activity of investigating the building site, it was Sunday evening before Eilidh finally got round to opening the email from FamilyFinder. They'd spent both Saturday and Sunday clearing vegetation out of the way. Although the trees had been felled the previous year, plenty of undergrowth remained, and it was that which was concealing the signs of occupation. With the bracken pulled up and the brambles cut away, it became clear there had been twelve buildings up at the top of the fields. Even though Eilidh wasn't usually one for overthinking, she couldn't help but notice the symmetry. The diggers would clear the remaining stones of the twelve forgotten buildings tomorrow, and they would eventually be replaced with twelve new lodges. Amongst the stones, they'd found fragments of broken pottery and a couple of rusted cooking pots. They weren't valuable objects, but they were reminders that the site had once been full of life, just as they hoped it would be again. Eilidh's limbs ached from the day's physical exertion, as she eased herself into her favourite seat by the window and clicked the email open.

There were no surprises in the genetic origin section of the findings—majority European, with a few tiny hints of more far-flung destinations. It didn't appear there were going to be any surprises in the family links section, either. Her sample had generated a few cousin matches, two were in Scotland, and the furthest match was only as far away as the English midlands. Eilidh had the sinking feeling that her parents had been right. The test had been a waste of money. She had learnt nothing about her family that she didn't already know. At the end of the results, there was a box to tick if you wanted to receive the contact details of any family links that had also consented. It seemed slightly pointless to Eilidh. She saw most of her cousins at least once a year, so there wouldn't be any emotional reunions, but she ticked the box, anyway. If nothing else, it'd be interesting to see which of her cousins had also been daft enough to take the test, and she may as well try to get something for her money.

As the construction workers packed up at the end of their first day on site, Eilidh realised she wouldn't be happy with the amount of progress possible in any one day: she was just too impatient to see the finished results. But although it was good that work was finally happening, it surprised her to find she was a little sad that all traces of the previous settlement had now disappeared. It wasn't like her to be sentimental, and it wasn't as if the site held precious memories. No one had known there were buildings up there until a couple of weeks ago. Then again, maybe that was why she felt sad. The houses had been forgotten for so long, and then, almost as soon as they were rediscovered, they were gone again. But people knocked down and rebuilt houses all the time, she reasoned with herself. They were simply bringing this section of land back to life. Also, Beth and Graham had meticulously mapped the layout of the buildings and they had carefully photographed everything. Nothing was going to be forgotten again.

There was just enough warmth in the air for Eilidh to be tempted to drag a chair outside when she got home from work. The weather had finally taken it upon itself to improve again, and it seemed as if the promise of a few weeks ago might be returning. Eilidh always liked this time of year. Not far enough on for the midges to be making their presence felt, but just warming up enough that you didn't fear turning into an icicle if you stood still for too long. The doors at the front of the kitchen slid open onto a large deck. Nothing marked the edges of it, so when the tide was in, the deck seemed to hang over the sea. It was what had made Eilidh really want to buy the house. It was like having her own private jetty, and she'd even toyed with the idea of getting a little boat to tie up next to it. They hadn't got as far as organising any outdoor furniture yet, so it was the armchair next to the window that found itself being manhandled through the sliding doors onto the deck. She sat watching the seals play for a while. Some ducks she didn't recognise were floating serenely in the distance and she made a mental note of their colours to ask Ali about at work the next day. Beth's husband might be the life and soul of any social event, but he had a lesser-known alter ego as an avid birdwatcher. Within a few minutes, her urge to be doing rather than watching had taken over, and she found herself checking her emails again. There was another message from FamilyFinder, one of her cousin matches wanted to meet up. It only gave the first name and an email address, but that was enough to get Eilidh interested. The name it gave was Sylvie and as far as Eilidh knew, she didn't have a cousin with that name.

Rich had phoned to say he needed to work late and would grab something to eat in Inveravain, so Eilidh decided to make the most of the beautiful evening and take a trip over to Strathglen. She wanted to see if her parents could shed some light on this new cousin. Her dad had a lot of relatives, so it was quite possible there were some branches of the family they just hadn't kept in touch with. Also, if Rich wouldn't be home to eat with, it made sense to enjoy her mum's amazing cooking instead.

Once again Alan had been called out to help a damsel in distress, only the damsel was actually the grumpy old man who lived two houses away and couldn't get his door to shut properly. So it was just Eilidh and Claire who sat down to bowls of spaghetti carbonara.

"Do you know of anyone in the family called Sylvie?" Eilidh asked between mouthfuls.

Claire paused for a moment, swallowing her forkful of pasta slowly before answering.

"In the family? No. Why?"

"I got a meeting request from one of my cousin matches on FamilyFinder, but the name given is Sylvie."

"I thought you weren't going to bother with all that," Claire queried, sounding almost cross.

"I just thought it might be fun. But you were right, anyway, my background is just bog standard European as you'd expect, and almost all the family matches it brought up are in Scotland. The only mystery is the name Sylvie."

"It's probably just an admin mistake," Claire

said confidently. "That request was most likely meant for someone else."

"I suppose it could be," Eilidh conceded. "But I thought that because Dad has so much family, there could be some people we've lost touch with."

"Maybe. But it doesn't seem very safe going off to meet someone you know nothing about, especially as it could just be a mistake."

Eilidh looked at her mum, surprised. It wasn't like Claire to be so negative and dismissive, but she'd been like this each time Eilidh had mentioned anything to do with FamilyFinder. Before she had chance to offer any comeback, Claire spoke again.

"So obviously you'll just leave it well alone," she stated in a tone that didn't invite any further discussion.

As Eilidh was driving home, she heard her phone buzzing on the seat next to her. Her car was far too old for her to be able to answer calls through the speaker system, so she had to do things the old-fashioned way and pull over into a lay-by. However, it wasn't much of a hardship when the view from the car window was distant hills bathed in the last light of the day. She saw it was her dad on the caller ID and smiled as she answered.

"Hi Dad."

"Hi sweetheart, are you back home already?"

Eilidh laughed. "No dad, I haven't saved up enough for my own helicopter yet. I only left Mum ten minutes ago. Of course I'm not home."

"Oh, so I really did only just miss you. I assumed when your mum said you'd left a bit ago that she meant half an hour ago or something."

"No, if I'd known you'd be back that soon, I'd have waited. I wanted to ask you if you knew of a cousin called Sylvie."

Alan thought for a minute before replying. Eilidh could almost see him scratching his head in thought.

"No one comes to mind. But I have a lot of relatives, and the names of some of their kids get mixed up in my head."

"That's what I thought, but Mum was really dismissive."

"Dismissive of what, my love?" Alan asked.

"Well, I did that FamilyFinder test in the end, and I had a request from a cousin match called Sylvie to meet up, but Mum was just 'oh it'll be a mistake you can't go'," Eilidh whined in a very unflattering impersonation of her mum's voice.

"I thought we'd agreed those tests were a waste of money. You know what? Your mum's probably right. I've heard they get a lot of false matches on those sites."

"Right," Eilidh said quietly, disappointed that her dad was showing the same lack of enthusiasm as her mum. "Anyway, was there something you wanted to talk about, Dad? Because if not, I'd better be getting home."

"There was actually. I heard from Professor Blake today. You know, she's the lady who was trying to identify the remains. I told you I went with her to get some DNA samples from Fergus's descendants, didn't I? Anyway, she rang me tonight to say that none of the samples matched the remains."

"But would they necessarily?" Eilidh pondered aloud. "It was so long ago there must have been all sorts added to the genetic mix since then, and you've just said you don't think DNA tests are very reliable."

"Well, I don't know how it works, but I think Professor Blake is a bit different from some money-making website, and she seemed pretty certain the remains couldn't be Fergus."

"So are you disappointed?" Eilidh asked.

"A bit, I suppose. It'd be nice to have found out who was buried up there. But in a way, I'm glad it's not him. My great-granny always talked about Fergus as if he was an absolute top lad. It's nicer to think he made a life for himself in Edinburgh, than to think he was lying forgotten in that hole."

"He's never been forgotten though," Eilidh

countered. "You've remembered his story, and everyone up at the building site over the weekend knows all about him."

"Aye, I suppose you're right. But overall, I think I'm glad it wasn't him. Anyway, I'd better let you get home. I just wanted to let you know."

After she'd said her goodbyes, and restarted her journey back to Ardmhor, Eilidh tried to identify what she was feeling. Deflated, she thought. She hadn't realised how much she wanted to know the identity of the remains, and now it looked as if she never would. It was then that she made up her mind. She was going to meet this unknown cousin, Sylvie. She might not be able to find out anything else about the skeleton from the building site, but she could find out a bit more about her own family. Even if no one else seemed interested.

CHAPTER NINE

The past

Esther

Before I even opened my eyes, I could sense something was amiss. I'd been lost in the most romantic dream. Everything was soft and warm, and I didn't want to leave, but something was pulling me away. I was fighting as hard as I could to stay in that beautiful place, but it was slipping from my grasp. Reality was creeping in at the edges. The voices of my sisters, the tang of the peat smoke, those were things that did not exist in that perfect dream world, but somehow, they were now present. One voice was calling my name.

"Esther! Esther! If you don't get out of bed right now, Mam is going to kill you. Esther! You need to get up NOW!"

I peeled my eyes open slowly, finally accepting that my dream was just that. My first sight of reality was my sister Cait, her face just inches from mine.

"What's going on? What's the rush?" Rubbing the sleep from my eyes, I pulled myself upright.

"We've been trying to wake you for ages. Mam has had to do the milking herself. She says you're not to be dancing with Hiram again if it means you can't do your work the next day."

I couldn't help but smile at the mention of Hiram. Thinking about the night before sent a shiver of excitement down my spine. Being in Hiram's arms, swirling around amongst the other dancers, had given me the same feeling I'd been enjoying in my dream. We hadn't just danced, either. Amidst the commotion of the dancing, we'd been able to sneak off into the woods together. The only thing better than dancing with Hiram is being kissed by Hiram. His lips are so soft, and he is so gentle, but last night there was something else too. He seemed powerful; he felt strong. When he kissed me, it was as if a fire was being lit somewhere deep inside me, a fire that spread throughout my body. We've kissed before, but not like that. Last night's kisses started as normal, just pecks really, but they got longer and deeper, until they melted into one long moment where I could hardly breathe. I can't wait until we marry, and I can start my proper life as Mrs Stewart. There'll be no work for me then, just kisses. And we'll travel together, to places far from here. Hiram's parents go to Edinburgh sometimes. I can only imagine how exhilarating it must be to walk amongst all those people, with buildings as far as the eye can see.

"Esther, come on! You're still not ready. I'll be getting told off too if you're not outside soon. Mam said I was in charge of getting you up."

Cait's words brought me back to the present, and I quickly made myself presentable, hoping I wouldn't be in too much trouble. As I stepped out into the sunlight, sunlight far warmer and brighter than it would have been at the time I was supposed to rise, it wasn't mother's voice I heard first. That was when I realised the situation was worse than a telling off from mother. It was going to be a telling off in front of Fergus. The pair of them were walking towards the house. Fergus was carrying our water bucket. Mother was laughing at something he'd said and thanking him for his help. It was Fergus that saw me first.

"So, you're finally back in the land of the living. I suppose all that dancing must have been exhausting."

"I can't help that I didn't wake up. Anyway, you were doing plenty of dancing too, with Isobel. It must have been tiring keeping a conversation going with her all that time."

"Esther! Don't be so rude," Mother hissed angrily. "Isobel's been a good friend to you, and it doesn't matter how much dancing Fergus did, he's been up doing your work while you've been lying about."

"I'm sorry," I offered, trying to ignore the smug look on Fergus's face. "I didn't mean to sleep so long."

"Well, maybe you could see to the bairns now, so that I can get on."

Mother took the bucket from Fergus and walked away into the house, but I could tell from her tone that I wasn't forgiven yet, it was only that she was too proud to carry on an argument in public, especially in front of her precious Fergus.

"I imagine it was whatever went on in the woods that wore you out more than the dancing," Fergus said, as soon as mother was too far away to hear.

So he'd seen me and Hiram disappear after all. I'd been careful to avoid being spotted by Mother or Father. Much as they tolerated Hiram now, the thought of their daughter alone in the woods at night with anyone was unlikely to please them. I knew we hadn't escaped totally unseen. As Hiram pulled me into the trees, Iain was just emerging into the open. He winked as he caught my eye, letting me know our secret was safe with him. I wondered now whether he'd told Fergus what he'd seen, or if Fergus had spotted us himself. I decided it was probably the latter. Fergus is so protective of Hiram he probably spied on him all night, and Iain isn't the type to tell tales. He's so tall and handsome, I imagine he's been sneaking off into the woods for many years. If good looks were the only thing to consider, I'd certainly be happy to spend a bit of time alone with Iain. However, a pretty face and a strong frame won't be enough to take me away from this life. Also, Iain is two years older than me and is to be wed to Rebecca, so it's not really worth thinking about. Anyway, Hiram's golden curls are far more unusual than Iain's dark locks and, if I'm honest, Hiram's face is probably more beautiful than mine. Yes, our children will be the loveliest anyone has ever seen, and Hiram and I will live happily ever after.

"So what were you doing out there, anyway?" Fergus pestered, interrupting my thoughts.

"What do you think?"

"I don't know, Esther. That's why I'm asking."

The cheek of him. After I asked him what he'd been discussing with Hiram and he told me it was none of my concern, what right did he have to ask about our private moments? I knew I should just walk away as he had done the night before. That would have been the right thing to do. But somehow, I couldn't make myself do the right thing. I wanted Fergus to see that what Hiram and I have is just as special as their friendship. In fact, I wanted him to know we have something much more than that. Also, I wanted to shock him, to take that smug smile off his face. So instead of walking away, I said,

"We were kissing, Fergus. Kissing and everything else that people do when they're in love. Not that you'd know about things like that. Isobel is so dull I imagine she'd rather sing than kiss."

It worked. Fergus wasn't smiling anymore. Instead, he looked positively angry.

"Isobel is worth ten of you, Esther, she wouldn't be letting her mother down or getting other people to do her work for her. The way you speak about other people shows me you don't know anything about love. I only hope Hiram doesn't end up with his heart broken, he deserves much better than you."

I didn't bother to give him a response. He thinks he knows so much about me, yet he barely bothers to speak to me anymore. When we were younger, it was always the three of us, Fergus, Hiram and me, but as we got older the games changed, and I was always left behind. They didn't need a girl on their adventures. Fergus can't stand that things have changed again. He hates that I am becoming more to Hiram than he can ever be. Well, Fergus can keep his smug smiles and everyone thinking he's wonderful because I'm not giving up Hiram. Fergus is wrong. I won't hurt Hiram, I love him, and I will marry him.

I looked back down the hill, towards the sea, as I rounded up my little sisters. Fergus was halfway down the fields, standing next to Isobel. They looked in my direction and then threw their heads back in laughter. I could do nothing but stamp my foot in exasperation. He really is the most hateful person I know.

CHAPTER TEN

The present

As soon as Eilidh arrived back from her parent's house, she fired off a quick email to arrange meeting up with Sylvie. A response came within the hour, and in the days since then, emails had flown back and forth between the pair. They had only been brief exchanges, trying to find a convenient spot in which to meet up, but Eilidh felt they'd already made a connection. Sylvie shared the same sense of humour. Maybe it was a family thing, Eilidh reasoned. Everyone knew her dad could bring laughter to any situation.

However, even though things were going swimmingly with Sylvie, the lack of enthusiasm from her parents was bothering Eilidh. They were usually so encouraging of any idea she had, no matter how hare-brained the scheme might seem, and family was so important to both of them. Really, she'd have expected them to try and muscle their way in on the meeting, rather than attempt to put her off. Her grandparents on her mum's side had been frequent visitors to Strathglen before they passed away, and her uncle and his partner often came to stay, or they visited his home in Edinburgh. Her dad had been raised by his gran, for whom family had been everything, and he made a point of keeping the extended family together. Eilidh couldn't work out why they weren't keener to add another sheep to the fold. The only explanation she could think of for their reticence was that they were concerned about their only child going to meet a stranger off the internet. Therefore, even though she felt she'd really clicked with Sylvie, she'd tried to keep safety in mind as they made their arrangements. Eventually they'd settled on meeting at a roadside café, midway between Eilidh's home in Ardmhor and Sylvie's in Glasgow. It was a popular spot with a craft shop attached to the cafe and plenty of parking, so Eilidh had no concerns about being dragged off unnoticed by some sort of ancestry obsessed criminal gang.

However, by the time the day of the meeting rolled around, Eilidh's enthusiasm was also waning. She woke up with a headache. Even though she'd had a very restrained Friday night, her body ached, and she felt exhausted. Her head was throbbing, and she wondered if she might be coming down with something. The thought of driving for an hour and a half didn't fill her with enthusiasm. The duvet felt so soft, and she much preferred the thought of snuggling underneath it for the rest of the day. She stretched her arm out towards Rich but found only empty space. Rolling over to look at the clock, she was surprised to find it was already after nine. As she tried to summon the strength to emerge from the covers, Rich appeared next to her with a steaming cup of coffee.

"Good morning, sleepyhead. I thought you might need this to revive you for your journey. You don't want to be leaving much later than ten, if you're meeting at midday."

"I don't know if I'm going to go, actually."

She reached out to take the coffee, blowing on the surface before taking a tentative sip.

"Why not? You've been excited about this all week. I thought you felt like you'd got lots in common?"

"I do, and I am excited. It's just I feel rubbish this morning. My head hurts and I'm exhausted."

"Well, the coffee will soon fix the tiredness, and I'll grab some tablets for your head. I reckon between them and a shower, you'll be sorted."

"Is there a reason you're so keen to get me out of the way?" Eilidh queried, as Rich headed towards the bathroom cabinet looking for painkillers.

"No, I just don't want you to miss out on something you've been looking forward to."

"Hmm," Eilidh began, with a note of suspicion in her voice. "I'm not sure I'm totally convinced. There was a definite twitch at the corner of your left eye, Richard Givens."

"Alright, you've got me, Eilidh McRae. I might have invited Ali and Andrew round to watch the match this afternoon."

"Fine," said Eilidh, pulling herself out of bed and planting a kiss on Rich's smiling mouth as he handed her the tablets. "You should have just said, a long drive has to be preferable to three blokes shouting at the telly, headache or not."

By the time Eilidh stepped out of the shower, the painkillers were kicking in and her headache was subsiding, and after half an hour on the open road with her favourite tunes playing, she was feeling her usual energetic self. She was glad Rich had pushed her to come. However, when she pulled into the car park of 'The Biadh Barn', the food and craft centre where she was meeting Sylvie, Eilidh wondered if meeting somewhere popular had been a mistake. The place was packed. Eilidh circled the car park twice, losing out on a couple of spaces to other drivers, before she was finally lucky. A huge four-wheel drive was struggling to fit into a tight spot and eventually gave up, giving Eilidh the chance to manoeuvre her much smaller car into the opening instead. She just hoped Sylvie had been lucky as well, or their meeting might not be happening after all. They'd agreed to meet outside the entrance at twelve. They hadn't gone as far as describing what they'd be wearing or making elaborate plans, like standing under a clock holding a red rose, but Eilidh had mentioned that her hair was currently bright blue, so she had a feeling Sylvie would identify her easily enough.

Walking towards the entrance, Eilidh realised she might have got that wrong too. Just to the side of the door, she could see a young woman pulling away from another woman's embrace. One of them seemed to be apologising profusely while turning bright red. The other, with a mane of turquoise hair Eilidh would have been proud of, appeared to be waving off the apologies while looking slightly confused. Eilidh had a sinking feeling she knew what was happening, but she approached the pair cautiously, aware she might have misread things. Gently, she tapped the shoulder of the non-turquoise haired lady.

"Sylvie?"

The lady in question broke off from her apologising and span round to face her.

"Eilidh?" she said, taking in the sight of another blue-haired woman with a smile. "If only you'd said electric blue! This is Ellie," Sylvie said, gesturing to the young woman stood to the side of her. "She was just waiting for her mum to finish paying when I accosted her."

Ellie laughed. "Honestly, don't worry, you don't usually get two people with blue hair in the same place! Anyway, I can see my mum coming, so I'll leave you to it."

She set off towards a woman who had just walked out of the cafe, saying to Eilidh as she left, "I do love that deeper blue. I think I might try that next."

"Oh, my goodness!" said Sylvie as Ellie vanished across the car park. "What an introduction. You must think I'm a total fool. I'm Sylvie, by the way, in case that wasn't obvious."

"Nice to meet you, Sylvie. I am definitely Eilidh, and I don't think you're a fool. I shouldn't have been so sure that I'd be the only person here with great taste in hair dye!"

Sylvie's face relaxed a little. "She was right next to the entrance, and it was almost midday, and her hair was bright blue. Then when I said 'Eilidh' to her, she must have replied Ellie, but it was noisy, and I was expecting her to be you, so I just thought she was confirming that yes, she was Eilidh. So, I started hugging her because I was so excited to meet you at last, but then I noticed she wasn't responding, so I let go, and she just looked at me and said, 'who are you?' I'm so embarrassed!"

"Well, now I know we're definitely related,"

said Eilidh, linking her arm through Sylvie's. "You don't really pause for breath either! Shall we go in?"

They were shown to an empty table by the window, and within a minute, someone was taking their drinks order. Eilidh supposed somewhere as busy as this had to be efficient. As Sylvie was being questioned on exactly how she wanted her coffee, Eilidh finally had the opportunity to study her properly. Sylvie was also petite, which made Eilidh wonder if their connection might actually be on her mum's side. She'd been assuming Sylvie would be another cousin from her dad's huge extended family, but petite didn't usually seem to happen amongst Alan's relations, her cousins all towered over her. Sylvie had straight brown hair, exactly as Eilidh thought hers might look if she ever stayed away from the dye. Not that she was sure. It had been over a decade since she'd last seen her hair in its natural state. Sylvie's facial features were dainty, like her frame. She looked as if she'd been sort of scaled down from average size, like a perfect pixie or a little fairy. Overall, Eilidh decided she seemed familiar, but she couldn't quite put her finger on why.

The confusion outside had well and truly broken the ice between them, so there were no awkward silences as they tried to look through the menu. In fact, they had to send the man who came to take their food order away the first time he appeared at the side of them, as they'd been too busy chatting to decide. By the time they'd finished eating, they'd covered everything from their jobs—Sylvie was an office manager in a builder's yard—to their partners, and where they lived. Eilidh had to admit that growing up on the coast around Inveravain had little in common with growing up in Glasgow, but their jobs had a lot of similarities, and they had both been with their partners since they were teenagers. They were eating cakes and sipping more coffee by the time they got round to discussing families. They were getting on so well, it was as if they'd forgotten the actual reason they were meeting. Eilidh explained she was an only child, which was also true for Sylvie, although she had been raised by her gran after her mother's death when she was young. When Eilidh asked about her dad, Sylvie finally went quiet. Worried she'd brought up something she shouldn't have, Eilidh quickly steered the conversation back to their reason for meeting: how were they cousins? However, that question didn't seem to bring Sylvie round either. Eilidh watched as Sylvie took a big gulp of coffee, and then an even bigger breath, before she eventually spoke.

"The thing is," she began quietly, forcing Eilidh to strain to listen. "I'm not sure how you're going to take this, but I don't think we are cousins. I think you're my sister."

CHAPTER ELEVEN

The past

Fergus

It wasn't until the evening that I spoke to Hiram about what was going on between him and Esther. When we'd talked the day before, I'd thought he'd accepted that there could be no future for the two of them, so I hadn't expected to see them disappearing into the woods together. Esther might have given me her explanation of events, but I had a feeling there was more to it than that. Hiram isn't the type to tempt girls away into the night for a bit of fun. I was sure he'd have been too protective of Esther's reputation to risk dragging her off when anyone could have seen—not without a good reason. It's not that I didn't understand how much a couple might want time alone together. Believe me, I understand the urges a typical man feels, but that's the point, Hiram isn't a typical man.

Anyway, I knew Esther was deliberately trying to anger me with her answer this morning. I have to admit I'd almost been glad she'd overslept and that I'd had to fetch the water for her. I knew how much it would irritate her to have to be grateful to me. So, knowing that my own motives were questionable, I had to wonder how much trust I could place in the words of someone as shallow as Esther. But it wasn't until the evening I got the chance to speak to Hiram himself. We're in the middle of cutting the peats right now. It takes weeks of hard work to make sure every home has enough fuel to last the year. No one minds doing extra to help those that can't provide for themselves, but it annoys me when people like Esther, who are perfectly able, don't do their share. Anyway, working away, rhythmically cutting, gave me plenty of time to think over Hiram's situation. Mr Stewart's plan to send him to Edinburgh wouldn't just affect Hiram: my life would change as well. Every single day for over ten years, I've spent time with Hiram. I tell him everything, just as he does with me. He's my best friend, the person who knows me better than anyone else. I can't imagine life without him. His cold acceptance of his father's plan had made me feel there was no alternative, that he really would have to leave, but his behaviour with Esther last night had got me thinking that maybe he'd come up with something. I knew I'd support him whatever he did, but try as I might, I couldn't imagine what he had in mind. When I finally saw him, it was late. The sun had already set, but there was still plenty of time before the light of the day would disappear. He was just passing the stream when I shouted for him to wait there. I didn't want him to reach the space where everyone was gathered. More specifically, I didn't want him to reach Esther before I'd had the chance to speak to him. He sat down on a rock that jutted out into the burn, looking slightly puzzled.

"Are you alright? Is something wrong?" he asked, clearly wondering why I was keeping us from whatever entertainments might await in the village.

"No, not really," I began. "It's just that I saw you disappearing into the woods with Esther last night."

I let the words hang, waiting to see what explanation Hiram would volunteer.

"I thought I'd been careful enough not to be seen," Hiram replied with a shake of his head. "I didn't want to cause any trouble for Esther."

"That's what surprised me. You're always so protective of her. I thought maybe you'd come up with a plan to stay and that you needed her help."

"I'm afraid you were thinking too highly of me, Fergus. Dancing with Esther made my worries seem a little less important. I just wanted that feeling to continue, and Esther seemed as keen as me, so I thought, why not? I thought perhaps I should try not to think so much and just act instead."

"But that's not like you, Hiram. You don't just act regardless of the consequences."

"And look at where being cautious has got me. My father thinks I'm too sensitive—that I'm not a real man. The reward for all my thinking is being sent away from everything I love."

"Yes, but your father said you weren't to come to the village anymore. If Esther's father had seen you last night and complained, it might have ended up with you being sent away even sooner."

"Well, that's where you're wrong," said Hiram, poking a stick into the mud at the edge of the stream. "My father sent me here last night, and tonight as well. He said he'd reconsidered: not about sending me away, that is definitely happening, but he no longer wanted me to keep away from the village. He said that as I would be leaving soon anyway, perhaps it would be good for me to have a bit of fun with a village girl. He said that acting like a real man might help me become one. So if my father had seen me last night, I'd have had his full approval."

"But you've not got mine, Hiram. This isn't you. This is the way your father or George might behave. Maybe it's even what some lads in the village would do. But it's not you."

"How do you know?" Hiram practically spat the words at me. "Maybe this behaviour is me. It felt great taking Esther off like that, knowing she was enjoying everything I was doing with her. I'm sick of everyone thinking they know who I am, and always finding something wrong with me. I'm too sensitive for my father, and now I'm not sensitive enough for you. Maybe I just want to enjoy myself. Anyway, Esther wasn't complaining."

"Well, maybe she wasn't, but it doesn't make it right. Esther thinks you're going to marry her. She wouldn't be doing those things with you if she thought you were just taking advantage and then planning to leave."

"Do you not think she's been taking advantage of me all this time, Fergus? I'm not a fool. I know she's only ever been using me as a way out of the village. She wouldn't have looked twice at me if I wasn't the factor's son."

"You don't know that," I said. It didn't matter that I'd wanted Hiram to realise this for years, for some reason, I couldn't let him say it out loud. I wasn't defending Esther: it was more that I wanted to protect Hiram from the truth.

"I do know," Hiram stated firmly. "You've been

warning me about her for years. We both know it'd be you she'd choose if there was no difference in status between us, just like every other girl in the area."

"Well, that is definitely not the case. Esther would no more want to be with me than I'd want to be with her."

"And now you're doing what you always do, trying to protect me. Well, I don't need that anymore, Fergus. I don't need you to look after me, and I don't need my father to tell me how to be a man. Just leave me alone."

Then he was gone. In over ten years of spending every day together, it was the first time we'd really argued. I didn't like the feeling of him being angry with me or the feeling of him leaving me behind. And I knew it would be a hundred times worse when he left for Edinburgh.

CHAPTER
TWELVE

The present

Eilidh's first reaction was to laugh. She could only think that Sylvie was making some sort of joke about how similar they seemed to be.

"What do you mean, sisters in what way?" she asked eventually, when it became clear from Sylvie's straight face that she was serious.

"Like sisters who share the same dad," Sylvie replied.

That was not the answer Eilidh had been expecting. She couldn't make sense of what Sylvie meant.

"I still don't understand. Are you saying that my dad had an affair? That he's got another family?"

"No, not an affair, just that he had another child after he was with your mum."

"I'm not getting what you mean, Sylvie. My dad is still with my mum. They're totally in love. There is no way he'd have been with someone else after I was born."

"Sorry. I know I'm explaining this badly. I don't mean that the person you think of as your dad is also my father. What I mean is that my dad, Keith, is your biological father. He and your mum were together before I was born."

Eilidh looked around as if someone might appear and explain to her what was going on. Was Sylvie actually trying to tell her that Alan wasn't her father?

"No, you're still not making sense. You must have got it wrong. Alan, my dad, is my mum's only love. She always says he was the only man for her. She moved away from her family because she was so desperate to be with him."

"Honestly, Eilidh, it's the truth. I'm not making this up."

Eilidh wondered if she should leave. That's what happened in films. When someone made a ridiculous accusation, the other person would storm out, disgusted that such a thing could even be suggested. But Sylvie was sitting there at the other side of the table shaking. She didn't look like she was deliberately trying to cause trouble. She looked vulnerable and a bit scared.

Also, Eilidh had never been able to get her head around people storming out without at least waiting to hear an explanation. Did these people not want to find out what was actually going on? She knew she was far too impatient and nosy for that. She needed to get to the bottom of this right now.

"Alright. You're going to have to give me a bit more detail. Maybe start from the beginning. What makes you think your dad is my father?"

"It's a long story," Sylvie began, "and I'm happy to tell you everything I know, but I'm going to show you something first. It might help you believe me."

With that said, she reached into her bag and pulled out a photo, pushing it across the table to Eilidh. It was a bit dog-eared, and the colours had faded slightly, giving it the yellowed look of the past. It showed a young couple. The man was unknown to Eilidh, although she could clearly see a look of Sylvie in his features. The woman at his side, though, the one with her head resting on his shoulder and a huge smile on her face, she was as familiar to Eilidh as her own reflection. She was obviously younger in the photo, but there was no denying that the woman was her mother. Eilidh looked back up at Sylvie.

"So I take it this is Keith, your father?"

"Yes, our father," Sylvie replied, emphasising the middle word of her statement.

"Okay, well, I believe you that he knew my mum, but this photo doesn't prove he's my dad. It only proves they used to know each other."

"Look at the date on the back," Sylvie prompted.

Eilidh obliged, picking up the photo and turning it over slowly in her hand.

"It's the year before I was born. But that still doesn't prove anything. My mum could have met my dad just after this was taken. Or maybe she was only friends with your dad?"

"Then how do you explain our DNA link?" Sylvie responded.

"But that said we were cousins. Maybe my mum and your dad are cousins. Maybe that's why they're in the photo together."

None of this was making much sense to Eilidh. She had so many questions whirling around her head, but she couldn't get them to stay still long enough to work out what she actually needed to ask.

"I don't know how much research you've done into the FamilyFinder tests," Sylvie began, "but half siblings will generally show up as cousin matches. I've known all my life that I had an older sister, and my gran said her mum was the lady in that photo. Being an only child, I've always wanted to find you. Everywhere I went, I'd be looking out for that lady, or someone around my age that looked a bit like me. I did the FamilyFinder test years ago as soon as I heard about them. I knew it was unlikely that my sister would have done the test as well, but I thought it was worth a try. Anyway, so far, I've had two other cousin matches, but both of them were too old. I didn't want to get my hopes up when your match appeared, but I was excited to meet you anyway because you seemed so nice. I just kept thinking how amazing it would be if you were actually her. Then, when you said your parents' names, it fitted with what I'd been told, and you were the right age, and we look alike—you must be able to see it—and it is your mum in the photo, so I have to be right. We're sisters, Eilidh, honestly."

Eilidh was reeling from Sylvie's words. She barely registered one of the staff approaching their table again, or Sylvie ordering them two more coffees. The idea that her mum might have had a relationship with someone other than her dad was shocking enough. Claire had always told Eilidh that Alan was her only love. But the thought that her dad was not really her father, that was something her brain couldn't even begin to compute.

"Okay, so if this is true," Eilidh began slowly, trying desperately to get her thoughts in order, "why didn't I know anything about it? And how does your mum fit into this? We can't be much different in age."

"I don't know why your mum didn't tell you. All I know is that ever since I was tiny, my gran has told me I had a big sister and that her mum broke my dad's heart by running away with his friend. My dad met my mum not long after that, and they had me, but my mum got ill after I was born, which is why we ended up living with my gran."

"So, is my dad, Alan, supposed to be the friend she ran away with?"

"Yes, that's the name I've always been told."

"But couldn't it be that my mum and my dad were having an affair, and they left because she knew she was carrying his child?"

"Our DNA matches, Eilidh. The only explanation is that what I'm telling you is true."

"I just can't see my mum and dad doing something like that," Eilidh mused quietly, more to herself than in response to Sylvie.

"I realise it must be a shock," said Sylvie, "and I'm sorry to be upsetting you like this. My gran always says my dad never got over it."

"But he must have met your mum quite soon after."

"Yes, and he really loved her, although I can't remember that much about the two of them together because I was pretty young when she died."

"That's really sad," Eilidh replied, wondering who it was sadder for, Sylvie's dad, going through the loss of two partners, or Sylvie, growing up without her mum. "What about your dad though? You said his mother brought you up after your mum died. Where was he?"

"Oh, he lived with us too, but he had to go away a lot."

"And where is he now?"

"I'm sorry, Eilidh. He died three months ago. That's why I was so excited to get this match now. I felt like he was somehow helping to bring us together. To give me something to fill the gap."

Eilidh left not long after that revelation. It was all too much to take in. Her dad maybe wasn't her dad, and her mum wasn't the person she'd always thought she was. If what Sylvie claimed was true, it changed so much of what she'd thought about herself. She wasn't an only child. She had a sister and a grandma in Glasgow, a whole different life. And on top of that, this possible father was already dead. There would be no chance to get to know him. Her head was spinning. She'd exchanged numbers with Sylvie and promised to get in touch soon. She'd liked her, there was no denying there was a connection between them. But even though a lot of Sylvie's tale added up, she couldn't quite bring herself to believe it. She was sure there had to be another explanation, and she knew the only person who could sort everything out was her mum. Eilidh picked her phone up as soon as she sat down in the car, but then she changed her mind: this wasn't a conversation to have on the phone, she'd have to drive to Strathglen and ask about this face to face. The text symbol was flashing on her notifications, so she quickly checked them before setting off. There was just one text, from Beth, telling her she'd discovered that most of the people cleared from the holiday village site had gone to Nova Scotia. She'd contacted a local history centre over there to see if they had any information about the Ardmhor villagers, and if there had been any rumours about someone going missing. Eilidh didn't hold out much hope —the Clearance had taken place almost two centuries ago. Anyway, the mystery in her own family had eclipsed that of the unidentified skeleton.

CHAPTER THIRTEEN

The past

Esther

All day my thoughts revolved around Hiram. I just couldn't stop thinking about him. All I wanted was to recreate what I'd been feeling when Cait woke me so rudely. Each time I've allowed my mind to wander back to the way he kissed me, I've felt hot, as if I'm standing in the burning midday sun. I don't know if it will feel the same once we're married and kissing is something we are supposed to do. Maybe I enjoyed it so much because I know it's wrong to sneak off into the woods, but imagine if it does still feel that wonderful! With each task I carried out,

I thought about Hiram and when I'd next see him—hoping we'd manage to sneak off and be alone. His kisses replayed in my head a thousand times, and I imagined what we might name our children. I daydreamed about us moving away—perhaps to Edinburgh. I'd have the most beautifully fitted dresses, and people would admire what a handsome couple we made as we visited the theatre. I wondered when he'd actually ask me to marry him. Yes, my thoughts were with him all day.

Well, they were with him most of the time. They might have wandered for a while early this morning, but I can hardly be blamed for that. After being wrenched from my dreams and having to suffer the indignity of being told off by my mother, as well as being laughed at by Fergus and Isobel, it was impossible to resist spending some time plotting elaborate ways to make Fergus disappear. Then this afternoon, I have to admit, I got lost in my hatred of Fergus again for a while. This time, I didn't even see him. I simply overheard old Annie and old Morag talking about what a godsend he was because he'd make sure they weren't short of peat for the winter. It made my blood boil. No one would ever be left without peat. The village always makes sure of that. They'd have got their peats regardless of Fergus. I don't see why people act like he's so wonderful when he's just doing the same jobs everyone else does. No one goes into raptures about how well

I've milked the cow. So, my thoughts were mostly taken up with how much I love Hiram, apart from when they were taken up with how much I hate Fergus.

It wasn't until evening that I finally saw Hiram. He was just on the other side of the burn, ready to walk into the village. I'd tried to make excuses for a walk down to the harbour earlier, to see if anyone needed any help. It was purely so I'd be able to walk past the factor's house and hopefully catch sight of him. However, Mam had seen straight through me.

"You know full well there's no help needed at the shore today, as all the men are off cutting the peats," she'd said. "You'll just have to wait until tonight to catch sight of those golden curls again. And that's only if you've made yourself useful. You'll be spinning with me tonight, if I've had to waste all day keeping an eye on you."

So I'd had to buckle down to work to avoid missing the chance of seeing him at all. At least Mother hadn't added something about Fergus's mam not needing to remind him of his responsibilities. She often does, so I suppose I should be grateful to have been spared for once. With a lot of effort, I finally completed everything I needed to, but it felt like the longest day of my life. I dropped things, and I nearly let the youngest of the bairns get burnt when I took my eyes off her and she strayed too close to the fire. Even the cow wouldn't settle and let down her milk. I had to sing every song I could remember to get her calm, and for someone with my singing voice, that was no easy task.

But finally, finally, I saw Hiram in the distance. I spent just one moment pinching my cheeks and straightening my skirts, so that I'd look my best when I reached him, but that one moment was all it took; when I looked back round, Fergus was already bounding towards him. I set off down to the stream, anyway. After the way Hiram had dragged me off into the woods the night before, I knew that he'd rather spend time with me than Fergus. But as I got nearer, something made me change my mind. I don't know what it was exactly, it's not like me, but suddenly I felt shy. The Hiram who took me off into the woods was different from the boy I've always known. He was commanding, and for once I hadn't been the one in charge. I'd been thrilling at the memories all day, but now I was near him all my confidence seemed to vanish. Hiram and Fergus were clearly deep in conversation. Neither of them noticed me watching them. They were totally engrossed in whatever they were saying to each other. It was then I realised they were arguing, something I'd never seen happen between them before. I was desperate to know what was going on, but somehow, I couldn't take a single step closer. Instead, I found myself edging away. Despite how curious I was, I knew I'd learn nothing by getting involved now. I'd have to be patient and bide my time. Slowly, I edged my way back towards the houses. By the time I saw Hiram rise to his feet and storm away, I was hidden from view.

The next day was Sunday, which meant less work and also the opportunity to slip away for a while. I'd already seen Hiram in church, but as usual, he was alongside his family at the front, and I was too far back to catch his eye. The sermon seemed to last forever. I couldn't even tell you what it had been about. The words drifted past me in one long, monotonous drone. My eyes wandered to the tall windows. For reasons I don't understand, probably just plain old meanness, they are set too high in the wall to see out of, instead they just torment me with the promise of sunshine outside. Then I focused on the back of Hiram's head, imagining my fingers tangling amidst his tumble of curls. For what felt like hours, my gaze flitted between the window and Hiram, then between Hiram and the window, both held much more interest than the words from the front of the church. When the service was finally over and we made our way out into the sunlit churchyard, I was dismayed to find the Stewart family long gone. Lord MacAird was away again, and Mr Stewart never lingers long after church when he isn't there to impress.

Later in the day, I finally got my chance to

take a walk down to the harbour. A walk that I obviously intended to take me slowly past the factor's house. Before the house came into view, I heard raised voices. They were too muffled for me to be able to understand the topic of discussion, but it was impossible not to notice the anger behind the words. I moved cautiously closer until I could see the owners of the voices. It was as I had suspected, Hiram and his father. It was no surprise to see the two of them in the middle of a disagreement. Everyone knows how often the two of them clash. However, it was a surprise to realise that the loudest and angriest of the pair was Hiram. Usually, he quietly accepts his father's criticisms, looking for all the world like an innocent bystander who has strayed into the path of a madman. But today it was the other way round, today Hiram had taken the role of the madman for himself. I kept out of sight. I knew this wasn't a scene intended for my eyes. Although Hiram was shouting, his anger distorted his words, and I couldn't work out what he was saying. His father, although quieter, was much clearer. His tone was calm, almost mocking, in the face of Hiram's obvious distress. Snatches of Mr Stewart's replies made their way to my ears.

"No concern of yours", "They'll be looked after", "They've got away with it for long enough", "It means you can have your fun without worrying", "Are you not even man enough for that?"

Each snippet made no sense without the words that should have surrounded it, but each carried just enough information to lead me to a thousand more questions. The last statement I'd heard had been the easiest to understand. It was a common refrain between Hiram and his father. Mr Stewart thought Hiram was too sensitive, too fond of his books, too keen on studying nature rather than killing it, and too full of concern for his fellow humans to be the son he wanted. In his eyes, it was his second son, George, who embodied everything a man should be. It would have been better for Hiram if he'd been the second born. There would have been less pressure on him if he didn't have to carry the weight of his father's expectations. However, it would be much worse for my dreams. If Hiram was the second son, he wouldn't be able to offer me the life I've been living in my head for so long now, and the prospect of marrying George is much less appealing. As the suggestion that Hiram lacks manliness is nothing new, his reaction shocked me. His face contorted, his fist clenched, his arm drew back, and then he hit his father. A swift punch connecting clearly with his face. I have never, in the whole time I have known him, seen Hiram resort to violence before. I almost didn't think that he could. Then Mr Stewart reacted just as oddly. He laughed, rubbing his face lightly, as if a drop of rain, or the tip of a bird's wing, had merely brushed against it. He laughed long and loud and clear. The pain that should have shown on his face was on Hiram's instead. Mr Stewart looked as if he didn't have a care in the world. It was with a smile on his face that he threw his first punch, and then another, and another. I gasped from my place in the shadows as the blows continued to fall. Hiram was on the floor in seconds. Mr Stewart continued to laugh as he kicked Hiram's stomach before walking away. This time, although his words were thrown casually over his shoulder, every single one was as clear as day.

"Even when you show a sign of what I want, you manage to let me down."

Hiram's response was no more than a whimper. With the door to the factor's house now slammed shut, I ran from my hiding spot to reach him. But as I moved, I noticed a figure running from the opposite direction. I wasn't the only witness to the argument. I think my heart sank at the sight of Fergus more than it had at the sight of Hiram on the floor. Why did he always have to be there? Why did he have to be involved in every moment that should have remained private between Hiram and me? Although I felt it should be me comforting Hiram, I slowed my pace. As Fergus finally registered my presence, he motioned for me to go, and my feet did as he asked before my mind processed why. Perhaps I knew deep down that Hiram wouldn't appreciate knowing I had seen him humiliated. No matter how much I hated Fergus, I had to accept that, in this situation, he was the person Hiram would want.

I fretted for him throughout the day. Anxiously watching out for Fergus arriving home so that I could find out how Hiram was. It was late when I finally spotted Fergus weaving his way through the lower houses, making his way up the edge of the fields. I was half-heartedly helping mother to ready the wee ones for bed, but I broke off from my task and ran to meet him.

"Fergus! What's going on? What were they arguing about? I've never seen Hiram react like that before."

"If Hiram wants you to know, I'm sure he'll tell you himself."

That was all he said, his voice as smug as usual. Fergus knew full well there had been no chance for Hiram to tell me anything because he himself had sent me away. Now he was using the fact I had followed his instructions to imply that Hiram preferred to talk to him. I was incensed, but I tried my hardest to bite down my anger. I knew snapping at Fergus would get me nowhere.

"Can you at least tell me if he is alright? I thought Mr Stewart was going to kill him."

"He's sore, but he'll survive. It's up to him if he wants to tell you anything else."

"Do you know what they were talking about though? Mr Stewart said something about people getting away with things for too long and that they'd be taken care of. I couldn't work out what he meant, but it didn't sound good."

"I've told you already, Esther, if Hiram wants to tell you about it, he will. Until then, don't you think you should see what your mother wants instead?"

I'd been doing well at ignoring Mam's calls. They'd been following me since the moment I'd run from the house. I suppose I had been in the middle of untangling little Mary's hair when I'd caught sight of Fergus and rushed off. I'd have thought Mam would have been pleased. She's always going on at me to make more effort with Fergus. Then when I do what she wants, she's still not happy. Just at that moment, Isobel appeared. It was no surprise that dull old Isobel, with her shiny gold flecked hair, had been keeping an eye out for Fergus's return. She's obsessed with him and has been for years. Despite living in our cluster of houses, she's never been part of our little group. At first, at a year older, I think she thought she was too grown up for Hiram, Fergus, and me. Then as we got bigger, she wasn't brave enough to join in our games. She never did manage to jump the burn in one leap, and after Fergus had to rescue her, she didn't try again. Also, by then, it was too late—our three didn't have room for anyone else. That was before Fergus ruined it all and started leaving me out as well.

"Your mother's shouting you, Esther," Isobel said, stating the obvious in the way that dull people do.

"I can hear her myself. Thank you, Isobel," I replied.

"Don't you think you should see what she wants, then? Don't worry, I'll keep Fergus company."

She was starting to sound almost as smug as he did.

"I'm sure you will," I muttered as I turned to head back up the hill.

So there were to be no answers to my questions. I was glad to know that Hiram was alright, that his injuries weren't life threatening, but I still had no idea what had led to them in the first place. I didn't know what they had been arguing about or what had caused Hiram to react so uncharacteristically. And somehow I was supposed to sleep with all these unknowns floating around my head. The fact I could hear Isobel and Fergus's laughter drifting up the hill did nothing to aid my gentleness as I finished my work on poor Mary's hair. Her tears matched my frustration, and I barely noticed when Mam removed the brush from my hand and pushed me out of the way with a long-suffering sigh.

CHAPTER FOURTEEN

The present

There had been an accident on the road to Strathglen. Although those involved had escaped serious injury and recovery trucks were now clearing the road, there was still a huge queue of traffic waiting to pass, and Eilidh was stuck right at the back of it. She flicked through the CDs that lived in a heap on the floor, but nothing grabbed her. It was at times like this she wished her car wasn't so old and that she could link her phone to the stereo. Instead, she had to make do with the radio, switching through the frequencies, trying to find a traffic report. By the time she reached Strathglen, she'd done a lot of thinking. She still couldn't grasp the idea that Alan might not be her father. Obviously, she could understand the abstract concept of it, it wasn't that uncommon a story, and if it was happening to someone else, she wouldn't consider it a particularly big deal. But it was impossible to accept it as a story about her and the people she knew better than anyone else in the world.

As she parked her car, Eilidh wondered how she was going to broach the subject with her mum. How could she possibly ask the questions that might tear their lives apart? Although Eilidh had a key to her parents' house, she always knocked and waited to be let in. It had been a long time since she'd lived with them, and it seemed the polite thing to do. When Claire opened the door, Eilidh thought she saw signs of worry around her eyes. Was that because her mum knew who she'd been to meet and was afraid of what she might have found out? Or was she just imagining things because of Sylvie's claims?

"This is a lovely surprise. How did your meeting go? It was Sylvie, wasn't it? The name of the girl you were meeting."

"Yes, she's called Sylvie," replied Eilidh, following her mum into the kitchen.

"And did she seem nice?" Claire prompted, flicking the switch on the kettle.

"She did. She seemed a lot like me, actually. In fact, she even looked a bit like me."

Claire put down the cups she had in her hands. She didn't reach for the tea bags as she usually would. She didn't turn around or look at Eilidh either, she simply stopped moving. That was when Eilidh knew she hadn't imagined the look of worry earlier. Something was wrong. The silence grew heavy and uncomfortable, and Eilidh's direct nature couldn't stand the tension.

"Sylvie said she was my sister, that her dad is my dad as well. There was a photo of you together. She said you ran away when you were pregnant and broke his heart. It's not true, is it, Mum?"

Claire stayed still as a statue for a moment longer, and Eilidh held her breath, waiting for her world to collapse. But when Claire finally turned round, she had a bright smile fixed on her face.

"Of course it's not true, sweetheart. She'll have just got something confused along the way. Why don't you have a look in the cupboard and see what biscuits we've got in?"

Eilidh felt no sense of relief. Her mum's reaction was too odd to be genuine, but she did as she was told and looked for the biscuit tin. She had no intention of letting the matter rest, but she needed to work out the right questions to ask.

Claire looked calm as she finished making the tea. She seemed steady as she put their drinks down on the table and reached out plates for their biscuits. However, how she felt was a different matter. On the inside, she was in turmoil. The moment she'd dreaded since before Eilidh's birth had finally arrived, and she needed Alan by her side to deal with it. They should have had a plan in place so she'd know what to say. Inevitably, this day had been coming, and they should have been prepared. Claire knew the wrong words could send her whole life crashing down. Alan should be back any minute, she told herself. She just had to bide her time and steer the conversation onto something else. If she could just hold out until Alan got home, he'd know what to do.

"So, have there been any more developments up at the holiday village?" Claire asked, reaching a custard cream out of the biscuit tin, trying desperately to hide the fact her life was crumbling around her.

"It's going fine," replied Eilidh, refusing to let herself get side-tracked. "So why did Sylvie have a photo of you if she's just confused? You looked very close to the man in it. The one she says is my dad."

"I don't know. I mean, I know I always say that your dad is my only love, but that doesn't mean he's the only boyfriend I've ever had. There were others before him. Maybe it's just a photo of me and one of them."

"But why would she be so certain? Why would she have been so determined to track me down, if it was simply a photo of her dad and some random ex-girlfriend?"

"I don't know, Eilidh!" Claire snapped, losing the calm reserve she'd been clinging to so desperately. "I wasn't there," she began again, more quietly. "It's hard to know what this girl is thinking when I haven't met her or heard what she had to say."

"But you knew someone called Sylvie, didn't you? When I first asked you about her, you looked funny when I said her name and then you didn't want me to meet her. Hang on, was her mum called Sylvie as well? Did you know her mum? Were you having an affair with her dad?" Eilidh's face fell as another thought occurred to her. "Were you cheating on Dad with him? Does Dad even know?"

"It's her gran," interrupted Claire, sounding defeated. "It's her gran that's called Sylvie, well, Sylvia actually."

"So you do know her? Am I right then? You had an affair and Dad doesn't even know I'm not his."

"No!" Claire shouted. "That's not it at all. Her gran wasn't a very nice woman. I've never forgotten her and that's why I reacted to the name. I knew as soon as you mentioned this girl that there would be a connection to Sylvia."

"Mum, I couldn't care less about her gran. I just want to know whether she was telling me the truth. Is Sylvie's dad, Keith, my father?"

Claire replied so quietly that Eilidh could barely hear.

"Yes."

"What? Did you say yes? You mean Dad's not my dad?"

"Yes," Claire said again, this time more definitely. "But it's not what you think."

They were both startled by Alan walking into the room. They hadn't heard his key in the lock, or him taking his boots off in the hall.

"Hello, my dears," he said, taking in their ashen faces with confusion.

Eilidh ignored him, fixing Claire in her gaze and saying bitterly, "It's exactly what I think. Everything you've ever said to me has been a lie, and you've robbed me of my chance to know him because he's dead. I don't want to speak to you ever again."

She pushed past Alan, shoved her feet back into her trainers and was reversing her car before he'd had the chance to work out what was going on. From his spot by the kitchen door, he could see the gravel flying under the wheels of Eilidh's car as it sped up the drive. To the other side of him, he could see his wife dissolving into a mess of tears. He tried to get her to explain what had happened, but he was struggling to get a response. He hadn't seen her like this since those dark days when they'd first left Glasgow. Even in the terrible days before that, when they'd been planning their escape, it had been Claire that had held everything together. It had been him that panicked every time his landlady's phone rang, terrified that something had gone wrong, terrified she'd been hurt. He reached for the tissue box and tried to dry her tears, but the flow was constant. He thought over Eilidh's words. Who was dead? A sense of fear gripped him. Please God, not Rich. Surely nothing had happened to him.

"What did she mean, Claire? Who's dead? Is Rich alright? Has something happened to Rich?"

He was panicking now, and his desperation somehow seemed to penetrate the bubble Claire had locked herself in.

"No, not Rich."

Alan breathed a sigh of relief and started again, still none the wiser.

"Just talk to me, sweetheart. I'm sure we can sort everything out, but I can't help if I don't know what's going on."

Alan felt as though hours passed before Claire finally spoke.

"It's Keith," she whispered, her voice still distorted by sobs. "That girl she met was his daughter. She knows Keith's her father."

Alan didn't hesitate. He'd tried to reassure

Claire that Eilidh's interest in the FamilyFinder tests was nothing to worry about, the chances of one of Keith's relatives having done the same tests seemed low, but it appeared he'd been wrong. He pulled Claire to her feet and grabbed the car keys.

Screeching to a halt outside Eilidh's house, Alan pounded on the door. Rich opened it within seconds. He didn't seem surprised to find Alan on the doorstep.

"She's already gone," he said simply.

"Where?" Alan asked.

"Somewhere in Glasgow. I'm not sure she knows where exactly."

"Why didn't you stop her? She won't be in a fit state to drive all that way," Alan shouted in frustration.

"I tried, but short of locking her up, there was nothing I could do, and I don't think you'd really want me to treat your daughter like that."

Alan rubbed his hands over his face. "I'm sorry Rich, I didn't mean to have a go at you. I know there's no stopping her when she's got a bee in her bonnet. Did she tell you why she was going?"

"Not in any way that made sense. She was obviously upset, which is why I didn't want her to go. But she wouldn't talk, she just kept muttering about Claire lying to her and needing to speak to Sylvie again, you know, the girl she went to meet today. I don't have a clue what's going on, only that she said she needed to leave right away. When I realised there was no talking her out of it, I tried to go with her, but she was adamant she wanted to be alone. Do you know what's going on? Everything's alright, isn't it?"

"No, son, I don't think it is. Did she give you an address?"

Rich shook his head. "I don't think she knows where she's going herself. But as soon as I speak to her, I'll let you know where she is."

"Thanks Rich. We'd appreciate that."

"Do you want to come in? Talk about what's going on?"

Alan could hear football on the telly and voices in the background.

"No, you're alright, I'd better get Claire home. To be honest, I'm not sure I know much more than you do at the moment. Just let me know as soon as you hear anything."

"I will," Rich replied, surprised to find himself crushed into a bear hug.

It was his mother-in-law that was the tactile one. Alan was normally more reserved when it came to physical contact, but it seemed that today was not a normal day. Rich watched their car pull out of the drive before he shut the door and returned to Andrew, Ali, and the match.

Picking up his beer, he tried to relax back into what had been a simple afternoon with mates, but he didn't let his phone out of sight. He needed to know that Eilidh was safe.

CHAPTER FIFTEEN

The past

Fergus

When I watched Hiram hit his father and then saw his father hit him back, I didn't know what to do. I was on my way home from the harbour when I heard raised voices and I slowed down to work out what was happening. As I rounded the corner, I could see Hiram and Mr Stewart clearly, but I couldn't work out what they were arguing about. The moment I saw Hiram lash out, I wanted to help him; I knew Mr Stewart wouldn't just walk away. But Hiram's words from the previous night made me hesitate. He'd said he didn't need me to protect him. Every instinct told me to help, but what about Hiram's wishes?

As I faltered the attack came to an end. Mr Stewart walked away, slamming the door behind him, and I ran towards Hiram, scared of what I would find. It was only once I was kneeling by Hiram's side that I realised Esther had also been watching. I was grateful that she listened to me for once and left us alone. Hiram might love her, but I knew the last thing he'd need was her overreacting and making everything worse. And, in fairness to Esther, my reaction had been extreme enough. The relief I felt when he opened his eyes was intense. His nose was bloody, and he was going to have a huge black eye, but remarkably it didn't look as though his nose was broken, and all of his teeth seemed to have survived. He winced as he sat up, so the kick to his stomach had obviously found its target, but he could move, so I hoped there was no serious damage.

"Do you want me to take you into the house?" I asked. "I could get your mother so she can clean you up."

"No," he replied. "I don't want to go in there. I can't face him yet."

We wandered into the woods at the back of the house instead, my arm supporting him with each painful step. A short distance away was a spot where we'd often played as children. The trees opened out into a small circular clearing with rocks scattered around the edges. Esther used to make us pretend it was a stone circle placed there by the fairies and destroyed by an angry monster of the woods. Sometimes we'd go along with her story, pretending to banish the monster with sticks as our swords. Other times Esther would have to play our game and we would be soldiers, the rocks acting as the ruins of our fort. A fort felt like what we needed at that moment, a safe place to keep everything else at bay while Hiram recovered. We arranged ourselves on the largest of the rocks, Hiram moving cautiously, trying to find a way to sit that didn't hurt, and I looked at his face more closely.

"You're going to have an amazing bruise," I said.

Hiram attempted a small smile, but he didn't speak.

"I'm sorry about yesterday," I offered. "You're right. It's not my place to question how you behave. I know you don't need that, and I know you can look after yourself."

There was still no answer from Hiram, just a sad little laugh.

"So what made you hit him?" I asked, trying again. "He's been on at you for so long and he's hit you so many times, but you've never hit him back. What made you hit first today?"

"I don't know," Hiram said eventually. "I honestly don't know where it came from."

"Well, what were you talking about? What had made you so angry?"

"It was just the usual things, me not being good enough, me being a disappointment."

"But he says those things all the time. I mean, they are awful things to say, and he deserved to get hit, but it's not like you haven't heard it all before."

"There were some other things to do with work as well, some changes Lord MacAird has planned."

"Well, they must be quite some changes to make you turn to violence after all you've put up with in the past."

"They are," Hiram stated flatly.

It obviously intrigued me what Lord MacAird had in mind that had riled Hiram so much, but it didn't seem right to push him if he didn't want to volunteer the information.

"Do you feel up to walking?" I asked instead, thinking perhaps we could go fishing off the rocks further along the shore. I thought it might help take Hiram's mind off things, and his pain seemed to be easing.

We walked through the trees and eventually emerged into the open just above the shoreline, picking our way across the rocks until we reached a large slab that jutted out into the sea. I only had my pocket-knife with me, so the chances of us being lucky enough to spear a fish were slim, but it was more about doing something than trying to catch a meal. I lay on my front, my face hanging over the water, and Hiram sat to the side of me, just watching. All was quiet except the lapping of the sea. When Hiram finally spoke we'd been silent for so long that the words sounded strange.

"You're the only person I can rely on," he said. "My father thinks I'm useless, George definitely agrees with him, and my mother doesn't seem to care either way. She's never spoken up for me when he's gone into one of his rages. In fact, she never really speaks to me at all. None of them do. You're the only person that cares about me, so I'm sorry I was rude to you last night. I know you were trying to help."

"I'm sure they care, really." I replied. That wasn't true. I was fairly certain that Hiram's description of how his family felt was accurate, but denying it somehow seemed the right thing to do. "I mean, your father is so set in his ways that your mother probably just finds it easier to agree with him. I'm sure they must care in their own way."

"Well, I'm glad that you're sure." Hiram plunged my knife into the water, narrowly missing a fish as it darted out of reach.

"I'm sure I'm not the only person that cares, either," I said. "What about Esther?"

I don't really know why I went down

that path. The last thing Hiram needed to be worrying about was whether Esther was someone he could trust. Maybe I just couldn't resist the chance to hear him speak badly of her.

"You know as well as I do what Esther really thinks of me. I'm not saying she doesn't love me —I actually think she does in her own way—but she doesn't love me because she's interested in me as a person. It's not even about what I look like. She loves the life she thinks she'll have if she marries me. I'm sure she'd always stand by me, but she doesn't care about me like you do."

Although I wasn't convinced Esther would always stand by him, I couldn't argue with Hiram's summary of her feelings, so I didn't interrupt.

"The thing that upset me most when my father told me I'd have to go away wasn't that I knew I'd lose Esther. It wasn't having to leave all this behind, either, because I know that one day I'll be back. What I was furious about was knowing I'd lose you. By the time I come back, everything will be different. I should be married. You'll probably be married as well, and I have no doubt Esther will be. Maybe you'll be married to each other. But that wouldn't even bother me. The worst thing about having to leave is that you and I are over. There won't be any more days like this."

I laughed before I replied. "I can guarantee you

130

I won't be married to Esther, and I am certain no matter how old we get, there will always be chances to sneak away for an afternoon and not catch any fish."

"I don't think there will be though. We'll be different people by then. You'll be the one paying rent and I'll be the one collecting it. And that's if nothing else changes."

"No, that's not true," I argued. "Whatever happens, we'll always be us, Hiram. No matter how much time goes by, that will never change. We'll always be friends."

Hiram didn't reply, but he did at least smile, so I hoped he believed what I was saying. I certainly meant every word. There isn't much I can be sure of, but I know Hiram will always be the person I'll want to talk to, the person I'll always be looking out for. For over ten years, we've spent every day together. I know our friendship won't change just because we'll get older, and Hiram will be more powerful than me. If anything, it's reassuring that he'll be the factor one day. It feels like our future will be in safe hands.

As the sun dropped in the sky, we trudged back towards the factor's house, following the edge of the shore. Hiram moved slowly, so he didn't jolt himself and make his stomach hurt more than it already did. As we reached his house, I asked if he wouldn't rather come back to the village with me, but Hiram didn't want to.

Instead, he reassured me he'd be alright and that he'd rather go to bed and try to sleep off the worst of the pain.

I could see Esther running down the hill towards me as I made my way out of the lower houses. I knew that if I was in her position, I'd be desperate to know what was going on, but I really didn't want to talk to her. The time I'd just spent with Hiram felt too personal to discuss with Esther, so it was an effort even to tell her he was alright. I was relieved that her mother was shouting for her, and I was even more relieved when Isobel appeared and forced Esther to go home.

But that wasn't the only reason I was pleased to see Isobel. It felt good to laugh with her as we stood looking out over the sea. The last rays of the sun picked out the gold in her hair until it shone like a halo around her face. I reached out gently, twirling a strand round my finger, and Isobel smiled up at me. Esther might be the prettiest girl in the village, but I know without doubt which girl I'd rather be with. Hiram has nothing to fear there.

CHAPTER SIXTEEN

The present

The majesty of the scenery on the drive south from Ardmhor had never failed to impress Eilidh. It didn't matter that she had known it all her life and that really a flat, urban expanse should have seemed more exotic to her. There had never been a day when she hadn't noticed the beauty that surrounded her. There had never been a time when the sea had failed to calm her. Today, though, the scenery barely registered as she made her way south for the second time. Her mind couldn't take in anything other than the road in front of her, and even that was forgotten the second she rounded the next bend. She had always been so secure in who she was. The idea of that identity being built on lies seemed to have rendered her incapable of thought. Perhaps that was what people meant when they described some discoveries as mind-blowing. She had already passed the southern end of Loch Lomond when it occurred to her she didn't know where she was going. She had exchanged numbers with Sylvie, but hadn't a clue where she lived. Also, she wasn't sure she was ready to meet the rest of a family she hadn't known existed until lunchtime that day.

As the dual carriageway swapped countryside for the start of urban life, Eilidh spotted the logo of a chain hotel. She indicated at the roundabout and pulled into the car park. It was already early evening, and the light was rapidly fading from the sky. She'd left home without a plan and suddenly it seemed important to have one. Finding somewhere to stay felt like a good place to start. She was in luck, as the hotel had availability. It was still early spring, before the tourist season had really begun. If she'd enquired about a room on a Saturday night in summer without a prior reservation, she'd probably have been laughed out of the reception area.

Making her way down the brightly lit corridor, Eilidh almost laughed at the strangeness of the situation. She'd expected to meet a new cousin and then end the day with a few drinks at the Ardmhor Hotel, not find herself alone on the outskirts of Glasgow. Shutting the door to her room, Eilidh rested her head against the cool wood. She knew she ought to phone Rich. He'd looked worried by her strange behaviour earlier, and he'd probably been panicking about whether she'd been fit to drive. However, she knew if she called him, there would be a whole host of questions to answer that she couldn't face yet. In the end she typed out a quick text letting him know she was safe and that she'd call him soon. The thought flashed through her mind that her parents would also be worried, but that soon led to her wondering if she could even call them that anymore. She decided against contacting them. Let them worry. This was all their fault, anyway

Or maybe it wasn't. Her mind was galloping off again. Certainly, her mum had to be to blame, but did her dad even know? Maybe she should try speaking to him? Or see what Rich thought she should do? But that would mean having to explain everything, and she didn't know if she could say out loud to anyone that Alan wasn't really her dad. She switched on the telly in a bid to stop herself from thinking, but nothing held her attention. She tried to read, but found it impossible to even choose a book from the app on her phone. It wasn't like her not to know exactly what she wanted to do. It was disconcerting and uncomfortable. She contemplated phoning Beth. Maybe it would be easier to talk to someone outside the situation, and Beth definitely knew how it felt to be unsure, but again, it would involve explaining everything, and she knew she couldn't put it all into words yet. Eventually, she decided to write down everything she knew about her parents, Keith, and Sylvie. She hoped that committing the details to paper would help them sink in; however, seeing the words mum and affair next to each other in stark black and white did nothing to help.

After a while, she grabbed her coat and left the room. She hadn't tried fresh air yet. Maybe that could help her make sense of things. She took a side street heading away from the dull roar of the traffic on the dual carriageway. Passing a park, empty and forbidding in the darkness, she found herself on a residential street. The lights were on in most of the houses, and some hadn't got as far as closing their curtains or blinds yet. All around her, Eilidh caught glimpses of families going about their business in their own private worlds. Were any of them being torn apart by secrets she wondered? It was odd to see life going on as normal, when it seemed to her nothing could ever be normal again. She watched a man swinging a pyjama clad child over his shoulder. The child laughed, burying their face into the man's neck. Eilidh imagined it was a dad carrying his precious daughter up to bed, something Alan had done for her many times when she'd claimed to be too tired to make it up the stairs. How could Alan possibly not be her dad?

Since Sylvie's revelations, Eilidh had either acted instinctively, like going to question her mum, and setting off for Glasgow, or doubt and indecision had crippled her. Now the instinct seemed to return. She'd taken out her phone and dialled her dad's mobile before she'd registered what she was doing.

"Sweetheart! Are you alright? We've been so worried."

Eilidh waited until he was quiet before speaking. There was only one question she needed answering.

"Did you know?" was all she said.

The line was quiet, and she wondered for a moment whether she'd lost her signal and been cut off, but then she heard his reply.

"Yes. I've always known, but it's not what you think. We had…"

Eilidh didn't let him finish.

"I never want to speak to you again," was all she said before ending the call.

So they had both been lying to her. The McRae's, the very image of the perfect family, were just that, an image. There was nothing real about them. Her whole identity was a lie. Being Eilidh McRae was so important to her she hadn't even considered changing her name when she'd married Rich, but now it seemed she'd never been a McRae in the first place. She didn't even know what her surname should have been.

That was the moment her usual decisiveness returned. She knew what she needed to do. She had to move forward. It was obvious now, there was only one option. She couldn't trust Alan and Claire for answers, not now she knew they'd both been lying to her. The only way to feel she knew who she was again was to get to know her new family. She reached her phone back out of her pocket and dialled her newest contact.

"Hi Sylvie, it's Eilidh. I know it's short notice, but I'm in the area and I wondered if I could come and see you tomorrow?"

By nine o'clock the next morning, Eilidh was listening carefully to the sat nav on her phone as it guided her to Sylvie's address in Glasgow. After two wrong turnings and subsequent u-turns, she finally pulled up outside a sandstone block of flats. Sylvie was by the door waving wildly, so she knew she'd reached the right place.

"I thought you should arrive about now, and it's not easy to work out how to get into this place," Sylvie explained before Eilidh had even shut her car door.

"Thanks so much for meeting me. I hope I'm not interrupting any plans you had."

"Not at all," beamed Sylvie. "This is what I've been dreaming about my whole life. Come in and meet Chris, and then we'll go round to Gran's when you're ready."

Eilidh noticed that Sylvie's use of the word gran was including her as a fellow granddaughter. It was surreal that she and this virtual stranger shared a family. She was definitely going to need a coffee before tackling any more introductions. Sylvie's flat was bright and modern with enormous windows overlooking the city. Her partner, Chris, stood to greet them as they came in. He was one of those people who made you feel instantly at ease. His huge smile made Eilidh think of Rich, and she resolved to phone him as soon as she got the chance. Alan had tried to ring her so many times the previous night that after sending Rich a text telling him she loved him, she'd turned her phone off. When she'd turned it back on this morning, she hadn't been brave enough to check any messages.

Although conversation flowed easily, and it was tempting to stick to small talk rather than risk ruining the atmosphere, Eilidh had questions she needed to ask.

"Do you have any idea why my mum left? Was she having an affair with your dad? Or was she cheating on him with mine? When I say your dad, I know he's my father as well, but I can't get used to thinking of it that way."

"This must be so hard for you," responded Sylvie, looking pained. "I've been so desperate to meet you that I hadn't really considered I'd be ripping your life apart in the process."

"It's okay," Eilidh said, smiling in Sylvie's direction, touched by her concern. "I don't know if you can destroy something that wasn't real in the first place. So, do you know why my mum left?"

"No, I don't. But Gran will be able to tell you more. All I know is that she disappeared, and Dad was heartbroken."

As Chris drove them across the city, to the house where Sylvie had grown up, and where her gran still lived, Eilidh was struggling to adjust the idea of the mum she'd always known, the woman who looked after everyone and loved nothing more than cooking for friends, to that of a wanton heart breaker. It felt like the world was shifting slightly.

Sylvia's house was a boxy semi, that looked as though it had been built from concrete in the sixties. Although it wouldn't win any beauty contests, it was well maintained, with clean windows, a shiny front door, and a garden full of ornaments. The door opened before they'd reached the top of the path. A short, stout lady, with a helmet of grey hair, put her hands to her mouth and promptly burst into tears.

"I've always hoped this day would come. I'd

have known you as Keith's bairn anywhere. You've a real look of him."

The lady, who had now been introduced as Sylvia, was still dabbing at her eyes as she spoke. They were sitting on a floral, velvet three-piece suite and Sylvie was pouring out cups of tea.

"I'm so sorry for your loss. I really wish I'd been able to meet him," Eilidh said, taking hold of the older woman's hand. She might have only just met her, but she instinctively wanted to comfort her.

"Me too, lass, he never got over your mum taking you away like that."

"Do you know why she did?" Eilidh asked tentatively, not sure the answer was going to be easy to hear.

"I can't answer that one for you. One minute she was here, and we were all looking forward to you being born. Then the next minute she'd disappeared. Keith doted on her, you know. He'd have done anything for her, anything. He never recovered."

"But he moved on? I mean, he met Sylvie's mum and started a new family."

"Aye, he did. He tried his best to get over being abandoned like that, but he was never the same. He always struggled afterwards."

Another thought struck Eilidh. "Did you know Alan as well? The man I've always thought was my dad."

"Yes, I did. I knew him very well. He was your dad's best friend. I always think that was what made it worse for him. The fact it was the two people he loved the most betraying him. You don't get over something like that."

"Did he try to look for me?"

"Oh, he tried everything. He knew Alan came from this little place up north, so he went there, trying to track them down. Eventually he found them, but Alan threatened him. He got a group of blokes to beat him up and then they moved again, and this time no one would let on where they'd gone."

Eilidh's head was spinning again. She had a father she'd never met who had tried desperately to find her. Her mum was some kind of floozy, and her dad, who might look like a bruiser, but who she'd always thought wouldn't harm a fly, had been handing out threats like a mafia boss. Her world wasn't just tilting slightly, it was totally off its axis.

Aside from the revelations, Eilidh actually found the afternoon at Sylvia's house lovely. Two of Keith's sisters came round, and then more and more of their adult children arrived, until the little house was bursting at its seams. Everyone was thrilled to meet Eilidh, and they welcomed her into the family like the prodigal son. It wouldn't have surprised her if someone had produced a fatted calf to sacrifice. She had always been in her element surrounded by people, and for the first time since her identity had been challenged, she felt a little like herself again. It made sense that this was the sort of family she should have had. They were noisy and loud and a bit in your face, and Eilidh felt she fitted right in. It was so different to the calm unit of three she'd grown up in, and she loved it. But she was angry as well, angry that she'd missed the chance to meet Keith, the most important piece of this family jigsaw. Alan and Claire's lies had denied her that, and they'd denied her the opportunity to be a proper part of this.

Before she set off home to Ardmhor, Eilidh promised Sylvie she'd be back the following weekend. She meant it too. This was her family now, Sylvie, Sylvia, and Keith's sisters and their children. She didn't think she'd ever be able to forgive Alan and Claire for what they'd stolen from her, and she certainly didn't want to speak to them again. Ardmhor was still home because it was where Rich was, but she no longer had the absolute conviction that it was where she belonged. Perhaps she didn't know where that place was anymore. Perhaps it was somewhere she was only just discovering.

CHAPTER SEVENTEEN

The past

Esther

I t was five days after our night in the woods, and three days after I'd seen his father attack him, when I finally got the chance to speak to Hiram again. I'd been thinking about him constantly; when his father kicked him as he lay on the ground, I honestly thought he might kill him. Although Fergus had told me that Hiram was alright, I only had his word for it, and I really wanted to see for myself that he wasn't badly hurt. The main reason I was desperate to see him, though, was because I couldn't get our time together in the woods out of my head.

I could barely concentrate on anything for

thinking about his kisses. If I'd just been clumsy or careless for one day, my mother probably wouldn't have noticed, but with my absent-mindedness stretching out for almost a week, Mam's patience had worn thin. She sent me off to look for Hiram before I'd even finished helping her ready the wee ones for sleep. That was something she'd never done before. She knew Hiram well, and she tolerated him, but she'd always made it clear he wouldn't be her choice. She had never encouraged me to seek him out. I think she'd grown so sick of the way I was moping around that she thought she had no other choice.

He was by the stream when I found him. I half expected Fergus to appear from nowhere and spirit him away, but for once it seemed I had Hiram to myself. He looked up as I approached. I fancied he'd sensed my presence because he'd been longing for my kisses as much as I'd been longing for his, but the reality was probably just that he had heard my footsteps. I was shocked by the state of his face, his stark black eye in such contrast to his soft, golden hair.

"That looks sore," I said to him, reaching out my hand to his face.

He stepped back quickly, turning away.

"Go away Esther. I don't want to see you now."

My heart was racing as I tried to work out what he meant. Did he regret what had happened between us on the night of the dancing? Had it changed how he felt about me?

"Why Hiram? Don't you like me anymore?"

"Of course I like you, Esther. I just don't want you seeing me like this. I don't want to talk about what happened."

"Oh, Hiram," I sighed, putting my arms around him and refusing to let go. "You don't need to explain anything. I was there. I saw what happened."

"I suppose that means you feel sorry for me as well," he replied angrily, sounding like a sulky child who'd been refused a treat.

"No!" I said hastily, before rethinking my answer. "Well, actually yes, I do, but only because you're unlucky to have a dad that's a horrible bully. I'd feel sorry for anyone who had to put up with that."

"But you saw what he did. You saw him beat me to the ground. You must have been laughing at me."

"Hiram, I wasn't laughing. I was scared. I thought he was going to kill you."

He shook himself free of my arms and looked me in the eye.

"So I'm right. You're just like everyone else. You don't think I can defend myself either."

"Hiram, stop it! I love you. I don't care if you can fight. It doesn't matter."

Then his face changed, and I couldn't read the expression in his eyes. He grabbed my arm and pulled me behind him. His grip was so strong, and he was moving so fast that I panicked he'd break my arm. I was struggling to keep up, stumbling over brambles and tree roots. For five days, I'd been dreaming of being alone with Hiram in the woods, and now I was there, I felt scared—something I'd never felt in his company before.

"Slow down, Hiram, please!" I cried.

His pace didn't alter though, even when I asked him again and again to stop.

"Please, Hiram, you're scaring me!"

Somehow that seemed to get through to him, although not really how I'd wanted it to.

"Oh, so I can make people afraid. I thought you'd just said I was some sort of coward who couldn't even stand up to his own father."

His voice was bitter, not at all like normal. I wasn't entirely sure how I'd angered him, but the person in front of me was not the boy I'd been feeling weak at the knees remembering all week. In all my many daydreams, I'd never once felt scared of him.

"That's not what I meant. You know that isn't what I meant. I don't think you're a coward. What I think is that your father is a horrible bully. I don't want you to behave like him."

"Well, he does. It's all he wants."

Hiram's voice was quieter by then, less like that of a stranger. I finally realised where we were. We were in the fairy circle, well that's what I'd always called it. Hiram and Fergus used to insist it was the ruins of an ancient fort. I used to love it there, hidden away from adult eyes. It used to feel like somewhere safe, but things were simpler when we were just children.

"Does it matter what your father wants? Surely you don't want to be like him. You always told me that if an argument was good enough, you could change people's minds without fighting. You're the clever one. You get what you want by knowing everything, not by using your fists."

Hiram shook his head. "You're just like Fergus. You both think you know what I am. Everyone either wants to change me or to tell me what I can't be."

He didn't seem unfamiliar or frightening now. He seemed like my normal head-in-the-clouds Hiram again, always sensitive and overthinking.

"I'm definitely not like Fergus, and I do know you," I said firmly. "We love each other, and I know that one day soon we'll be married. No one will be able to say you're not a proper man then."

We'd been sitting on separate rocks a little way apart from each other, but at that point, I moved across to him and positioned myself on his knee. It felt exciting to be so bold.

"I've been thinking about being alone with you ever since you took me into the woods on the night of the dancing," I said.

My heart was beating faster as I spoke, knowing how forward I was being. I moved closer to him, slowly edging my mouth towards his. Hiram's lips were just as soft as I remembered and they parted against mine, responding to the pressure. My hand reached behind his head, my fingers tangling into his curls, just as I'd been picturing as I sat in church. My thoughts at that moment definitely weren't suitable for church though.

"I've been wanting to do this all week," I said breathlessly. "I hope you've been wanting it, too."

I didn't get an answer in words, but I didn't need one. His actions made it clear he felt the same. He crushed himself against me. His tongue was in my mouth, and his hands were wandering to places where I knew I was supposed to push them away, but I didn't want to. I never wanted this feeling to end. It was like being consumed by a fire, and it was everything I'd been imagining.

"I told you I'm not like Fergus," I whispered into his ear, shivering as I felt his hand travelling up my leg. "I don't think you'd be wanting to do this with him."

It was a silly thing to say. There had been no need to say anything, but I always have to take things too far. I felt the change in Hiram instantly. His hand only paused for the smallest of moments, but when it resumed its journey, inching its way above my knee, everything felt different.

"Stop," I said, struggling to get myself under control. "We shouldn't be doing this, not until we're married."

"But it's what you wanted," Hiram said into my neck, still planting kisses between words.

"It is, but not now, not like this. We have to wait until we're married."

"Why Esther? You've already said we're in love, so what does it matter if we're married?"

His hand was still moving in slow circles on my thigh, making it hard to think.

"You know why it matters, Hiram. It's not right. What if someone sees us?"

"No one's going to see us, Esther. No one ever comes out here."

I don't know whether I was thrilled or terrified to realise that what he said was true. No one ever went out there other than Hiram, Fergus, and me. No one was going to come along and discover us.

"It's still wrong though. We shouldn't. What if we make a baby? This is how it happens, isn't it? This is what they're warning us about when they tell the story of Quiet Janet's daughter."

I was fairly sure I knew how babies were

made. There wasn't much opportunity for privacy when your whole family essentially lived in one room. All of us village children had quietly discussed the strange things we'd seen, or heard, our parents doing when they thought the rest of the household slept: things that sometimes resulted in your mother's swollen stomach and another brother or sister. Also, Quiet Janet's daughter, Ann, had been used as a cautionary tale in the village for as long as anyone could remember. The story was told both on Sundays in church, to remind us of the consequences of the desires of the flesh, and by mothers who were worried their daughters might become too bold for their own good. The story went that Ann had been close to a local boy for a long time, but then her head was turned by a handsome stranger passing through the area. Anyway, Ann let her desires overcome her, with one or both of her young men, and found herself expecting a child. She could have got married and tried to cover her sins, but the stranger had vanished, and her local boy had gone away to fight in some conflict that no one can quite remember. So Ann was all alone, trying to hide what was happening to her. The first her mother knew of it was on the night the child was born, when she found Ann doubled up in pain. When it finally emerged, after a long and difficult struggle, the child didn't look as it should have. The body had formed all misshapen. They weren't even sure if it was a boy or a girl, and it only took a few breaths. People said it was for the best. The child wouldn't have to suffer for the consequences of its mother's sins. The sins which had surely caused it to be born so wrong. But Ann didn't want to suffer either. The next day she dragged herself from her bed, walked out into the sea and never came back. When the minister tells the story, he doesn't say her suffering ended there though. He makes it clear she'll pay for her sin for eternity. It makes me shiver to think of Ann walking out to her watery grave and then burning in the fires of hell. The minister doesn't seem to worry what Quiet Janet thinks of it all when he sets out on his story of hell and damnation. She is very old now, some say over one hundred, and she hasn't spoken a word since it happened. Apparently, she wasn't quiet before her grandchild was born, but no one alive now can remember the sound of her voice.

"Well, yes, this is what they're talking about," Hiram replied, halting his kisses while he spoke. "But I don't believe it's a sin. I don't think God would mind. If he really created everything, he created the animals too, and they don't bother getting married. Also, you can't make a baby the first time. I've heard my dad say that, so you don't need to worry. Unless..." Hiram stopped speaking, something obviously occurring to him. "This is your first time, isn't it?"

His hand finally stopped moving.

"Yes, of course it is."

"So is it that you don't love me? Is that why you want me to stop?"

"I love you more than anything, Hiram, but we have to stop. Even if I won't end up with a baby, I know it's a sin unless you're married. Why else would everyone say that? If it wasn't true, why would the minister talk about Ann spending eternity in the fires of hell?"

"If you really loved me, you wouldn't tell me to stop, Esther. You wouldn't be worrying about what the minister, or anyone else, thinks." His voice was changing again. "I bet you wouldn't tell Iain to stop, or Fergus. Is it because you think I'm too weak? Maybe you've already done this with them and that's why you're worried about babies? Is it another thing you all laugh about?"

"Hiram, of course not!" I stammered. "You know I've only ever loved you. I've never kissed anyone but you."

And then, because I wanted the other Hiram back, because the moment had been perfect and now it wasn't, I kissed him again. I didn't stop him when his hand reached the top of my thigh, and I didn't object as he lifted my skirts out of the way. All week I'd been imagining what would follow on from his kisses, so surely this was something I wanted to do. Maybe, I thought as he started pulling at his own clothes, it was normal to find the reality a little frightening. So I didn't say a word as he shoved me backwards until I was lying on the rock. I didn't complain when the kissing stopped and his face creased with concentration. I didn't make a sound as I felt him pushing into me, and I didn't cry out when it hurt. Instead, I just lay there, waiting for the kisses to start again, hoping the fire I'd felt earlier would return. And I lay there because I loved him, and I wanted to be Mrs Hiram Stewart, and if this was what it took, it was worth it. Eventually, he stopped moving. I waited for him to put his arms around me, to hold me tightly to him, to bring back the excitement I'd felt earlier. But he didn't hold me or kiss me. He didn't speak to me or even look at me. He just pushed my skirts back down, stood up, and walked away.

I sat there on the rock, getting colder. I didn't call after him or ask him to come back. It was obvious I'd done something I shouldn't have. That was why everything had suddenly felt so wrong. I should have tried harder to stop him. That was probably how it worked. The boy was supposed to push, and the girl was supposed to say no. I'd got it all wrong. I didn't want to lose him, so I'd gone along with it, but I was going to lose him, anyway. I'd shown I wasn't the type of girl anyone would want to marry. That explained why he couldn't look at me. What came after the kissing hadn't been what I'd expected, and it probably wasn't what Hiram had expected either. He'd expected me to stop him. He'd thought I was better than I was. I wished more than anything that I hadn't gone out to find him. If I'd stayed at home, helping mam with the bairns, my dreams would still have been safe. If I wasn't so impatient, I wouldn't have ruined everything. I knew what I'd done was terrible, and there was nothing I could do to change it. I slid down from the rock and let the tears fall.

CHAPTER EIGHTEEN

The present

One thing that Eilidh found hard to deal with over the next week was the fact that everyone she knew also knew her parents. As she went about her daily life, almost every interaction involved an enquiry about how they were, what they were up to, or what they thought about the latest hot topic of local news. It was something she'd always loved before, being part of a tight- knit community and having genuine connections with everyone she met. But it felt different now, now that she knew Alan and Claire had been lying to her. Now, every time someone asked her about them, she felt the walls closing in a little. For the first time in her life, she found herself avoiding people she knew.

What was she supposed to say? If she smiled and said everything was fine, she'd be a liar like Claire and Alan. But how could she tell people what was actually going on? The local grapevine could spread news faster than wildfire. She'd experienced it personally when the rumour mill went into overdrive about why Jay MacAird was leaving Ardmhor almost as soon as he'd arrived back. The gossip had died down eventually; however, the experience had left her careful to only be interested and concerned when she heard local news, rather than looking for the next person to pass the scandal onto. Alan and Claire were very much pillars of the community. The McRaes were seen as a perfect family. Eilidh knew finding out all was not as it seemed would be big news. While a part of her thought her parents deserved to reap what they'd sown, she also knew that she wasn't ready to face the whispers and the pitying looks yet. The only solution was to lie low for a while, but she was rapidly discovering how impossible that was.

She'd explained everything to Rich in as much detail as she could when she'd arrived back from Glasgow. He'd been totally supportive, making sure she didn't need to leave the house apart from going to work. He'd encouraged her to listen to what Alan and Claire had to say, just to make sure she knew the full story, but he'd accepted that she didn't want to and hadn't pushed it any further. She was aware she couldn't avoid people for ever though.

A couple of days after Eilidh had arrived back from Glasgow, Beth had texted to invite her to lunch. The short distance between the factor's house, where Beth lived, and the building site meant there was no problem fitting in a quick lunchtime visit. Also, she hadn't seen baby Grace or Rory for a while, and much as she didn't want children of her own, Eilidh enjoyed spending time with them. So she'd decided now was the time to brave seeing people and accepted the offer. She knew it'd mean having to tell Beth the truth, but if she continued hiding away, that could become gossip in itself.

As it happened, Beth didn't start the conversation with polite enquiries about family. Instead, she thrust Grace into Eilidh's arms the minute she opened the door and disappeared at speed into the house. Eilidh headed in the same direction, making her way through the kitchen and into the glass fronted extension.

"Sorry about that," said Beth, reappearing a minute later. "I've been dying for the loo, but then Rory spilt his drink over the rug and by the time I'd cleared that up, you were knocking on the door."

"It's no bother. Getting a squeeze of this one is hardly a hassle," replied Eilidh, stroking the downy hair on the top of Grace's head.

The wet patch spreading across the rug

couldn't detract from how lovely the space was. The room soared up to meet the pitch of the roof, and the windows spread across the front flooded every corner with light. Rory's toys lay scattered across the floor and Grace's Moses basket was on its stand next to the settee.

"Are you ready to eat now? Or do you want to cuddle Grace for a while first?"

Much as Eilidh was tempted to sink into the cushions of the settee and enjoy the view out to sea, she knew that she only had a short time until her lunch break was over.

"We'd probably better eat now, if that's alright. It smells great, by the way."

"It's only vegetable soup, but they had those crusty rolls in at the shop this morning, so I bought loads. They were warm when I got them, and I have to admit not all of them have survived 'til now!"

"I'll let you off as long as you've saved at least one for me," said Eilidh, laughing.

With Grace succumbing to sleep and safely tucked into her Moses basket, and Rory showing how grown up he was as he perched on his tall chair, they settled down to eat.

"I've found out some more information that fits with your dad's story about the day of the Ardmhor Clearance," said Beth.

Eilidh swallowed her mouthful of soup a little too fast at the mention of her dad, but she relaxed as she realised Beth wasn't pausing for her to respond.

"I found an old ledger which says the factor at that time had a few days off when he received news of his son's death. It says the son died of sickness on a ship called the Mary Ann and was buried at sea."

"That's the same as we thought then, isn't it? The factor's son and my million times great-gran's sister died before they reached anywhere new."

Eilidh struggled a bit with that sentence, very aware that the girl in the story wasn't a distant relative of hers after all. It was just another way in which Sylvie's revelations had changed everything. But Beth was too engrossed in telling her story to notice.

"Yes, it is, apart from everyone else from the village sailed on a different ship. They were headed for Nova Scotia, but the Mary Ann was sailing for New Zealand. The factor's son and his girlfriend didn't sail with everyone else."

"Surely that makes sense though. The story said the girl ran off with the factor's son, deliberately separating herself from her family. They wouldn't have been very separate if they'd then spent the next month on the same boat, would they?"

"Oh," said Beth. "You're totally right. That hadn't even occurred to me! I was thinking I'd discovered something important. I blame the baby brain."

Eilidh smiled at her. Beth was so clever, but she did sometimes totally miss the obvious, baby brain or not.

"But you might still get some information from your contact in Nova Scotia. Someone might have passed on stories about what happened on the day everyone left. Although, I suppose we don't actually know that the remains are connected to the clearance."

"True," said Beth "What happened to the factor's son and his girlfriend could be a totally separate story, and, as they both died before reaching New Zealand, I probably can't find out much more about them or why they didn't want to travel with the others."

"I think the answer to that is probably obvious," replied Eilidh. "Either her family, or his family, or both, will have disapproved, and the pair of them will have thought it was easier to disappear and start again where no one knew them. Unfortunately for them, they died before they got that chance."

It hadn't escaped Eilidh's notice that she could have been describing Alan and Claire's situation. They'd clearly felt their only option was to run away and start again, but in doing so, they'd ruined her father's life and deprived her of the chance to know him. Usually, she'd have been sympathetic to a story of people following their hearts, but with all that was happening in her own life, she was seeing things from a different perspective. All she could feel was anger at how selfish people could be, and sadness at what their families would have lost. Even with Beth's small child induced brain fog, the change in Eilidh's demeanour was impossible to miss.

"Aww, it's not like you to get soppy, Eilidh! But it is sad, isn't it? And I'm still disappointed that finding out they went on a different ship doesn't actually tell us anything."

"It confirms the story of the runaway sister was true though, and it's interesting in its own right."

"Yes, I suppose so," said Beth. "I'd just been hoping it was a clue to something. Maybe I'll have a look if there's a historical association where the Mary Ann was sailing to, just in case they can tell us anything else. After all, someone must have let the family back here know what had happened."

"Wouldn't the shipping company have done that?" asked Eilidh.

"Yeah, I suppose they might have. I don't really know how all that would work. I'll see what I can find out."

They'd talked all the way through the soup, and they'd continued through some particularly nice cupcakes that Rory had apparently insisted on Beth buying. A glance at the clock told Eilidh she'd be late back if she didn't leave soon. It was as she was saying goodbye, thinking that perhaps she might escape without having to talk about her family, that Beth asked the fateful question.

"Are we still on for lunch at your mum and dad's on Saturday?"

Saturday lunch at Alan and Claire's house in Strathglen had been a regular event for Eilidh and Beth ever since Beth had moved to the area, but this arrangement had totally slipped Eilidh's mind.

"I don't know," Eilidh stammered. "I mean, you'll be very welcome, but I don't think I can go."

"I couldn't go without you. It'd be too weird," said Beth, looking slightly panicked by the prospect. "If you've got something else on, I think we should rearrange."

"It's not that," began Eilidh. And then she dissolved into tears.

Beth rushed to fold her into a hug, and the words Eilidh had been so desperate to avoid came spilling out. In the end, she didn't make it back to work for the afternoon. Beth phoned Ali, and Ali told her to reassure Eilidh he could handle anything that came up at the building site. Eilidh spent the rest of the day curled up on Beth's settee, cuddling Grace, drinking tea, and helping

Rory with his train set. Like Rich, Beth suggested it might help to talk to Claire and Alan, but she also knew Eilidh well enough to see there was nothing to be gained by pushing the issue. Eilidh was grateful for the distraction Rory and Grace provided—almost three-year-olds don't care how upset you are if they need your help to build a railway bridge. But Rory's demands weren't enough to stop her from thinking entirely. She knew that Beth and Rich were right. She did need more answers. However, she thought they were wrong about where she should get them from. How could she possibly trust anything that Alan or Claire had to say? No, the answers would have to come from her father's family, the people who hadn't been lying to her for her entire lifetime, but unfortunately, that meant waiting until the weekend and her next trip to Glasgow.

CHAPTER
NINETEEN

The past

Fergus

I don't know what led me to our old fort in the woods. Until I went out there with Hiram after his fight, I hadn't thought about it for years, but something made me set off in that direction. It had been one of our favourite places to spend time when we were little. It always seemed full of adventure, but that last visit had been full of sadness instead. Maybe I went because I wanted to remind myself it was a special place after all. But I wish I'd stayed away. Perhaps I could have strolled down to the harbour, or just sat up at the houses listening to some of old Annie's stories. But I didn't. I went out to our fort, and there I found Esther.

I almost didn't notice her. She was curled up in a tight ball, her back against a rock, as if she'd slid from it, unable to hold herself up any longer. From the angle at which I approached the clearing, the rock hid her from view. It was only the strange sniffling sounds that made me look closer. She was so tightly furled that I couldn't see her face, but I didn't need to in order to know it was Esther. You can't live next to someone your entire life and not be able to identify them in an instant.

It's no secret that Esther and I don't see eye to eye. Apparently, we got on well when we were children, but as we've got older, that's changed. I don't know if it's because she doesn't treat Hiram well enough or if it's because she's thoughtless, lazy, and has such a high opinion of herself. Perhaps I just don't like the fact she takes up Hiram's time when I'd rather he spent it with me. Anyway, we don't like each other, and I have to admit that I usually quite enjoy seeing her get in trouble. I always try to be a good person, but I just can't help being pleased when things don't go her way. However, this seemed different.

She wasn't making much noise. Only a quiet sniffling gave away that she was crying, but her whole body shook with each sob that passed through her. This wasn't Esther showing off for attention, crying prettily so everyone would ask her what was wrong. She wouldn't have expected anyone else to be out in the woods, so I knew this was genuine, and I knew that instead of being petty and silly, I had to help. I slowly lowered myself down to the ground, not wanting to give her a fright. Then I gently put my hand on her back. Despite the warmth of the evening, she was cold as ice. I tried to pull her towards me to share the heat from my body.

"Esther, it's alright," I whispered. "I'll look after you, it'll be alright."

"Hiram?" she asked quietly, lifting her head a fraction.

"No, it's not Hiram. It's me, Fergus."

The sound she made then was like a low moan. I'd not really heard someone cry like that before, and I wasn't sure what to do. I moved closer, sort of wrapping my body around the ball she'd made of herself. Rubbing her back and whispering in her ear that everything would be alright. It was what my mother would have done when I was upset as a child, what I still watched her doing to comfort my younger sisters and brothers. I didn't know if it was the right thing to do, but after a while, she stopped shaking so much. Eventually, she shifted a little, pulling herself up to sit alongside me.

"Do you want to tell me what's wrong?" I asked.

"No."

"It might help."

"It won't," she replied.

"Fine, you don't have to tell me anything."

And then, typical Esther, on being told not to do something, she decides that's exactly what she wants to do.

"It's Hiram," she began. "Something happened with Hiram."

Immediately I panicked. Had his father attacked him again? Was he badly hurt? Had something even worse happened to him? Was that why she was so distraught?

"What happened, Esther? Is he alright?"

"Yes, well, he was fine when he left. I think it's us, me and Hiram, that aren't fine anymore."

"Have you argued? Is that why you're so upset?"

"No. It was the opposite of arguing, really, but I did something I shouldn't have. Or I didn't stop Hiram from doing something we shouldn't have, and now he's disgusted with me. He couldn't even look at me, and he'll never want to see me again."

Another sob escaped her, and then another, and I thought I finally understood what might be going on. After Hiram disappearing into the woods with Esther during the dancing the other night, and then our disagreement when he'd told me his father was encouraging him to 'have some fun' with her, I wondered if perhaps things had gone too far between them. Although that still didn't explain why she thought he'd never want to see her again.

"Did the two of you, well, you know, did things go further than they did the other night, during the dancing?"

Esther nodded sadly. "I know I should have made him wait until we're married, but Hiram said it didn't matter as long as we loved each other, and I wanted to make him happy. But then when it was over, he didn't say anything, he wouldn't even look at me, he just walked off. He must think I'm disgusting, Fergus. I was supposed to say no, I was supposed to make him wait, wasn't I?"

"I think you were both supposed to wait, Esther. You can't be to blame for something Hiram did as well."

"Then why didn't he speak to me at the end? If it wasn't a test where I was supposed to say no, why did he walk off like that? I thought I was doing it to make him happy."

"I don't know, Esther. I have absolutely no idea what he's thinking at the moment. Did this happen here? Have you been lying here since?"

She nodded again. I'd never imagined being disappointed in Hiram, and I'd certainly never imagined taking Esther's side in a disagreement between the two of them, but that was what seemed to be happening. He'd brought her to a secluded spot in the woods, somewhere he knew they wouldn't be disturbed, and then he'd left her upset and alone. If he hadn't planned for this to happen, why bring her somewhere so lonely? Hiram never did anything without thinking it through. He knew he was leaving, and he'd followed his father's advice to do whatever he wanted with Esther, regardless of the consequences. And seeing as Esther was still talking about marriage, he clearly hadn't been honest with her about what was going on. It wasn't behaviour I'd have expected from Hiram, and as Esther sobbed in my arms, I felt my anger rising. I'd always worried for Hiram, thinking that Esther was taking advantage of him, but tonight had made me look at things very differently. I didn't say any of this to Esther, though, what would have been the point? Instead, I told her what I thought she'd want to hear. The words I thought would help get her off the ground and back to the safety of home.

"I'm sure he's not disgusted with you. How could he be? He loves you. Hiram's always loved you, ever since you first met. He probably just panicked. Maybe he was afraid he'd hurt you. I'm sure you'll sort it all out as soon as you see each other again."

"Do you really think so?" she asked, looking up at me hopefully.

I didn't think so. In fact, I knew things wouldn't work out as she wanted because I knew Hiram was leaving. But I also knew that wasn't what she needed to hear.

"I'm sure everything will be alright."

"Will you speak to him for me? Explain how sorry I am?"

I didn't think there was anything for Esther to apologise for. For once, I didn't think she was the person in the wrong. But I was more than happy to agree to talk to Hiram. I was ready to find him right away and tell him exactly what I thought.

"Of course I will, but you don't need to keep saying sorry. You haven't done anything wrong."

And with that, she let me lead her back to the village. I talked all the way about useless nonsense, trying to make sure she looked less broken and dishevelled before she entered her house. But while I forced myself to think up those silly stories, I couldn't help wishing I'd not gone out into the woods. I didn't like the way my feelings had shifted. Since the moment I'd found Esther sobbing on the floor, everything had felt wrong.

CHAPTER TWENTY

The present

Since the Saturday night in Glasgow when Eilidh had told Alan she never wanted to speak to him again, she'd received twenty-six calls from him. Sixteen of them had been that same night, when she'd ended up turning her phone off, and ten had been the next day. Then she'd asked Rich to speak to Alan on her behalf and ask him to stop calling. She didn't know what Rich had said, but it had worked, and the calls had stopped. They'd been replaced with two text messages per day, one each from Alan and Claire. The messages always said essentially the same things: they loved her, they understood why she was so angry, they were sorry, and they'd like to explain. Eilidh deleted each one as it popped up on her phone. She wasn't interested in what they had to say because she knew she couldn't believe them. She hoped her lack of response would send its own message and that they'd give up and leave her alone.

On Thursday afternoon, Eilidh was busy working in the office. Things were progressing nicely at the holiday village site, and the construction team had assured her they wouldn't need her for the rest of the day. The office was quiet. Ali had gone out to check on something at the wind farm and everyone else was busy catching up on admin. When Ali returned, he slowly made his way over to Eilidh's desk, looking as if he'd rather be going in any other direction.

"Are you alright, Ali?" she asked. "You look worried."

"I'm fine, it's just…" He rubbed his jaw anxiously. "I don't know if it's my place to say anything, but the thing is, your dad's outside. I know you don't want to speak to him, but he was there when I left to go up to the wind farm and he's still there now. He wouldn't listen when I told him he was wasting his time, he just said it's his time to waste. I don't think he's going anywhere. So it might be better to go out there and get it over with."

"No. Thanks for letting me know, Ali, but I've told him I'm not interested. He can sit there all night if he wants, but he won't be talking to me."

An hour later, as she got ready to head home, Eilidh wasn't feeling so confident. It was easy to say she didn't want to talk to Alan, but the reality was different. The last time she'd seen him, he was still her dad. Yes, she'd been aware as she pushed past him that he wasn't her biological father, but there hadn't been time for the knowledge to sink in, and she hadn't known then that he'd been lying to her as well. Now she didn't know what their relationship was. She didn't even know what to call him anymore. Facing the man that had always been there to protect her suddenly seemed the most difficult thing in the world. She made excuses not to leave until everyone else had gone. She hoped Alan would get the message she wasn't coming out and give up, but as she walked through the door and twisted the key to lock it, she was immediately aware of his presence. Alan was a big man. He wasn't the sort that could sneak up on someone. Instead, his being filled any space he inhabited. Eilidh had always loved that in the past, but now she wished his presence was smaller, something she could sneak round and pretend she hadn't seen.

"I've told you I don't want to speak to you. Just leave me alone." She pulled her jacket tight, as if to shield herself from his response, and hurried to pass him.

"Eilidh, wait!" he shouted, quickening his pace to walk alongside her. "Please, just listen to what I've got to say, and then I promise I'll never bother you again."

"As if I can trust your promises," Eilidh spat back at him, walking faster.

"Well, I'll just wait here then, every night and every morning. Or I'll wait outside your house. You need to know the truth."

"And I'll just call the police. You need to listen to what I've said. I can't trust you, and I don't want to hear what you have to say. I'll get the truth from Sylvie."

"Sylvie doesn't know everything, Eilidh. I'm not trying to threaten you, sweetheart, and you're right, I can't force you to listen. But I want you to hear both sides. I thought you'd have wanted to hear both sides. You usually need to know everything."

Eilidh was incensed by Alan suggesting it was her that was acting out of character, rather than accepting the problem lay squarely with him and her mum.

"I'd love to know everything," she said, slowing down slightly. "Of course I would. But how can I believe a word you say? Our whole family, my whole life, is based on lies. Lies that you've been telling. What would be the point in me listening to you now?"

"I don't know," Alan said, holding his hands

up in submission. "Maybe there is no point. Or maybe it'll help you make sense of things. If nothing else, it'll mean you'll get rid of me."

"Fine, you've got five minutes, but if you try to speak to me again after that, I'm calling the police."

Alan moved towards the wall that surrounded the office carpark, sitting down on it as he prepared to tell a story he knew he should have told many years before.

"It's hard to know where to begin," he said.

"You're down to four minutes now, so you'd better figure it out quickly," Eilidh snapped. Her tone was still angry, but she sat down beside him none the less.

"You know I grew up here and I love living here now, but I didn't always. Living with my gran was stifling at times, and although I loved her, I couldn't wait to get away. As soon as I got the chance of a job in Glasgow, I leapt at it. I hadn't always wanted to be a brickie, but I'd have taken anything I was offered, and it turned out I loved it. Seeing a building take shape before your eyes, there's nothing like it. I was on top of the world, and that was when I met Keith."

"My real dad?"

"Your biological father, yes. We got talking on my first day on site. He had the gift of the gab, did Keith. He could talk to anyone about anything. You're like him in that respect."

Alan paused and looked at her, as if checking for other signs of Keith he'd been ignoring over the years.

"I always thought I got that from you," Eilidh said quietly.

"Aye," Alan sighed. "We were alike in that way, which was probably what drew us together. We started going for a few drinks on a Friday. Then we got into the habit of having a swift one in the pub after work each day. He was so quick-witted and funny, Eilidh. I loved spending time with him. In fact, I loved him full stop. I thought he was the greatest person I'd ever met. He knew everyone, and everything, and soon I was spending every bit of spare time with him. I met his mum and his sisters, his dad had died a while before, and then finally I met his girlfriend, Claire—your mum."

Eilidh's head lifted at the mention of her mum's name, but she didn't interrupt.

"She was stunning, Eilidh, absolutely beautiful. She still is now, but back then, she couldn't walk into a room without everyone looking at her. Meeting Keith had turned my head, made me realise how sheltered my life had been up here, but meeting your mum just blew me away. I could hardly string two words together in her company, and it made complete sense to me that they were together. They were the perfect couple. Him so charismatic and her so pretty, and both of them so quick—she gave him a run for his money when it came to things to say. Anyway, we fell into spending a lot of time together, the three of us. It didn't occur to me they might have preferred the time to themselves. Keith was always encouraging me to join them, and your mum didn't seem to mind. But after a while, something changed. We were working on different sites by then, and Keith started disappearing. We'd arrange to meet, but he wouldn't show up. It'd just be me and your mum left on our own. When he was there, he was different: he was quieter, or he'd get wound up over nothing and storm off. After a while, I stopped turning up as well. It didn't seem right to be spending so much time alone with my best friend's girlfriend. But one night your mum turned up at my house in tears. My landlady was huffing and puffing about no visitors, so I had to take her to the pub round the corner. By the time we'd got there, she'd stopped crying and said she was fine. We had a drink and a chat and then she went home to Keith. I wouldn't have thought much of it, but then it happened again, and again. By then I knew I was falling for her, but I'd never have acted on it. Even though I wasn't seeing much of Keith, I still thought of him as my best pal. Anyway, the last time she turned up in tears, she had a black eye as well. Eventually, she told me that Keith had hit her. Even though I was head over heels for her by then, I didn't want to hear what she was saying. I tried to excuse it, thought maybe he'd been drunk, but it turned out it wasn't the first time. It was just the first time he'd hit her somewhere she couldn't cover. It was obvious she wasn't lying, and in some ways, it made sense. Keith had been acting oddly for a long time by then. I told her to leave him, to go back home to her parents, but she was adamant she couldn't. She said it was too complicated, and that she loved him. So she walked out of the pub and back to their flat, but I couldn't stop thinking about her. I knew where she worked, so I hung around outside over a couple of lunchtimes; that's when I found out how complicated it was. She was expecting, almost three months gone, and she was frightened he wouldn't let her leave with the baby. I couldn't get over the fact that he'd hurt her while knowing she was carrying his child. All the respect I'd had for him vanished in an instant. I told her that I'd help her get away, and that's what I tried to do. I came up with a plan for the pair of us to disappear; I thought we'd head up here, where I knew there'd be people we could count on. We didn't want to make him suspicious, so she went home to him until I got paid—Keith had been taking her money 'to keep it safe'. Then, once I'd got my money, and she'd got all her things together, we left and came up here, to a tiny house in Inveravain. Up until the day we left, I wasn't sure if she'd change her mind. He had such a hold over her, and I didn't think it'd take much for him to talk her round. I'd known that I loved your mum for a long time by then, but as far as she was concerned, we were just friends. It wasn't until a while after we left Glasgow that she started to see me differently. I think she needed some distance from Keith to be able to see that the way he treated her wasn't love. Anyway, by the time you were born, five months later, we were together. But I know I'd have loved you as my own, even if me and your mum had only stayed as friends. I'm so sorry we lied, Eilidh. It was wrong, but at the time it seemed like the right thing to do. You always felt like mine, so it didn't seem like a lie to keep saying I was your dad."

"But what about my real dad? You didn't give him the chance to be my father."

"He didn't want to be your dad, Eilidh. If he'd wanted to be a family with you and your mum, he wouldn't have treated her like he did. He wasn't the man I'd thought he was. The more your mum told me about their life together, the more I realised how difficult he was. He didn't just hit her, he controlled her."

"So you say."

"Aye, I do. Besides, we did give him a chance. He turned up here about six months after you were born. We weren't that well-hidden, I suppose; he knew I came from round this way, and he'd have only had to ask round a bit to find us. Anyway, he seemed like he'd changed. He said that he'd been drinking too much and that he knew he'd behaved badly. He said he'd given up booze and that he was desperate for a second chance. There were lots of tears, and I believed him. He seemed genuine. We offered to move nearer to Glasgow, so he could see you more easily. But that wasn't what he wanted. He wanted your mum to leave me and go back to him. When he realised that wouldn't happen, that if she went back to Glasgow it'd be with me, the tears stopped, and his attitude changed completely. He offered to sell you to us. He said he'd give up his rights and never try to see you again if we gave him enough money. I told him we weren't going to buy you, and that he was welcome to see you whenever he wanted, but he got really angry. He said he was going to take us to court to get custody of you. Your mum was distraught, so in the end, I gave him every penny I'd got saved, just to get him to leave. A while after that, we moved to a bigger house further down the coast. I don't know if he couldn't find us there or if he just never bothered looking. He knew where your mum's parents were in Glasgow though, and he could always have tried asking them, but none of us heard from him again. So he had his chance to be your father, Eilidh."

"Again, so you say," Eilidh replied bitterly. "But

Sylvie's family tell it differently. They say he was devastated by losing mum and me. They say that you threatened him and had him beaten up, and that he never stopped searching for me. So someone's lying, and I know you've got plenty of experience at it."

"I know we should have told you, Eilidh. I can see now that we got it totally wrong, but you always felt like my daughter. It didn't seem like a lie to keep saying that. I just wish we could turn back the clock and do it differently."

"Well, you can't, and I don't think I can believe a word you say. Just like I probably can't trust you to stick to your promise of leaving me alone now I've heard you out. But I really hope you do because what you've said hasn't changed anything; I never want to see you again."

CHAPTER TWENTY-ONE

The past

Fergus

I tried to find Hiram the same night that I found Esther crying in the woods, but he was nowhere to be seen. Usually, I try to avoid his house, but my need to speak to Hiram was stronger than my dislike of Mr Stewart. However, Hiram was not at home, and it was made clear that I was not welcome to wait. I was desperate to find him. I wanted him to give me an explanation of events that would allow me to place all the blame on Esther, a version that would put the world back in order. But it wasn't to be. Hiram had disappeared.

There was not too much work to be done the

next day. We'd finished bringing the peats down to the village and stacking them for each house, and the fields needed little attention until the harvest was ready. Some of the men were taking a boat out fishing, but they had no need of my help. My mother was busy spinning, and the oldest of my sisters was keeping the little ones in line. I avoided Esther's house. I didn't know what I'd say to her. We'd shared something so personal the previous night, whereas all we'd shared for years before that had been dislike and insults. I'd seen that she was up and about though. She'd milked the cow, and been across to the stream to collect water, so she'd obviously put on a good enough show to convince her mother nothing was wrong.

It was a pleasant morning. There was no sun, but it was mild, and there was just enough breeze to keep the flies at bay. Isobel was busy with her spindle, keeping an eye on her brothers and sisters. She asked me to join her, and it was tempting to sit and enjoy the company of someone who was always cheerful, especially when that person's hair shone gold in the light, but there was too much chance of being confronted by Esther, so I said no. Instead, I set off in search of Hiram.

Although I found him in the end, he was definitely trying to avoid company. There were several places we tended to meet, and I'd tried all of them. I'd wandered the length of the stream and looked under the bridge that carried the path to Ardmhor House. No one was resting on the fallen tree near the harbour, and the men patching their nets said they hadn't seen Hiram. I checked the old fort in the woods, where I'd found Esther the night before, and I even tried his house again, but there was no sign of him anywhere. Then I wondered if he'd be at the flat rocks, where we'd attempted to fish a few days earlier. From a distance I could see there was no one there, but I carried on towards them anyway, thinking perhaps Hiram had headed further along the shore. As I picked my way around the giant outcrop of rocks which blocked the next bay off at high tide, I heard pebbles shift to the side of me, and there he was, hidden in a gap in the rocks, looking almost as distraught as Esther had the night before. I edged myself into the gap, just fitting onto the rock beside him, and then I did nothing, waiting to see if he was going to tell me what the problem was. After a while, I ran out of patience. I couldn't wait any longer to find out what had been going on.

"I was looking for you last night," I said.

"I've been trying to keep out of people's way until all of this has gone," he replied, gesturing at the bruises on his face.

"But you saw Esther."

Hiram didn't confirm or deny what I'd said, he

just sat there staring off in the other direction, leaving me with no choice but to continue.

"I found her out in the clearing. She said you'd been there."

Hiram remained silent.

"She was crying, Hiram. She was almost inconsolable."

I was losing my temper by then. I couldn't believe he wasn't offering any explanation. He was deliberately looking away from me, and I had to resist the urge to shake him and force him to speak. But then I noticed the slight tremble of his shoulders, a barely discernible movement up and down. Instead of trying to make him look at me, I adjusted myself instead, so that I could see his face. He hadn't been silently ignoring me after all. He'd been crying. Since the first time I saw Hiram, when he'd been so determined not to cry as his father pushed him aside, I'd watched him subdue his emotions many times. Each time I'd seen his father attack him, I'd also seen Hiram bring up a sort of barrier around himself. He was more sensitive than any other man I'd known, but he refused to let a single tear escape his eyes. To see him weeping now, knowing that I'd forced him to show me those tears, was as unsettling as the sympathy I'd felt for Esther the night before.

"Do you want to tell me what's wrong?" I asked quietly.

"No."

Hiram's reply came quickly, and I couldn't help but think of the identical conversation I'd had with Esther the previous night.

"It might help," I tried again.

"It won't," Hiram rebutted instantly.

"I had almost the same conversation with Esther last night. Do you want to hear what she said in the end?"

"I don't think I need to, Fergus. I can imagine. She must hate me, and you must think I'm a terrible person."

My relief that he was finally talking was short-lived because I knew our conversation wouldn't be easy. Esther might not hate him, but I did feel that his behaviour had been terrible. I decided to start with Esther.

"She doesn't hate you, but she's very confused. I have to admit that I am too. She doesn't know why you just walked off, so she's afraid that she did something wrong and that you're disgusted with her. She's scared that you won't want to marry her anymore because of what happened."

"She should hate me, Fergus. She's right that we won't be getting married, but it's not because I'm disgusted with her. If I'm disgusted with anyone, it's myself. I can't marry her, and I knew that before I pushed her into this. I don't know what came over me. We were kissing, and it felt so good, just like the other night. I wasn't thinking about leaving or anything else. All I could think about was how good it felt. But then she asked me to stop, and I was so angry. It was like this dark cloud came over me. I thought maybe she was laughing at me like my father does—that she'd been leading me on, just so she could turn me down. Or even worse, I worried I was doing it wrong. I thought maybe my father was right, maybe I wasn't a proper man, and that was why she wanted to stop. I just wanted the cloud to go. I wanted to feel good again. So I kept going on at her, saying that she'd do it if she loved me, and eventually she started kissing me again. I should have listened when she told me to stop."

"Yes, you should have."

Part of me wanted to comfort him, look after him like I always had. But I was angry as well. I felt like he'd let me down by behaving in a way so different from what I expected. That part of me didn't want to let him off

"What if she ends up with a baby, Hiram? What will you do then?"

"She won't. I know I shouldn't have pushed her, but she doesn't need to worry about that. I've heard my father say plenty of times that a girl can't end up with a child the first time."

"I don't think that's true, Hiram. You've heard the story of Quiet Janet's daughter enough times."

"Yes, but we don't know she only did it once, do we? After all, she was involved with two different men. Or are you saying that Esther's been with other men?"

"No, well, I don't think so. Not going by how upset she was last night."

Hiram was quiet for a while.

"I don't think we need to worry about a child, but I still know it was a terrible thing to do. Esther wouldn't have backed down and started kissing me again if she'd known I'm not going to marry her."

"Can't you though? Can't you just ignore your father? You could run away and marry her. By the time he found out, it'd be too late. That'd show him you're your own man and not to be pushed around."

"Perhaps. The thing is, though, and this is why you'll think I'm really awful. I don't think I want to."

"Oh."

I honestly couldn't think of anything else to say. Ever since we were children, Hiram had loved Esther. He'd talked about how beautiful she was, and said he was going to marry her, since before we really knew what it meant. At first, I used to laugh at him. I just couldn't understand seeing Esther in that way, but he said it so often that it just became how things were. Hiram loving Esther was one of life's unquestionable truths. So the idea that he didn't love her after all was unfathomable. He'd turned away from me again now, his gaze fixed determinedly on the distant horizon.

"I don't really know when things changed," he said. "But I've wondered for a while if I really love her in the way you're supposed to. I can still see how beautiful she is, and she's always going to be special to me, but I don't think she makes me feel what I should be feeling for the person I'm going to marry."

"I don't understand, Hiram. You've just been telling me how good it felt to kiss her, and last night you..., well, you know. Isn't that exactly what you're supposed to want to do with someone you want to marry?"

Hiram stood up and started pacing back and forth on the shore. "It's just too hard to explain. It feels wrong talking about this. I'm not sure I even know what I mean."

"We've always talked about everything, Hiram, so why would this be different? There's no rush," I reassured him. "I'm not going anywhere."

And I wasn't. We had discussed every embarrassing thing that had ever happened to us, usually at great length. We'd talked about every girl we'd liked, or I'd liked, as Hiram had only ever cared for Esther, and we'd analysed every unexpected change that happened to us as we grew. We were closer than brothers. There had never been a secret between us. Eventually,

Hiram took a deep breath and started talking.

"When I took Esther off into the woods on the night of the dancing, it wasn't because I'm in love with her, it was because I was angry about what my father had said. He'd said I should 'have some fun' before I left, and then he'd laughed at me. He said he was laughing because he knew I wouldn't be man enough to do anything. I wanted to prove him wrong, and I wanted to prove myself wrong as well because, to be honest, I wasn't expecting to enjoy it as much as I did."

"But why weren't you? Surely it's what you've always been dreaming about."

"That's the thing. It's never Esther in my dreams anymore. I want it to be, but it's not. I thought maybe my father was right, maybe I'm not a real man. That's partly why I was so angry, and it's why I took Esther off like that."

"So you like someone else, and even though you enjoyed being with Esther, you don't want to marry her. Is it because you like this other person more?"

"I don't know. When I was kissing Esther, it felt like I thought it was supposed to, like it does when I'm dreaming. So I thought everything was going to be alright. But last night when we…, well, you know, when we did it, it just felt wrong. I knew I wasn't supposed to be with her, that it wasn't right, and that's why I ran away."

"But you think it might have felt right with

this other person?"

"Maybe, I don't know. I know I shouldn't have treated Esther like that though. I still don't know what came over me. One minute everything was great, then I was angry, and then I felt like I had to prove something. But I don't know whether it was to me, or to her, or to my father. And then it had all gone too far, and everything felt wrong. I've made such a mess of things."

Hiram had stopped pacing by then and returned to his seat next to me. He looked as upset as Esther had the night before, and I put my arm around him, comforting him like I did my younger brothers and sisters.

"Things will be alright, Hiram. Esther is going to be really upset when you leave, but she'll get over it, it's not like she'll be short of other offers."

"But what about her reputation? Will people see her like Quiet Janet's daughter?"

"You said you can't end up with a baby the first time, and no one knows apart from us three. None of us are going to say anything, so no one else need ever know. It was a horrible thing to do, Hiram, but I think Esther will be alright."

"I hope so," he replied sadly. "I never wanted to hurt her."

We were still for a while, watching a gannet circle overhead before dropping like a stone to claim its prey from the sea.

"So who is this other person you like? Is

it someone your father might actually let you marry?"

"Definitely not," Hiram replied with a bitter laugh.

"But who is it? Tell me," I pleaded.

I was desperate to know who had turned Hiram's head away from Esther after all these years.

"You don't want to know. It's not something that will ever happen."

"Oh, I do." I replied, laughing.

I grabbed him in a headlock and squeezed a little, rubbing his hair with my knuckles, chanting 'tell me, tell me.' I was so full of how funny I was being that it took me a while to register the anger behind the 'no' he'd shouted in reply. Immediately, I let go of him.

"I'm sorry," I said, shocked by his fury. But my apology didn't seem to reach him or calm him.

"It's you!" he shouted. "I said you wouldn't want to know."

It took me a minute to understand what he meant.

"You dream about kissing me?"

Hiram didn't say anything, he just stared at me, and then he moved closer. It was as if I was rooted to the spot, powerless to move. His face was just inches from mine, and then his mouth was on my mouth. He was kissing me in a way I'd never kissed Isobel, and I did nothing. It was probably only seconds that passed with me as still as the rocks surrounding us, but it felt like much longer. Then suddenly, something snapped inside me, and I was free again. I knew this was disgusting. It was wrong, and it shouldn't be happening, not between two men. I pushed Hiram away with every bit of strength I possessed. He slumped backwards, and I ran.

"Fergus, wait. Fergus, I'm sorry, please wait."

I could hear Hiram's pleas as the rocks slipped beneath my feet and my hands grasped at the air to steady myself, but I didn't turn around. What I'd always known was changing yet again. I ran as fast as I could, and I didn't look back.

CHAPTER TWENTY-TWO

The present

Eilidh practically ran home from work. It was a good job it was only a short journey, as her heart was pounding by the time the top of her drive came into view. It was difficult to know whether her breathlessness resulted from the exertion or if it resulted from her anger, but from the moment she'd turned her back on Alan and his lies, she'd been desperate to reach the sanctuary of home. Unfortunately, as she passed the trees that marked the turning to her house, it became clear Alan hadn't been working alone. It seemed her parents had planned a two-pronged attack instead. Perched on the doorstep, looking older than she'd ever seen her, was the lonely figure of her mother.

"I know you don't want to speak to me, sweetheart, but we need to talk. You need to know what really happened."

Eilidh felt something twisting inside her. This week had been horrible, probably the worst of her life. She'd felt cut adrift from everything she knew. And now, sitting in front of her, was the person who'd always made everything right, the person she'd been able to turn to when things were going wrong, the person whose opinion she valued the most. A huge part of her wanted to throw herself straight into her mother's arms and cry her eyes out. But she reminded herself that she was only this upset because of Claire's lies. She couldn't let all that go because she needed comfort.

"Go away. I've told you enough times to leave me alone."

"Eilidh, I can't. I know you've spoken to Dad, but I think you need to hear my side of things as well."

"No, I don't. There's no point. I wouldn't trust what you said, anyway."

"Well, I'm not moving from here until you listen, so you won't be able to get in the house until you do."

"Fine, I'll just go across to the pub instead."

"And I'll still be here when you get back. You can't avoid me forever."

As much as Eilidh was angry, and wanted to

escape rather than talk, she didn't fancy having to repeat this later on. Inevitably, she'd have to return home at some point, especially as she'd forgotten her purse that morning. Perhaps, she reasoned, it was best to get this over with.

"You've got the same five minutes he had, and then I want you gone."

She sat down at the other end of the doorstep, as physically distant from her mother as she could manage without sitting in the gravel. She deliberately didn't look at Claire. There was no way she could meet her eyes at the moment, but she could sense her mother's expression as she tried to summon the words needed to explain.

"The thing I want you to remember, Eilidh, is that I really did love Keith. I know now, now that I'm with your dad and I can see how things should be, that our relationship was all wrong, but I would never have hurt him. I was only young when I met Keith, about the same age you were when you met Rich, and he just bowled me over. It was like I'd been blind until I met him, and then suddenly everything in the world was different and brighter. He was so clever and funny, he could put anyone at ease, just like you can. And he was so handsome, the best-looking boy I'd ever seen. You have a real look of him sometimes, in certain expressions. I think I've always tried to ignore it, but there's no denying he's there in you."

Claire's story continued much the same as Alan's. They approached it from different perspectives, but the content was the same. However, they'd had three decades to work on it, Eilidh thought to herself, it would have been more surprising if they hadn't got the details straight. In Claire's account, after Keith caught her attention with his good looks and confidence, she fell in love with him when she realised he wasn't actually as self-assured as he appeared—and because he seemed to always put her first, because he made her feel special, and because he said they belonged together. A few years down the line, Alan became part of their group. She'd liked him from the start, but he'd only ever been Keith's friend. Then, as time went on, Keith changed.

He'd always liked to be in control, looking after both of their wages, deciding where they should go each night and who they should spend time with, but that had always seemed fine. He'd just been taking care of her. It wasn't as though she wanted to see her old school friends, they didn't really have much in common anymore, and she spent enough time with her colleagues when she was working. She only noticed something was wrong when Keith started disappearing. He'd not show up when they'd made arrangements. Sometimes he'd not come home for a couple of nights. If she questioned him about it, it made him angry. If she didn't question him, he became angry anyway, saying that she obviously didn't care. That was when the violence had really started.

He'd hit her a couple of times before, but that was during arguments, when they'd both been riled up—and it was hard to know who'd started lashing out. This was different, the blows sometimes coming out of nowhere before he disappeared again. It was at that point she'd first turned to Alan. It had brought home to her that she no longer had any friends of her own. She didn't feel she could go to her parents, either. She'd barely seen them over the last few years and Keith had always said they didn't like him, surely they'd say she only had herself to blame.

When Alan finally had everything in place for them to leave, she'd still not been sure that she should. There was still a part of her that hoped Keith could change, that maybe with a baby to care for, he'd go back to how he'd been when they first met. But then he'd hit her again, and she'd known she had no choice.

After a few weeks in Inveravain, away from Keith and with someone who treated her as an equal, she'd seen their relationship differently. Keith didn't love her, he just wanted to control her. Then gradually, she'd seen Alan differently as well, building a relationship with him that was worlds away from what she'd experienced with Keith.

Eilidh didn't respond once during her mother's speech. She didn't interrupt or ask for clarification. The story was familiar now. It sounded pretty plausible: young girl falls for controlling man before things turn sour and she makes her escape with the reliable best friend. It would have been nice to believe it, she thought to herself, but it was so at odds with what she'd heard in Glasgow. And there were inconsistencies. Claire had said Alan was the only person she could turn to, but Eilidh knew that wasn't true. Her grandparents, Claire's mum and dad, visited all the time when she was growing up. Which must mean Claire had simply wanted to run away with Alan, if she hadn't, she could have gone to her parents for help instead. Why make out like they were the sort of people who'd have turned her away? It felt as if she had two different voices in her head. One was telling her she should listen to Claire and Alan. After all, she'd known them her whole life and she'd always seen them treating other people well, whereas she didn't really know anything about this new family in Glasgow. But the other voice was asking her if she really knew her parents? If they'd kept this massive secret from her, what else hadn't they been honest about? And Sylvie, and her gran, and the rest of her family had been so kind and welcoming. Why would they bother to lie? It wasn't like they stood to gain anything from adding her to their family. No, she told

WHAT WAS HIDDEN AT ARDMHOR

herself, she couldn't forgive Claire and Alan's lies just because they were telling a good story now, especially as that story didn't fit with anything else she'd been told about Keith.

"Right, well, you've said what you came to say, but it doesn't change anything. You lied to me, and you took away my chance to know my real dad. I'll never forgive you."

"Eilidh, please..." Claire pleaded.

Eilidh was already on her feet. Her arms were tightly folded across her chest, and her keys were in her hand. Claire got up slowly. It seemed to take her a long time, as though she was broken and the movement was beyond her. She took a step towards Eilidh, but Eilidh pre-empted the move, stepping backwards, out of reach. Claire finally seemed to accept defeat. She didn't come any closer, rushing towards her car instead. Eilidh didn't let her mind dwell on the tears she'd seem streaming down her mother's face. It wasn't her fault, she reminded herself. They only had themselves to blame.

CHAPTER TWENTY-THREE

The past

Esther

Since that night in the woods, I'd been avoiding both Hiram and Fergus. I'd kept as close to the house as possible, only going as far as the stream to collect water and finding excuses to be inside whenever I heard Fergus's voice. I couldn't face either of them. After Hiram's rush to leave me, I knew I wouldn't want to hear anything he had to say. There was no way he could want to marry me, not now he knew the sort of person I was. But even though I knew my dreams were over, I didn't want to hear that from Hiram. I wasn't ready to accept that my life wouldn't be as I'd planned.

I couldn't bear to hear the confirmation that I would never be Mrs Hiram Stewart. Fergus, I was avoiding for different reasons. He'd surprised me with his kindness that night. It would have been the perfect opportunity for him to point out all the things I'd done wrong, for him to once again show how superior he was, but he hadn't. He'd listened, and he'd cared, and he'd done everything he could to make me feel better. However, we'd had too many years of hating each other for me to feel comfortable owing him anything. I couldn't escape the fact Fergus was now the keeper of my worst secret and could be planning to use it against me at any time. Although, maybe I'd have preferred that to being indebted to him; it was too much to have to let go of my dreams with Hiram and accept that Fergus wasn't the villain I'd thought. It was easier to avoid them both and pretend all this had never happened.

The problem was that avoiding them could only work for so long. Eventually, there would be a point when I'd have to face them. Even though a week had passed by the time my luck ran out, it hadn't been long enough. I was just setting off home from the harbour when Hiram appeared in front of me. Immediately, I span round as if I'd been heading in the opposite direction, despite that leaving me nowhere to go but the sea

"Esther, wait," he called out, putting his hand on my shoulder and turning me around.

I pulled myself out of his grasp.

"I'm in a rush, Hiram, I can't stop to talk."

"You've just changed direction completely, and you've already delivered whatever you had in the basket. So you can't be in too much of a hurry."

"Have you been spying on me?" I asked, surprised.

After his desperation to get away from me the previous week, it wasn't what I'd expected.

"Maybe," he answered with the smallest hint of a smile. "I've been trying to speak to you all week, but I got the impression you were avoiding me."

"Can you blame me after what happened?"

"No, not really. I'm so sorry, Esther. Can we go somewhere, please? Just to talk."

And although I hadn't wanted to, although this was the moment I'd so wanted to avoid, I found my feet following his, stepping off the track and into the woods. As soon as we were out of sight, he stopped and turned to face me. There was none of the fear I'd felt last time I'd been alone with him. He was my Hiram again, the Hiram who made me feel I was the only person in the world.

"Esther, I'm so sorry about what happened…"

"No, don't say anything else," I interrupted. "I understand that you won't want to marry me after the way I behaved. No one would. I know that what I did was sinful and wrong, but I don't want to hear you say it."

"That's not it, Esther, you've misunderstood."

My heart leapt. Was he going to tell me we could be together after all? But then he continued.

"Well, you've not misunderstood everything. You're right, I can't marry you, but not because of what we did. I should have listened when you asked me to stop. I shouldn't have kept pushing you. That night in the woods was my mistake entirely, and I'm so sorry. If I could turn back time and change things I would, but it has nothing to do with why we can't get married. I can't marry you because my father won't allow it. I'm being sent away. He wants me to attend the school he went to, and he expects me to find a suitable wife by the time I finish."

"But I can be a suitable wife."

I was feeling more hopeful again. Hiram didn't hate me, and he wasn't disgusted by me. He was just worried about going away.

"No, Esther, in my father's eyes you can't. He wants me to have a wife that Lord MacAird would be happy to invite as a house guest, and you know that Lord MacAird would never see a girl from the village as anything other than a servant."

"Well, who cares what your father thinks? You

don't always have to do what he says. We could run away together, move to a city like Edinburgh or Glasgow. We could have a whole new life."

"But I'd be penniless, Esther. Can you honestly say you'd still feel the same about me if we were living in one room? Crowded into a building bursting with other people, short on food and working every hour in a noisy, dirty factory?"

"Why would it have to be like that, Hiram?"

"Because it would, Esther. I don't have any money of my own, or any qualifications. You don't either. It wouldn't be the life you've imagined us having unless my father approved, and that will never happen."

"Well, I might enjoy working in a factory. It has to be better than staying here forever and my life never changing."

"You know you'd hate it, Esther. You might want something different, but you definitely don't want to work hard."

Finally, a smile escaped me. I couldn't deny that. I'd been complaining about how hard and unfair my life was since before I was expected to work.

"And," he continued, "forgive me if this isn't true, but I've always suspected you wouldn't be quite so keen on me if I didn't offer the prospect of living in a nice house, with someone else to do the hard work."

This I thought perhaps I could deny. Although

I'd found some other lads as attractive as Hiram, they weren't as kind as him, or as clever. Obviously, I'd always longed to be Mrs Hiram Stewart and live in a house like his—I couldn't pretend I hadn't been dreaming of a life like his mother's—but it was impossible to separate out all the different pieces of Hiram and know what had made me love him. However, it was also possible he was right. It hadn't taken much for me to see that running away with him was no more my dream than being here without him. But regardless of where my feelings had come from, it didn't make the idea of losing him hurt any less.

"So even after everything that's happened between us, you're still going to leave? You must have known this last week, and yet you still did those things in the woods. You said it was alright as long as we loved each other, but you already knew we were over."

That was when I realised I was angry as well as hurt. Maybe I didn't love Hiram as much as the idea of a better life, but that didn't make the knowledge he hadn't valued me as much as I'd thought any easier to take.

"I really am sorry, Esther. I've been so angry recently, and I've done lots of things that I can't explain. Things that I wish I hadn't. I should have listened to you when you first told me to stop, and I am truly sorry. Like I said, if I could do things differently, I promise I would."

He looked so sad then. So sad, and so young. More like the Hiram of my childhood than the Hiram of the last week or so. I believed what he was saying, but I wasn't ready to stop being angry with him.

"You can't though, Hiram. It happened, and you're still going to leave me here alone."

"That's the other reason I needed to talk to you, Esther. There's something else you need to know. Something more important than what happened between us."

I couldn't imagine how that could be true. Nothing could be more important than the fact we were over. I couldn't form a response. I just looked at him, waiting to see what he could possibly have to say. In my mind, unless a mythical beast appeared alongside him and rampaged through the area, tearing down all in its path, nothing could seem more worthy of discussion than the fact he was leaving me behind.

"Lord MacAird wants to clear the village. I heard my father discussing plans with him."

"Our village? Clear it as in making us leave? But he can't. These are our lands. We've always paid our dues. He can't be so short of money that he needs to get rid of us and fill the place with sheep. He's got enough money to build his big house. How can he need more?"

"I don't think it's about money. It's about a road. He wants to build a new road to the harbour, so it's easier for his guests to enjoy the scenery. The simplest way to do that is to follow the track, but that goes right through the village and the houses are in the way."

"Not ours, though, at the top of the fields."

"I think he feels it will be easier to remove everyone at once. Lots of landlords have had problems with poor harvests and tenants needing support. I think he's decided that clearing you all would remove any potential problems."

"But where would we go?"

"Lord MacAird is going to arrange passage to Nova Scotia for anyone that wants it."

"And what if we don't want to go?"

"I don't know. They didn't talk about an alternative."

"So I won't have you, and I won't have my home?"

"But you've never wanted to stay here, Esther."

"That doesn't mean I want it taken from me though. Why are you telling me this, Hiram?"

"I don't know when they plan to tell the tenants, or how much notice they intend to give you. I thought you could warn your father. He could get everyone organised. Maybe they can do something."

So I'd been right to avoid Hiram. Speaking to him had destroyed everything, although not in the way I'd expected. I hadn't been able to imagine anything more significant than my relationship with Hiram ending, but Lord MacAird's power over our lives made him just as frightening as any mythical beast. That we would all have to leave was so shocking, so beyond what I'd expected, it never even crossed my mind to wonder why Hiram had come to me instead of Fergus.

CHAPTER TWENTY-FOUR

The present

Eilidh didn't sleep well the night her parents had ambushed her. It seemed to take hours for her mind to switch off, and then her dreams were a disturbing rehash of the stories told by Alan and Claire. She'd expected to feel exhausted the next day, but fortunately, her excitement about travelling to Glasgow that evening carried her through. She'd been in the office first thing before heading up to the building site to sort out a couple of issues. As she clicked out of a call with a building supplies yard, she noticed a figure waving to her from lower down the fields. The red hair billowing in the breeze and the tiny person weaving around their legs told Eilidh it was Beth. The issues she'd been called out to deal with had all been sorted, so she made her way down to say hello.

"What are your plans for lunch?" Beth shouted as Eilidh got closer.

"I thought I'd probably skip it today, so I could finish a bit earlier and get sorted for Glasgow."

"Oh, we'll not keep you then. Get on with what you need to do. You must be itching to get down there and find out more."

"Well, I am, but if there was a lunch offer about to be made, I'm totally up for changing my plans. It'll not take long to shove some things in a bag later, and I'm not getting the train until six."

Beth smiled as she leant down to retrieve a bag from the floor by her feet, a protective hand on Grace's head as she did so.

"Seeing as the sun's shining, we thought we'd have a picnic, and we may just have picked up your favourite sandwich from the cafe as well, so if you're sure you can spare ten minutes, we'd love you to join us."

Eilidh adored the sandwiches at the Ardmhor House cafe. It was a running joke between her and Beth that while Eilidh was generally very adventurous, she still ordered the same thing every time they met for lunch. The mere mention of her favourite had set Eilidh's stomach rumbling, so there was no way she was turning down Beth's offer. Instead, she helped spread a rug on the ground, and opened up Rory's sandwich for him, while Beth fed Grace.

"I may have had a slight ulterior motive for our lunch," confessed Beth as she sat rubbing Grace's back a few minutes later.

"You mean that spending time with me isn't reason enough?" said Eilidh, with a look of mock indignation.

"Well, of course!" said Beth, laughing. "But I wanted to tell someone what I found out this morning, and it turns out that Rory and Grace just don't care."

"How do you know I will?"

"Good point! In fact, you probably won't, but I'm hoping you'll be polite enough to pretend."

"I'll do my best," Eilidh said between bites.

"So, you know I told you that the factor's son and your ancestor went on a different boat to everyone else?"

"Yes, except the girl isn't my ancestor, after all."

"Oh, I'm sorry, Eilidh. I didn't think. Is it going to upset you to talk about this?"

"No, carry on, it's fine. I'm still interested in what happened."

"Alright, so I did a bit of research and I found out exactly which port the Mary Ann, the boat they died on, was sailing to. There's a historical society there and they have lots of records detailing everyone who disembarked from the ships. The factor's son was called Hiram Stewart, and as you'd expect, seeing as they died before reaching New Zealand, there's no record of him arriving, but there are members of the historical society who are descendants of people who survived that journey. They're going to put out feelers and see if anyone kept a record of their experiences on the boat. Someone might have mentioned Hiram and his girlfriend, they might know if they really were running away or if something else happened."

"Wow, you've worked quickly on that. You'd only just realised they went somewhere different from everyone else the other day."

"It's night feeds," said Beth. "Whenever I'm up with Grace, I keep myself awake by researching stuff on my phone. It's not likely anyone will have any information though."

"Well, you never know. You've found enough diaries and letters in the past. There must be other people writing them as well."

"That's true. I suppose all I can do is wait and see. Anyway, how about you? How are you feeling about going to Glasgow?"

They both feigned amazement at the worm Rory brought over to show them before Eilidh answered.

"I'm excited about finding out more. But I am nervous. I stayed in a hotel last time, but this time I'm staying at Sylvie's grans, well, my gran's,

I suppose."

"No wonder you're nervous. The idea of getting to know new people as family would definitely scare me."

"Yeah, but in fairness, everything scares you."

"Oi, cheeky," replied Beth. "But if you're going down that route, I suppose I can be cheeky too. Have you spoken to your parents yet?"

"I'm not sure I can really call them that anymore, but yes, I have. They both turned up after work yesterday, so I couldn't avoid them."

"And? What did they have to say?"

"Well, basically, they both said that Keith, my biological dad, had been abusive, and that they'd had no choice but to run away."

"So, do you believe them?"

"It doesn't fit with anything Sylvie and her family, I mean my family, have said."

"But they could be the ones that are lying," said Beth "After all, you've only just met them, so you don't really know them."

"I have thought of that," Eilidh replied abruptly, showing her frustration.

"Oh, I didn't mean to make it sound as if you wouldn't have. I just meant it's impossible to know who's telling the truth."

"Don't worry, I know what you meant. But my family in Glasgow has no reason to lie. There are loads of them. It's not as if they need to recruit new members, and it's not like they'll gain anything from getting to know me. I'm not loaded or anything. Whereas my so-called parents have been lying to me for years, so I wouldn't put it past them to lie about Keith, if they thought it'd help justify what they've done."

"Hmm, I suppose the only thing you can do is keep an open mind. You can't know exactly what happened, so you don't want to jump to any conclusions."

Beth handed Grace to Eilidh as she started folding up the picnic rug and gathering their rubbish into a bag.

"Fine," sighed Eilidh, inhaling the scent of Grace's soft hair. "I mean, you're right. Sorry for being so defensive before. I should approach this more like you would instead of jumping in with both feet."

"No, don't apologise." Beth reached out and took Grace from Eilidh, carefully wrapping the carrier around her and readying them for the journey home. "And don't do anything differently. I'd never be brave enough to go off and stay with people that are essentially strangers, so I'd completely miss the opportunity to find out the truth. You'll figure it all out, eventually. Just try not to take anything at face value."

CHAPTER TWENTY-FIVE

The past

Fergus

After leaving Hiram, I ran for a long time. I didn't know where I was heading. I was simply trying to outrun the memory of what had taken place on the shore. It was an impossible task though. My breathing was ragged, and my legs ached, but the image of Hiram leaning in towards me, the sensation of his lips meeting mine, the sound of his voice saying it was me he dreamed of—those recollections never dulled. I couldn't outrun my shock, my disgust, and my confusion. I knew what Hiram had done was wrong. The Bible says that for two men to behave together as a man should with a woman is detestable. It had never occurred to me to consider a man in that way. When my thoughts turned to those things, it was Isobel that I saw myself with. Or more troublingly, it was sometimes Esther who appeared in my mind. But despite my difficulty with controlling my thoughts, I'd never once imagined doing anything like that with another man. When Mr Briggs, the schoolmaster, had made a point of reading Leviticus to us, reminding us of the things that could put our eternal souls in peril, I'd found the idea of men lying together funny, I hadn't comprehended that some men might actually want to do that. I'd wondered instead what the Bible thought of four siblings having to make do with one bed between them.

As my muscles burned and I left the shelter of the woods, moving up the higher, barer reaches of the hills, I tried to make sense of what I was feeling. I was definitely shocked. When I'd been pushing Hiram about who he had feelings for other than Esther, I'd had no inkling of the direction events would take. I'd always known Hiram was different from the other lads in the village. He was quieter and more sensitive. Reading and learning weren't chores for him, they weren't simply things to endure before being released to the fun of sport and games. Also, he'd never wanted to solve a problem with his fists. But he wasn't that different. He'd always been in love with Esther, and because everyone thought she felt the same, he'd had the quiet respect of the other lads. It seemed impossible that Hiram could have been having thoughts like that.

I lost my footing on a patch of scree and skidded to a halt, my heart pounding in my chest as I righted myself. But I couldn't stop. Alongside my shock, there was anger. How could Hiram have involved me in something like that? He'd kissed me, actually kissed me. He'd made me do something sinful and wrong. I wasn't just angry at Hiram though. I was disgusted by the fact that I hadn't stopped him, not initially. When I'd felt the pressure of his mouth on mine, the force of his lips parting, I hadn't instantly shoved him away. In the moment before my arms found their strength and my legs started to run—I'd felt something stir. I might have been motionless, but something had been moving inside me, in the same way it did when Isobel smiled at me and pulled me closer when we danced or when I remembered Esther curled up against me in the woods. Surely I shouldn't have felt that? Did it mean I'd wanted it too, even though I'd never thought of it before? Was Hiram really one of those disgusting sinners Mr Briggs had warned us about? Was I? More than anything, I wished I could turn back time. I wished I'd not gone looking for Hiram that morning, and I wished I hadn't found Esther in the woods. I wished

I could go back to when things seemed less complicated, when I could happily antagonise Esther and enjoy my time with Hiram. Instead, I found myself avoiding them both.

It wasn't a simple task avoiding people you usually saw daily in a small community, but I managed it for almost a week. Obviously, I'd seen Esther. Living practically next door meant it was impossible not to, but I'd avoided being in a position to talk to her. It didn't surprise anyone. The days of us being inseparable had been over for years. People perhaps noticed the absence of Hiram more. He had been a fixture in the village each evening for as long as anyone could remember, but if they did notice, no one found it significant enough to comment on. After all, lovers tiffs happened, and everyone knew Esther wasn't easy to please. I was holding Isobel's drop spindle when my luck ran out. We'd been talking as she worked, and when her mother quickly called her inside, she'd shoved the spindle into my hands. It meant I was trapped waiting for Isobel's return when I saw Esther approaching.

"I need to talk to you urgently," she whispered. "I've just been speaking to Hiram."

A dread filled me. Surely Hiram wouldn't have told Esther about what had happened on the shore. But what else could have left her looking so shaken? I didn't want anyone overhearing what she had to say. I placed Isobel's spindle onto her stool as gently as I could, hoping I hadn't upset her progress, and steered Esther away into the woods.

"How much has he told you?" I whispered as we cleared the edge of the houses.

"Everything, I think," replied Esther, looking a little confused. "I didn't realise he'd already spoken to you, although I suppose that makes more sense. I just don't know what to do, Fergus. It's going to destroy everything."

Knowing Esther as I had for so long, I hadn't expected her to react so calmly. I hadn't thought that Hiram would ever tell her what had happened between us, but seeing as he had, I'd expected more anger. I wondered if she was struggling to make sense of things in the same way I was.

"It doesn't have to destroy anything, Esther. Nothing really happened. Hiram was just mixed up. I've already forgotten about it, and I'm sure Hiram will too. Nothing needs to change."

"What, so you think Hiram's just got things wrong? That Lord MacAird won't do anything?"

"What does this have to do with Lord MacAird?" I asked.

The feeling of dread had turned to absolute fear. I knew what we had done was wrong, that it was illegal as well as sinful, and that it must have hurt Esther, but surely there was no need to involve Lord MacAird. It had only been a kiss lasting a moment. Esther was looking at me as if I was crazy.

"Well, it's him that wants to clear the village, isn't it?" she said. "None of this would be happening if it wasn't for him."

That was when things stopped making sense. Was Esther talking about something different from the events on the shore?

"Lord MacAird wants to clear the village?" I asked incredulously.

"Yes, to make way for a new road to the harbour, the lower houses are in the way." Esther's reply sounded exasperated. "You did know, didn't you? Or did you think I was talking about something else?"

"No" I said quickly. "I was just confused, that's all. I don't understand why a new road needs to affect our houses at the top of the fields?"

"That's what I said, but Hiram said Lord MacAird thinks it would be easier to get rid of all of us. Then he can do what he wants with the land around Ardmhor House and not have to deal with any unwanted neighbours."

"But he can't do that. What we pay him might be called rent now, but he knows he doesn't really own our land. He promised after the last rent increases that the land would always be ours."

"I think it was just easy for him to say those

words, Fergus. He's hardly ever here, he doesn't know any of us. He'd probably quite happily see the back of us if it meant he could have a nicer garden."

"So, what are we going to do?"

I couldn't take it in. Esther was right. If Lord MacAird wanted us off the land, there probably wasn't much we could do to stop him. Our fathers had tried to stop the rent increases when Mr Stewart first arrived in the area, but the rent had gone up all the same.

"Hiram said he was trying to persuade his father that it made sense to keep the top houses —that the rent from us would help to fund the new road. He said we should try to get our fathers to organise a resistance, like they did with the rents."

"But that didn't work," I said hopelessly.

"Well, I know that, but we still need to try, don't we? Maybe you should speak to Hiram again, see if he's found out anything else. Then we could speak to our fathers together."

Speaking to Hiram was the last thing I wanted to do, but losing my home was a more frightening prospect than a tough conversation.

"Do you want me to come with you?" Esther offered.

"No," I replied quickly. The conversation would be awkward enough, and as it appeared Esther knew nothing of what had taken place between us, I wanted to keep it that way. Speaking to Hiram was something I needed to do alone.

I found Hiram in the clearing in the woods. It seemed to have become the place for difficult and upsetting moments. He got up as he saw me approach, but he didn't speak.

"What do you know about the plans for the village?" I asked as soon as I was close enough for him to hear.

"Fergus, I'm so sorry about what happened the other day. I don't know what came over me."

I held up my hands in front of me as if they could act as a barrier to his words.

"I don't want to talk about it, Hiram. I don't even want to think about it. Just tell me what Lord MacAird is planning for the village."

Hiram looked hurt, but perhaps a little relieved, too. Maybe he had been dreading the moment we'd meet again as much as I had.

"I don't really know any more than I told Esther," he said. "Lord MacAird wants the entire village gone. Most of the bottom houses would need to be removed to create the new road, and he thinks clearing the top houses at the same time will protect him from any future obligations. Some landlords have found dealing with famines on their estates troublesome over the last few years, and he seems keen to avoid that. I've been trying to plant the idea with my father that keeping the top houses would both allow the new road and provide a revenue for building it, but he's not keen. He thinks the village is just too close to Ardmhor House for Lord MacAird's comfort. He wants to enjoy the scenery, not be reminded of the people who live in it."

"But where will we go?"

"Well, Lord MacAird has agreed to pay for passage on a boat to Nova Scotia. Although he is planning to sell whatever you leave behind to meet the costs."

"We've got to stop this, Hiram. I can't leave here. This is my home. I don't want to start again somewhere else."

I suddenly felt an overwhelming urge to cry. If Lord MacAird wanted us out, how could we possibly fight it? But at the same time, how could I possibly leave? I knew every part of the land, every hill, every tree, and every rock. It was all a part of me, and I didn't see how I could exist away from it. I realised I wouldn't see Hiram again either. We saw each other every day, but that wouldn't be possible if I was beyond the far mountains and across the ocean. Everything I knew would be gone. It felt beyond hope.

"I'll never see you again," I said, defeated.

Hiram put his arm around my shoulders, and I didn't stop him. We'd comforted each other a thousand times before and despite what had happened, this didn't feel any different.

"No one else knows me as well as you do. Who will I talk to?" I asked.

"I suppose at least Lord MacAird will pay for everyone to travel together, so you'll still have the same people around you, even if it is a different place."

I knew he was trying to be helpful, but the place felt as important as the people. And no matter how I'd felt over the last few days, I knew it didn't matter who else was with me. I didn't want to be without Hiram, the best friend I'd ever had.

"I don't want other people," I retorted.

Hiram sat down and looked at me. He stared at me for so long that I eventually sat down beside him.

"Are you saying you feel the same as me about what happened the other day?" he asked quietly. "Because I meant every word I said. I am sorry if I made you uncomfortable, but I'm not sorry I kissed you. I love you, Fergus, and it's still you that I dream of."

Then it was my turn to be silent. I wanted to explain to Hiram that I loved him too, but I knew I didn't love him in the way that he meant. It was still a struggle to accept that he felt like that.

"I'm sorry," I began. "You know me better than anyone else. Whenever anything happens, it's always you I want to talk to about it. There is no one I want to spend time with as much as you, but I don't feel like that. The idea of kissing you feels wrong. It is wrong, Hiram. The Bible says so. Men aren't supposed to do those things together. Perhaps it's better that we're going to be separated."

"Yes, perhaps it is," Hiram said bitterly, as he stood up and began to walk away. "I can see that you wouldn't want to be tarnished by someone as sinful as me."

"Hiram, come back," I called after him.

I didn't follow him though. I didn't try to catch him as he disappeared further into the woods. There didn't seem to be any point. It felt as if distant mountains and an ocean wouldn't make any difference. It felt like the distance between us was already too great to overcome.

CHAPTER TWENTY-SIX

The present

"**I**s this all a bit much?"

Sylvie's voice was a mere whisper, but it wasn't difficult for Eilidh to hear what she was saying. They were both snuggled up under floral quilts in Sylvia's spare room. The last of the other family members had braved the rain and set off for their respective homes an hour or so earlier, leaving Sylvia, Sylvie, and Eilidh to clear up before heading for bed themselves.

"Is what a bit too much?" Eilidh asked in reply.

"Well, everything. All the aunties and cousins, and singing, and you and me sharing a room. Is it too much too soon?"

The glow from the streetlight outside the window gave enough light for Eilidh to see the concern on Sylvie's face. A narrow three drawer chest separated the two single beds. There was a tiny wardrobe at the foot of Sylvie's bed, and the door to the room was at the end of Eilidh's. There was no space for anything else. It meant that her proximity to Sylvie could only be described as intimate, but it didn't feel too much. It felt nice. In fact, the whole evening had been everything she could have wished for. She'd stepped out of Glasgow station into chilly wind and heavy rain, but the atmosphere in Sylvia's little semi-detached couldn't have been warmer. Keith had been the eldest of four siblings and the only boy. Each of his sisters had married, some of them more than once, and as a result Sylvie had ten cousins on that side of her family. Four of those cousins had little children of their own, so Sylvia's house had been bursting at the seams with all of her daughters, grandchildren, and great grandchildren present. There had been laughter, teasing, a couple of disagreements, lots of eating and drinking, and a fairly raucous sing song. Eilidh might have grown up with plenty of cousins, but it was rare for them to all gather in one place. The physical distance between them kept things slightly more reserved, and most of the time, it had just been her and her parents. Sylvie's family was different. They were tight knit. Most of them lived within walking distance of each other and were in and out of each other's houses frequently. It was completely alien to

Eilidh, but she was absolutely loving it.

"No, it's not too much," she reassured Sylvie. "It's great. I want to be part of everything."

"Alright, but make sure you say if it gets too overwhelming. I've grown up with them, but I still find them a bit much at times. Why do you think I chose a flat that was a drive rather than a walk away?"

Eilidh could tell Sylvie was smiling as she said the last part, but she appreciated the way she was trying to put her at ease. As she let the rain lull her to sleep, Eilidh was smiling too. It meant so much that this woman, her sister, who she hadn't even known existed two weeks ago, was determined everything should go well between them.

Saturday was another day that passed easily with her new family. The rain had stopped during the night, so Eilidh, Sylvie, and Sylvia caught a bus into the city centre and wandered around the shops for a while, before eating lunch in a cafe. They'd spent the afternoon looking through old photo albums. Eilidh had seen a resemblance between her and Keith in some of his childhood pictures, and she could definitely see she'd been very similar to Sylvie when she was little. Sylvia had spent the afternoon fussing over both Eilidh and Sylvie. She couldn't get over the fact that the two sisters were finally together, but she found it easier to express her feelings through tea and biscuits than she did through words. Keith's youngest sibling, Gail, had booked a table at a local pub for them that evening. This time it was just the six of them, Keith's three sisters, along with Sylvia, Sylvie, and Eilidh. It made for a much quieter gathering than the night before, but it gave Eilidh more opportunities to learn about her father.

"He would have loved you," stated Susan, the eldest of the three girls.

"Do you think?" asked Eilidh, fishing for more.

"Oh yes, definitely. You're so like him. He was always laughing and joking, and he always knew exactly the right thing to say. Not that he was perfect or anything, he got up to his fair share of mischief, but because he had the gift of the gab, he'd talk his way out of trouble, and the rest of us would take the blame. But we never minded, he'd usually talk us out of being cross with him before we'd had time to go running to mum!"

"He sounds like quite a character," Eilidh said with a smile.

"He was," sighed Susan. "He'd light up any room would our Keith. As soon as he arrived, you knew the party had started. It hit mum really hard when he died. He was the apple of her eye."

Eilidh was wondering how to ask what had caused Keith's death, but the arrival of their food interrupted them. The young woman who carried their order out to them on a huge tray didn't seem to have worked there long. She struggled to offload each item to its recipient without upending the entire tray. Once everyone had been served and conversation resumed, Eilidh found herself talking to Amanda, the middle of the three sisters, who was sitting at her other side.

"Sylvie says you're overseeing a building site at the moment, Eilidh."

"Well, I'm the project manager, but the construction team is so experienced that it's been really easy so far."

"That's good, love. It's funny you working with builders and Sylvie working for a builders' merchant. Your dad worked as a brickie, too. It must be in the blood."

Eilidh chose to focus on the connection to Keith, rather than the fact she'd grown up living with a builder. She loved how proud Keith's sisters were of him. It made her feel proud to be his daughter. Everything she heard from Keith's family was about how kind, how loving, how generous, and how funny he had been. No one had a bad word to say about him. Eilidh tried to remember Beth's advice to approach things with an open mind, but nothing she heard here fitted with Alan and Claire's stories. It seemed obvious to her who had been lying, and it wasn't the people surrounding her now.

On Sunday morning, after a full fry up, Sylvia asked Eilidh to look in the top drawer of the sideboard for another photo album. As she retrieved it, a birth certificate became dislodged from the stack of papers underneath. Eilidh saw it had Sylvie's name on and was surprised to find their birthdays were only days apart. She was about to remark on the coincidence when she noticed the year of Sylvie's birth. For some reason, she'd never asked Sylvie her age, she'd just assumed there were a couple of years between them. However, according to this birth certificate, they'd been born in the same year, with Sylvie's birth just two days after Eilidh's. Somewhere in the back of her mind, an alarm bell sounded. How had Keith, who was supposedly heartbroken by her mother's departure, had another daughter just days after her own birth?

"Sylvie's birth certificate was underneath this," Eilidh said as she handed the album to Sylvia. "It says she was only born two days after me. I don't understand how that's possible."

In the short walk from the sideboard to the settee, Eilidh had decided there had been too much secrecy already. She needed to know exactly what was going on.

"Oh, I hadn't realised that was in there," replied Sylvia a little shakily, sidestepping the real issue.

"Did you know this? That we were born two days apart." Eilidh directed her questions at Sylvie this time. "I don't see how my father could be devastated by my mother leaving him, but also have another baby at the same time."

Sylvia jumped in before Sylvie had a chance to respond. "Keith was the best son any mother could have wanted. He was everything anyone could have wanted, but as I'm sure his sisters told you last night, he wasn't an angel. So yes, there were only days between the two of you being born and yes, Sylvie knew, but it doesn't make your dad a bad person, or mean he was any less upset by your mother leaving. He just made a mistake, that's all."

"But he did cheat on my mother?" Eilidh asked, wanting to be absolutely sure, trying to remain open-minded as Beth had suggested.

"Aye, he did," sighed Sylvia. "But that's what men do, isn't it? They get easily tempted. It doesn't mean he didn't love your mam. I don't think any of us can say we've never made a mistake."

Eilidh wasn't sure where to go with that information. She certainly wouldn't see Rich cheating on her as proof of his undying love, but she knew first-hand how tempted she'd been by

Jay. Nothing had really happened between them in the end, but she'd wanted it to, and it easily could have. Could she really condemn Keith for a mistake she'd nearly made herself?

"And it turned out for the best," Sylvia continued. "It meant I got my little Sylvie, and Keith had Janey, her mam, to turn to when he was left all alone. He never really got over the betrayal, you know. The love of your life running off with your best friend would change anyone."

Eilidh's internal alarm bells were ringing again at the way Keith's betrayal of her mum was being written off as a simple mistake. It seemed that was no big deal, just what men did. Whereas her mum leaving Keith was apparently enough to ruin his life. She was also concerned how this conversation might feel for Sylvie. It must hurt to hear her own mother being referred to as someone Keith just turned to for comfort, when Claire was being called the love of his life. Sylvie didn't seem too perturbed though, and Eilidh got the impression she might have heard this view expressed many times before.

"Do either of you fancy a bit of a walk?" Eilidh asked suddenly. The walls of Sylvia's front room seemed to be closing in on her, and she felt a desperate urge to escape.

Within half an hour, the three of them were

strolling through the gates of the park at the end of Sylvia's road. They followed a path leading to a small boating lake, avoiding children on scooters and over exuberant dogs as they walked.

"Dad used to bring me here to feed the ducks," Sylvie said after a while.

She'd been quiet since the revelation about their birthdays, and Eilidh was relieved to see her relaxing again.

"What was he like as a dad? Was he a down on the floor, playing games and reading bedtime stories, kind of dad? Or was he more hands off?"

"He was away a lot, but when he was here, he was really involved. We'd spend every minute together. He'd make up games for the two of us to play. Even when I was older, he wanted to know everything I'd been doing."

Eilidh felt a pang of jealousy, imagining all the things Sylvie and Keith had done together. All the things that she'd missed out on, all the things she'd never get to do. Not that Alan had been distant or anything, but he wasn't actually her father, and no matter who was right or wrong in all this, that would never change.

"He wasn't that keen when I started seeing Chris, was he Gran?" Sylvie continued with a laugh. "He'd hardly let him in the house at first, would he?"

Eilidh had always been aware there was a stereotype that fathers didn't want their daughters to date: that they'd say things like 'no one's good enough for my princess' or threaten to do potential boyfriends serious harm. But she'd assumed it was just that, a stereotype. Alan had welcomed Rich into their home with open arms. At the time, she'd been pleased her dad was so laid back, but now she wondered if it was because he wasn't really her father. Maybe he just hadn't felt the same need to protect her.

"He was always looking out for you," Sylvia said, lovingly.

"He'd hardly let my mum out of his sight when he was home, would he, Gran? He'd make sure anywhere she wanted to go he could go with her. That way, he knew she wouldn't be lonely or get hassled by anyone. I think she found it hard when he was away. I was only little when she died, but I'll never forget how much they loved being together."

"Aye, they did pet," Sylvia said sadly. "He had to go through a lot of tragedy, my Keith. And you're right. He looked after her so well. Not like these fellas you two have got. Letting you out all weekend without even checking up on you. Keith was like his dad in how protective he was. I'd have seen the back of my Reggie's hand if I'd gone off gallivanting for days, leaving him to fend for himself."

"Gran!" Sylvie exclaimed, with a touch of exasperation in her voice. "How many times do

I have to tell you that things like that aren't acceptable anymore?"

"Well, maybe they should be," Sylvia huffed in reply. "We've got you and Chris not married, and Eilidh not even taking her husband's name. In my day, the men were in charge. That's just the way it was. My dad laid down the law to my mam, Reggie did to me, and Keith knew that was the way it was supposed to be. The world's all mixed up now with this women's lib stuff, and we're not any better off for it, are we?"

"Alright Gran! Let's get you home for a cup of tea, before you do yourself a mischief," Sylvie said, laughing.

Eilidh wasn't sure this was something she could laugh off though. Today she was hearing more and more that could support the stories Alan and Claire had told. She'd been so convinced they were lying—that Keith was this great bloke that could do no wrong. But perhaps that was only because Sylvia didn't actually see domestic violence as a problem. In fact, she seemed to think it was the proper way of things. Who to trust was becoming less and less obvious.

CHAPTER TWENTY-SEVEN

The past

Esther

The atmosphere in the village had been sombre and tense for a few weeks. To be honest, it had matched my mood. The weather had remained mild, but there were no impromptu dances as the light faded on balmy evenings. No one was in the right frame of mind. Fergus and I had approached our fathers with Hiram's revelations, and they'd quickly organised a deputation to speak to Mr Stewart. He, however, denied all knowledge of a plan to clear the village and shut the door in their faces. Mr Stewart's words did not convince anyone. Given a choice between believing Hiram or his father, the village was far more inclined to trust Hiram. A smaller delegation approached Lord MacAird directly, but unsurprisingly, he declined to see them. They didn't even make it across the threshold of Ardmhor House. So everyone was existing in a state of uncertainty.

Some people tried to believe there was no problem, but you could see the idea was still niggling at the corners of their minds. They couldn't ignore the fact that their rights to the land hadn't been strong enough to protect them from change before. Others felt the need to organise and fight. They came up with plans to defend the houses, to refuse to leave, but it was difficult to get the support they would need when the threat hadn't yet been confirmed. In many ways life seemed to carry on as normal, summer was drawing to a close, there was harvesting to be done, and animals needed to be cared for, but the thought that something bigger might happen, that all this work might be in vain, was always hovering in the background.

Amongst all this, I realised I had a problem of my own. A more personal one. One that seemed bigger to me than the thought of the entire village disappearing. My courses hadn't started when they should have. For a week I expected to find blood or feel the pains, but there was nothing, and now another week and a half had gone by. Fortunately, with everything else that was going on, my mother hadn't noticed anything amiss. Usually, I suffered from such terrible stomach cramps, I struggled to function on the worst days, and while I wasn't missing that pain, I knew what its absence could mean. I knew it had to be connected to what I'd done with Hiram. That was when I realised he'd been wrong. It seemed it was indeed possible to create a baby the first time. Once again, I wished I could go back and do things differently, but those wishes were futile. I knew that not every swollen stomach resulted in a baby, that things could go wrong, and I wondered if there were ways to make things go wrong. But who could I speak to about a thing like that? The story of Quiet Janet's daughter rolled continuously through my head. I couldn't stand the shame of having a child outside of marriage. There was no way I could bring that shame upon my family. But if I didn't act, a child was going to arrive regardless of how I felt about the idea. The only possible solution was to get married and to do it quickly, but I didn't know if that could be arranged without having to tell someone why; and having to admit to the mess I was in was what scared me the most. I knew I needed to talk to Hiram. Perhaps he'd view marrying me differently once he was aware of the situation. At the very least, I wouldn't be dealing with this alone.

After four visits to the factor's house, being told each time that Hiram was not available, I began to doubt my plan. I spent every spare minute wandering between the places where we used to meet, but it was to no avail. Eventually, I had to admit to myself that Hiram was not going to share my burden. After another week with no bleeding, all hope deserted me. I wondered about telling Fergus. He had been so kind the night he found me in the woods, so unexpectedly sympathetic. I allowed myself the comfort of a daydream where he immediately volunteered to marry me. Some days I embellished the dream a little: Fergus would confess he'd always wanted to marry me, that I was the reason he'd been arguing with Hiram by the stream that day. I pictured us leaving church, a crown of flowers atop my shining hair, people whispering that I was the most beautiful bride they'd ever seen. Those dreams were my only solace. In reality, I knew that apart from that one occasion in the woods, Fergus had usually delighted in my downfall. The likelihood was he'd go straight to my parents with the truth. Also, it was obvious that outside my daydream, his heart belonged to Isobel. If he really was as good as everyone claimed, if he offered to marry me just to save me from shame, he'd be doing it at the expense of their happiness. Could I really ruin both of their futures in order to save my own? So for days, I did nothing but wrestle with indecision, much as the rest of the village seemed to be doing.

Then, one day, as the harvesting was almost complete, something finally happened. It was evening, just as the sun was setting, a great fiery ball sinking behind the distant hills, tinging the sky with orange and pink. It was the one time in the day when you could rely on most people being in the same place. There had been no dancing or singing for weeks, but people were still milling about, trying to enjoy that bit of peace before their labours began again the next day. A sudden hush spread through the houses. The factor had been spotted approaching, and he wasn't alone. Mr Stewart and the small party of men stopped in the centre of the lower houses, leaving those of us from the top houses to rush down the path to find out what was going on. Most of the women were supervising their children, readying them for sleep, and couldn't leave their homes, but Isobel and I followed Fergus down the path. We could sense this was something important, and we wanted to hear it for ourselves. As we drew near, we saw it wasn't Mr Stewart at the centre of the group: it was Lord MacAird himself. He was flanked by Mr Stewart and a few of his men. It seemed they had purposefully chosen the bigger ones, the ones with the hardest, least open faces. The men weren't what drew my eye though. Even Lord MacAird's presence barely registered with me. My gaze was drawn solely to Hiram. He stood alongside his father, his face blank, devoid of any emotion. I knew he must have seen me making my way down the hill, but he stared straight ahead, not even looking Fergus in the eye. The remains of bruises clung to his face like dirty marks, but he didn't look down or try to hide away. He just kept his eyes fixed forward, focused on something no-one else could see.

Lord MacAird raised his hand for silence, and all noise ceased. He said little, just thanked people for their time and said he had important news, before handing over to Mr Stewart. However, his presence alone told people most of what they needed to know. This was not good. Mr Stewart cleared his throat and stepped forward with a smile on his face, enjoying his importance. His smile didn't falter as he informed us we would have two weeks in which to prepare to leave our homes. He announced that Lord MacAird had generously offered to pay for passage to Nova Scotia, although he also accepted that people might prefer to make other arrangements. But amongst all his smiles, the message was clear: no one was to be permitted to remain. There was stunned silence as Mr Stewart stopped speaking, but gradually a sea of voices rose up, clamouring to ask questions, trying to make sense of the incomprehensible. Lord MacAird simply raised his hand again.

"As my man Stewart has said, have your belongings ready to leave in two weeks' time. There will be no exceptions. Any changes will be communicated to you. Goodnight."

Then he turned and strode away, Mr Stewart and the other lackeys following in his wake. Hiram was gone too. I looked around at the shocked faces. We'd had an inkling of what was to come, but the confirmation was still enough to take our breath away. I saw my father looking up towards our house, the house that had sheltered him throughout his life, where at that very moment his wife was soothing his children to sleep. I saw Fergus slipping his arm around Isobel's shoulders, drawing her closer to him. And I saw myself alone. How could I bring my problem to anyone now? A fate no one had expected, and that no one could avoid, had befallen the village. My problem was entirely of my own making. How could I expect sympathy? It felt like my life amongst these people was already over. I wondered if it would be better for me to disappear quietly into the sea. Perhaps that was the example I was supposed to take from the story of Quiet Janet's daughter.

CHAPTER TWENTY-EIGHT

The present

On the walk back from the park, Eilidh replayed Sylvia's words in her head, wondering if she was reading too much into them. Sylvia was clearly a product of a very different generation, and just because Keith had grown up in a household where it seemed violence was accepted and that a wife had to know her place, it didn't mean he would automatically have repeated the same behaviours. Perhaps growing up with a heavy-handed father had been something he'd hated. Perhaps he'd rebelled against him by treating the women in his life with more respect. But there was no denying the fact that Keith had cheated on her mother. How much respect could you see in actions like that?

There were still a few hours before Eilidh needed to be at the station for her train back to Inveravain, she'd packed her bag so she wouldn't need to worry about it later, and Sylvia was bustling around the tiny kitchen preparing what looked like enough shepherd's pie to feed a small army. As Eilidh had witnessed the week before, Sylvia liked to feed her whole family on a Sunday. Her daughters, her grandchildren, their partners, and her great-grandchildren were all invited, and most of them were present each week. The little semi-detached wasn't big enough for everyone to sit down at once, so people just arrived whenever they fancied. For each person that came through the door, Sylvia would disappear off and return with a piled-up plate of reheated food. Eilidh was looking forward to things feeling as they had on Friday night again. The stories she'd heard about Keith that night, about the things he'd done for others, the friends he'd bailed out of trouble, and his unfailing generosity, had made her feel proud to be his daughter. The knowledge he'd cheated on her mum, and that it was possible he'd found domestic violence acceptable, had since dulled his shine.

In the lull between the food preparation and the arrival of the first guests, Sylvia, Sylvie, and Eilidh were in the front room, each sipping at yet another cup of tea.

"You said Keith was away a lot. Was that because of his job? Did he have to go to different areas to find sites to work on? Or did he go into travelling sales or something like that?" asked Eilidh.

Sylvia and Sylvie looked at each other warily, as if Eilidh had asked a question they'd been hoping to avoid. It was Sylvia who carefully replaced her teacup on its saucer and began to speak.

"No, pet, it wasn't. After your mam left, he found things hard, and that meant he struggled to cope at work as well. Some days, he just couldn't face being around people, so he didn't go in. After a month or so, he got laid off from the firm he'd laboured for since leaving school. He'd always gone above and beyond to please them, but they just washed their hands of him. It makes me sick to think of. Anyway, he got another job, but he struggled to fit in. Then he had another and another, but none of them seemed to last. He was finding it hard. His best friend and the woman he'd thought he was going to marry had abandoned him, and he could hardly afford to look after Janey and the baby that was on its way. So, when a lad in the pub made him an offer that seemed too good to be true, he went along with it and made a bit of money. Then he did it a few more times until he got caught. They charged him with handling stolen goods and sent him to prison."

Eilidh was shocked. She'd never met anyone who'd been to prison. It was totally beyond her usual frame of reference. It was something that happened to other people, people on the news, not people in her real life. Sylvie was looking at Eilidh anxiously, worried this information was going to spoil everything.

"When did this happen? How long was he in prison for? Was that why he took a while to come up to Inveravain to find me and mum?"

Eilidh wanted to know everything. She needed to make sense of this new aspect of her father, another element that didn't fit with the image she wanted for him.

"He was only in for a short time, less than a year. He was out before Sylvie was six months old. Janey was living here with her by then."

"Which would have been around the time he came up to Inveravain," interrupted Eilidh. "My mum said I was about six months old when he found them."

"Aye, that sounds about right," Sylvia continued. "He was heartbroken to have finally found you but not be able to bring you home. He managed to pick up some work while he was looking for you, though, so at least he had some money for a while. He tried so hard to get another permanent job, but it was difficult now he'd got a criminal record, and it really got him down. Eventually, he was tempted to do another dodgy job, but he got caught again, and this time they put him away for longer. Then it kept going like that. He'd get out, try so hard to find work and make things right for Janey and Sylvie, but no one would give him a chance. Then he'd end up so desperate he'd have no choice but to get involved in things he shouldn't again."

The way Sylvia told the story, Eilidh almost felt sorry for Keith. She'd heard how hard it was to get a fresh start after a prison sentence, with many people ending up trapped in a cycle of crime. Some parts didn't ring true though. What had Keith been intending to do if her mum had agreed to come back to Glasgow with him? He already had Janey and Sylvie living at his mother's house. Was he seriously expecting them to squeeze in together like one happy family? Her mind suddenly flashed back to Alan's words, when he'd said that Keith had offered to give up his parental rights in return for money. A horrible thought stole its way into her head: had that been Keith's real reason for looking for them? Had he been relying on the fact that Claire wouldn't agree to return so that he could try to extort money instead? Sylvia had said that Keith returned from his trip with money. It was possible it was from odd jobs along the way, but it could also mean Alan was telling the truth—that Keith had blackmailed them in to handing over cash. She was about to ask Sylvia what would have happened if her mum had agreed to return with Keith, but the sound of the door opening, and the thud of feet in the hallway, robbed her of the opportunity.

Sylvia's great-grandchildren worked the magic little children always did on Eilidh. She had never once felt the desire to have children of her own. She'd never imagined herself as a mum, nurturing a tiny life and being responsible for another human being. But she loved being around children, and she loved handing them back to their parents once they'd got too tired and wound up to be fun any longer. She swore that children in that golden phase—somewhere between two and five, when they'd developed a personality, but not even the smallest hint of a filter—could take anyone's mind off their troubles. Their demands didn't give you any time for your own worries and what they asked of you could be pretty entertaining. At the moment she was embroiled in an intense game of snakes and ladders. Bobby, at the grand old age of five, was incensed that three-year-old Amelie wasn't taking things seriously enough as she kept moving her counter down a ladder.

"You're a natural with them," Susan, their granny, said as she sat down alongside Eilidh on the floor. "Have you got any plans for having some of your own?"

Eilidh hid her irritation at the familiar

question behind a smile. She knew people didn't mean to cause offence when they asked about children. They were simply making conversation, but she really wished the question could be made illegal. If you could answer 'yes, we'd love some soon', it was all great, but if you desperately wanted children and had been trying for years, it wasn't something you could so easily convey in the trite little soundbites people expected, and why should people have to share something so personal with strangers? Eilidh had learnt from experience that if you replied you didn't want children, people either didn't believe you, insisted you would change your mind, or ended up getting defensive, as if you were criticising their life choices. However, she didn't see why she should have to lie to avoid the discomfort of others. That was why she wished the question would disappear. Unfortunately, her imaginary future ban wasn't going to save her from having to answer it right now.

"No, having children isn't for me," she answered, trying to convey that this was a decision she was happy with rather than something she needed sympathy for.

"What does Rich think about that?" asked Sylvia, somehow having overheard despite moving between the front room and kitchen bearing plates loaded with food.

"He's fine with it. He's never been interested in

having children either."

"That doesn't seem right to me," Sylvia responded. "All blokes want to have children to carry on their name, but I suppose you've not taken his name anyway, so he must be a bit of a funny one, like Sylvie's Chris."

Eilidh couldn't think how to respond. Fortunately, another arrival needing food saved her the trouble.

"You'll have to excuse Mum," Susan said, leaning in close, making sure Sylvia wouldn't hear. "She's quite set in her ways, but she means well."

"It's fine," replied Eilidh. "Lots of people find it strange that we don't want children."

Then, encouraged by the fact Susan was still smiling sympathetically at her, Eilidh took the chance to find out some more about Keith.

"Your mum told me that Keith had some trouble after my mum left and was in prison a couple of times. Did things settle down for him in the end? I'm sorry if I'm bringing up bad memories, but I don't actually know what happened to him, or why he died."

Susan took a deep breath, seeming to consider whether it was her place to tell the rest of the story. Eventually, she spoke. "He never stayed out of prison for more than a couple of years after that first time, Eilidh, but don't let that make you think less of him. Whenever he was out, he'd do anything for any of us, and if he had a bit of money in his pocket, he'd always try to spoil us. He couldn't get himself straight, but he wasn't a bad person."

"Was he in prison when he died?" Eilidh asked quietly.

"Sort of. He'd been out for a while, but he'd got involved in another scam and he'd just been arrested. Anyway, they put him in the cells, and when they next checked on him, he was dead. Just like that."

"Oh, that's awful," Eilidh replied, genuinely saddened. The thought of her father dying alone in a cold police cell was heart-breaking.

"They don't really know what happened. It seems he had some sort of seizure, but they hadn't checked on him as often as they should have, so it's possible he'd have been alright if it'd happened when he'd been at home and we'd been able to get him help."

There were tears in Susan's eyes and Eilidh felt moved by the strength of her emotion. Whatever faults Keith might have had, his family had clearly loved him dearly, and Eilidh wouldn't wish dying trapped and alone on anyone. But the version of Keith she was hearing about today was so far removed from the fantasy she'd been building in her head. She'd been picturing her father as a hero. Not only as a man who'd never given up on his daughter, but as someone who was funny, kind, and clever, a real people's person. Everyone kept telling her he could light up a room. The image she'd built was what she wanted to be true. She wanted Keith to be a man who'd missed her, but who had also been happy. She couldn't reconcile her fantasy with a troubled man who was constantly in and out of jail. And then there was Sylvia herself. Eilidh was loving being part of this big, slightly chaotic family, and her grandmother had welcomed her with open arms, but some of Sylvia's views were so different from Eilidh's own values. Could she really fit in here? But if she couldn't, then where did she belong?

CHAPTER
TWENTY-NINE

The past

Esther

Once the initial shock of Lord MacAird's announcement had worn off, the village seemed to divide; not between the lower houses and the top houses, as it sometimes had in the past, but between those who thought they should accept Lord MacAird's offer, setting sail for a new life, and those who thought they should fight to stay. Mine and Fergus's fathers fell into the group that wanted to fight. They both said they were too old to start again in a different world, and they also couldn't see why they should have to: this land belonged to the clan, not just to the chief himself. When they'd tried to resist the previous rent increases, Lord MacAird had assured them they would never have to leave. He'd said it would be worth all the effort it would take to make a living on our now smaller and more expensive pieces of land because it would be ours forever. That promise had been the only shred of victory back then, they'd still had to hand over the extra money Lord MacAird wanted. Now it seemed that promise was worthless, no more than pretty words to appease the crowd, hollow words that meant my father was struggling to persuade my mother to fall in with his plans. That broken promise proved it was impossible to stand up to Lord MacAird, and that had been with the entire village working together. As my mother pointed out, how could they expect to succeed now, when they were already divided amongst themselves?

So while my fears for my own future grew, fear and worry also spread across the village. It wasn't just in my home that there was disagreement over the right course of action to take. Harsh words drifted on the breeze as families struggled to convince each other. Maybe it would be sensible to accept Lord MacAird's offer and go willingly to a new life, one that might be better than what they knew here. That was exactly what my mother kept saying to my father. She didn't want to leave, but she could see it was inevitable, and she wanted to be prepared. She wanted to walk out of her home, the place she'd thought she would end her days, with everything she needed to begin a new life, and she wanted to do it with dignity. But like many others, my father couldn't see any dignity in giving in. So our little house became a very uncomfortable place to be. After a couple of days, my mother staged a tactical retreat. On the surface, it seemed as if my father had won the argument, but my mother was quietly carrying out her own plans, gradually packing her most treasured belongings into the hidden space beneath their bed. Father had dug that hole into the ground years ago, so that precious things could be hidden from the factor if necessary. It was intended to be used if things got hard and we couldn't meet the rents. Now my mother was discretely using it to hide the things she'd need to start again.

Those that intended to resist had come up with several plans, depending on which direction the factor and his men approached the village from. We'd heard no more since that initial announcement, so it seemed the original eviction date still stood. They intended to place lookouts at all the logical entrances to the village. Then, as soon as the evicting party was sighted, all those resisting were going to rush to that spot and defend it using whatever tools they had as weapons. If they held Lord MacAird's men back that day, and then the next, and then the next, the hope was that he'd give up, that he'd see the strength of feeling and adjust his plans. He seemed the type to favour the easy option, so they simply had to make things difficult. They just had to make him see it was easier to let us stay than it was to force us to go.

As the day drew nearer, people's nerves were on edge. The slightest provocation was enough to nudge anyone into anger. Neighbours that had never had a cross word between them were suddenly arguing about exactly who owned that spade. I knew I definitely wasn't making things easier for my parents. I was terrified about what was to come. Would my father be injured if it turned into a proper battle? What if they killed him? What would we do without him? And what would happen if we got on that boat instead? My condition would become obvious soon enough. How would my parents cope with that on top of everything else? My fears meant that someone only had to look in my direction before I unleashed my anger on them.

That the divide in the village was almost equal made the tension worse. Those wanting to fight felt their chances were being undermined by those who were giving in. Whereas those wanting to accept were worried any resistance might see Lord MacAird's offer to help with resettlement withdrawn. The village had ceased to be the peaceful place I'd known long before the day of the eviction arrived. For the first time, I appreciated how lucky I'd been growing up in a place where nothing ever seemed to happen.

When Lord MacAird's men arrived, it wasn't on the day we'd been told. They swept into the village at daybreak three days earlier than we'd expected. It meant there was no lookout to warn those wanting to resist. It meant there was no row of impassioned villagers brandishing their makeshift weapons and throwing rocks to prevent their approach. Fists pounding on their doors and shouts saying they must leave immediately awakened the families in the lower houses. Then, the screams and shouts from lower down the fields awakened those of us up at the top. Those like my father, who had been readying themselves to fight, rushed from their beds, still hoping to drive the evicting party back, but it was too late. The dawn light was only just filtering into our house as I followed my father in his dash to the door, but the scene that greeted us was one of devastation. People and possessions were being dragged out of houses, their own efforts apparently not fast enough to satisfy Lord MacAird's men. Little children were crying as they became separated from their mothers in the chaos. Women were being thrown aside as they tried desperately to cling onto their treasured possessions, screaming as Lord MacAird's men dragged their husbands away. Below us in the harbour we could see a boat, a huge sailing ship, which dwarfed the fishing boats. Despite knowing it would come, the sight still filled me with dread.

My father immediately grabbed his rake and charged down the fields to help. My mother retrieved her carefully stored bags from the space under the floor, and I helped to dress the little ones. Following my father's instructions, Mam led them quietly into the woods. Instead of following her, I hesitated outside our house, watching as people scurried about. Perhaps it was having my own disaster growing inside me that made me oddly calm. Regardless of what happened to the village, my life was already ruined.

I watched Isobel's family carrying their belongings carefully out of their home. They had already decided to accept Lord MacAird's offer of passage to Nova Scotia. Over the last few days, I'd witnessed intense discussions between Isobel and Fergus about what they should do. Isobel wanted Fergus to go with them, but Fergus didn't want to let his father down by refusing to fight for the village. Fergus asked Isobel to stay, but she couldn't imagine a future without her family. Lord MacAird's desire for his pretty little road, with no unsightly human life alongside it, meant heart wrenching decisions for so many.

Down the hill, I could just make out the sight of my father, with Fergus and others alongside him, shouting angrily at Mr Stewart.

Mr Stewart sat mounted high on his horse, safely removed from the surrounding chaos. Mam and the bairns were already in the woods, hidden by the trees. I barely noticed my mother, with her gentle eyes and her hair escaping from her shawl, as she calmly led my siblings to safety. I don't know whether the little ones were scared, or if they thought they were embarking on an exciting adventure. Was Cait being helpful, or was she acting as selfishly as I was? I don't know because my focus was elsewhere. I didn't even notice someone knock my father to the floor. The surrounding houses were emptying rapidly, people were fleeing into the woods away from Lord MacAird's men, and others were readying themselves to sail for a new life. All of them moved with hurried steps, hoping that swift action could avoid the scenes that were playing out at the bottom of the fields. I suppose I could be forgiven for being distracted by sights like that, but it wasn't the devastation around me that had stolen my attention from my family. Instead, it was a man heading up the field away from the worst of the violence. He wore a cap, and a scarf was pulled up over his face. The air was full of smoke from where the thatch had been set alight, but regardless of scarves or smoke, I knew it was Hiram, and he was all I could see. As he came closer, I called out to him.

"Hiram, Hiram, help us, please! You have to help us."

He didn't respond straight away, and I wondered if he hadn't heard me. My senses were so focused on him, my ears tuned out the panic surrounding me. My eyes didn't see the other figures following Hiram up the hill. I could only comprehend the existence of Hiram and me

"Hiram, please!" I shouted again.

This time, he replied.

"You need to find your family, Esther. I can't help you."

"Hiram! You have to be able to stop this. You have to!"

"Esther, you know I can't. I can't stop my father or Lord MacAird."

"But you don't have to work with them, Hiram. Are you really so desperate to please your father that you'd turn us out of our homes?"

"We both know I'll never be able to please him, and I have tried to help you. I've done all I could think of to persuade him to leave your houses alone. He knows it was me that warned you all. He blames me for all the trouble and resistance. I didn't just back down and agree with him."

"Well, it looks like you've given in now. You're working with him instead of with us today. Don't we mean anything to you? Don't I mean anything to you?"

His eyes were all I could see of his face, but I could tell he was anxious and upset.

"I told you there can't be anything between us. You need to find your family. It's over, Esther."

"Apart from it's not," I said quietly, finally saying out loud what I'd been afraid of for so long. "It can never be over between us because I'm having your baby."

CHAPTER THIRTY

The present

Despite the noise and general chaos of the Sunday afternoon open house at Sylvia's, the whole place fell silent when the doorbell rang. Everyone else had walked straight in, shouting their hellos as they made themselves at home. The doorbell was the sign of a newcomer, a stranger, someone who perhaps didn't belong, and all activity ceased while they established who was there. It was Sylvia who opened the door, not particularly because it was her house, but mainly because she was passing on her way to the front room with more gravy. Every other arrival had brought noise, feet stomping down the hall, drinks requests shouted through to the kitchen, but this one was different. After a sharp intake of breath from Sylvia as she opened the door, the only sound was silence. Eilidh had been midway through her fifth game of snakes and ladders. She'd sorted the argument between Bobby and Amelie by making the three-year-old play as a team with her and ensuring they didn't overtake Bobby too often. Amelie was more than happy to team up if it meant getting to sit on the blue-haired lady's knee. Eilidh was trying to stop Amelie from moving Bobby's counter when she heard her name. But that wasn't what made her rise to her feet. It was the voice saying her name that made her get up. She could hear her mum.

"Sylvia, is Eilidh here?" Claire asked for the second time.

Sylvia turned and passed the gravy to one of her grandchildren before responding.

"I've been wondering when you'd turn up. How many years is it since you last darkened this doorway? I'm surprised you've got the cheek, though, after all the trouble you caused."

Claire took a deep breath before she replied.

"I haven't come to argue, Sylvia. I just want to speak to my daughter. Is Eilidh here?"

"Oh, so you want to speak to your daughter, the daughter you've been lying to for years, and I'm just supposed to do as you say. Do you know what I'd give for a chance to speak to my son again? But I'll never get to do that, thanks to you.

You as good as killed him. Now get out of my house."

Claire stuck her foot out, forcing her way into the hall before Sylvia could slam the door.

"You can't hold me responsible for what happened to Keith, Sylvia. So, do you want me to go over the truth of what happened right here in the hallway with everyone listening? Or do you want to just answer my question and tell me whether Eilidh is here?"

"I'm not afraid of the truth about my Keith. Everyone here knows the truth. He was a good man, and you destroyed him. That's all there is to it."

"Oh, I destroyed him?" Claire replied, incredulous, losing control of her voice. "So it was me that ruined his life and left him stealing to fund his addictions? Obviously, it had nothing to do with the father that beat him every day and told him he'd never amount to anything. You're right about one thing: Keith was a good man, or he could have been, but he was broken long before he met me."

"How dare you? How dare you even suggest that what happened to Keith is Reggie's fault? Reggie always did right by his family. He'd never have run off like you did."

Sylvia's voice was shrill now, and her face was red. One of her grandsons tried to intervene, putting his hand on Sylvia's shoulder and suggesting forcefully that Claire should go. But Sylvia shrugged him off, saying that some things needed to be said. The interruption gave Claire a moment to compose herself.

"I ran off because I was pregnant, and even though he knew I was carrying his baby, your son was beating me regularly. I ran off because I was afraid of him. And I ran off because I knew he was seeing other women as well. He didn't even deny it, Sylvia, he was happy to tell me how much better they were than me, but he still wasn't willing to let me go. Running away wasn't something I'd wanted."

"Come off it, Claire. Keith didn't beat you. Yes, he lashed out occasionally, but that's what real men do. You were always so pathetic and spoilt, wanting to eat your fancy foods and wear your fancy clothes, expecting Keith to pay for everything. No wonder he needed a drink, and no wonder he got angry and had to teach you a lesson."

"No, he hit me because that was what he'd seen his dad doing to you when he was growing up. He cheated on me because he constantly felt the need to prove that his dad was wrong, to show that he was good enough and that people wanted him. You're right that I wasn't perfect, Sylvia, I was just a kid when we got together and I'd got a lot of growing up to do. But Keith wasn't hitting me because I needed to be taught a lesson, he was hitting me because that's what his dad had taught him about how to treat women."

"That's it, get out. I'm not listening to any more of this. You always were an ungrateful bitch. Making out that Keith hurt you when he treated you like a princess. He put up with all your whims and your silly ideas. He even let your dirty brother stay when your own parents kicked him out. And you repaid him by running off with his best friend. The pair of you betraying him destroyed him. He never got over it and now he's dead. I don't know how you can live with yourself, but you're not welcome in my house for a moment longer."

Eilidh had been listening to the exchange from the corner of the hallway. She wasn't sure if her mum had even noticed she was there. It seemed that the things Claire had said about Keith, the things that Eilidh had thought were just an attempt to bad mouth him, were true. In fact, it seemed her parents had tried to shield her from some of it. Claire hadn't mentioned Keith's affair with Sylvie's mum, even though it was clear she'd known about it. Hearing Sylvia order her mother out of the house destroyed any sense of belonging Eilidh felt. She grabbed her bag from next to the coat cupboard, grateful she'd packed earlier.

"Well, that means I'm not welcome either," she said as she pushed past Sylvia to get out of the door. "Come on, Mum. Let's get out of here."

CHAPTER THIRTY-ONE

The past

Fergus

The morning that Lord MacAird's men arrived in the village, was like nothing I'd experienced before. We'd made so many plans about how we'd stand up to them, all the ways they might attack and all the ways we'd be able to thwart them, but when it happened, it was sleep that defeated us. They'd told us we'd be informed if the eviction date changed. But just as they couldn't trust us to leave quietly, we should have known not to trust their word. We should have been keeping watch constantly as the day drew closer, but we were sleeping in our beds.

By the time I followed my father down the

fields, it was already too late for us to make a difference. Those not moving fast enough had their thatch set on fire, forcing them spluttering from their homes. Those who had accepted their fate were treated no better than those who tried to fight. Furniture built with love and handed down between generations was smashed and burnt. The air was thick with smoke and screams. One woman, due to give birth any day, refused to leave her bed, screaming that the baby was coming. MacAird's thugs simply picked up her bedsheets and carried her out on them. Dumping her on the ground as they set her home alight in front of her. We tried our best to stop them. We had our tools to use as weapons and we weren't afraid, but there were so many of them and we were too late. Our efforts were in vain. We couldn't fight the flames, and we were easily pushed aside. My father spotted Mr Stewart, sat high on his horse. He rushed over to him, attempting to unseat him. I don't really know what he was hoping to achieve. Hurting Mr Stewart would have made no difference, except perhaps make us feel we were doing something. However, we couldn't even manage that. Seeing us surround Mr Stewart, some of Lord MacAird's thugs came over. One of them shoved my father to the ground and began kicking him. I rushed at him, holding him back just long enough for my father to get to his feet, but then I saw Esther's father bleeding on the ground. Father told me to run. He shouted that I should get myself safe, that I needed to look after the family. Then he turned away to help his lifelong friend. When I had run far enough to risk looking back, I saw them both; their hands were bound, and they were being dragged towards the harbour.

I wanted to turn and help them. I wanted to free them, so they could run with me, but I knew that wasn't possible. There was no way I could take on those men alone. All I could do was follow Father's instructions and make sure Mother and the children were safe. I saw Esther's mother first, weighed down with bags, her children clinging to her skirts.

"We should get back into the woods to stay safe," I said to her.

"Bless you, Fergus," she replied. "But it's too late. They won't let him go and neither will I. We have to follow him to the boat. Do you know where Esther is?"

"I saw her in front of your house a few minutes ago. She was with Hiram."

A small smile played on her lips, completely at odds with the chaos around her.

"You're such a good lad," she began. "Will you tell her to come and get on the boat with us? But Fergus, if she isn't coming, if she wants to stay with Hiram, will you tell her I love her and that I understand?"

I nodded, not knowing what else to say as she

pulled me into a fierce embrace. I knew it was meant for Esther rather than for me. As I ran up the fields, I saw my mother making her way down, my brothers and sisters following close behind.

"They've got Father," I said.

"I know, I saw. I've gathered all I could carry from the house. We're on our way down to join him. There's nothing to fight for if they've got him, Fergus. There's nothing for me here without your father. And you'll be with Isobel this way."

That was typical of my mother, seeing the positives in the worst of situations.

"Is there anything else you want me to bring?" I asked quickly.

"No, just get yourself on to the boat with us. I don't want to leave here without you."

"I said I'd fetch Esther, but then I'll be straight down. Don't worry, I won't be long."

She smiled at me, and then, even though I had every intention of seeing her again in a few minutes, I told her I loved her, and I let her stroke my hair, something I'd not done for years. I don't know if it was the encounter with Esther's mother that had unsettled me, or if some unconscious part of me knew what was about to unfold.

As I burst into Esther's house, I was shouting. I knew that time was running out, and we needed to move fast. I paid little attention to Esther's red and tear-stained face, or the fact that Hiram was white as a ghost. It made sense that they'd both be struggling to cope with the day's events.

"We need to move fast, Esther. They've already got our fathers and the rest of them are on their way down to the boat. Do you know what time it's setting sail, Hiram?"

"They want to be going well before noon," Hiram replied, clearing his throat. "Then it'll put in at Inveravain, briefly, before continuing to Glasgow and eventually on to Nova Scotia."

"Right," I said, not really sure how much time that gave us. "Why didn't anyone say it would happen today, Hiram? Why are they burning the houses?"

Hiram shrugged. "Lord MacAird didn't want anyone left behind or anyone trying to come back. He thought it might be easier with an element of surprise. They're burning the thatch and the furniture to make sure there's nothing for anyone to come back to."

"But why didn't you warn us?" I asked.

"My father knows who told you about this in the first place. I haven't been able to get out of the house for weeks. Besides, we don't need to keep pretending that we mean anything to each other."

It was then that I realised Esther hadn't said a word, and that the redness on her face wasn't the result of her tears, it was the shape of a hand.

"What's going on?" I asked, looking between them. "Did you do this to her? Have you hurt her, Hiram?"

"Have I hurt her?" Hiram gave a bitter laugh. "I think it's more a case of her hurting me, just like you always used to say she would. All those days I spent worrying about how I'd taken advantage of her, when the whole time she was laughing at me with whoever else she was doing it with."

"There hasn't been anyone else," Esther cried. "There's only ever been you, Hiram."

"I know that's not true. We were only together once, so it's not possible. That baby can't be mine."

Now it was me turning pale. Esther was expecting a child. I knew it had to be Hiram's. She'd been heartbroken that night when I found her in the woods. I was certain there wouldn't have been anyone else.

"Oh, didn't you know?" Hiram said coldly. "Are you so shocked because it might be yours? Is that why you were so quick to defend her honour? Were you just covering your back in case this happened? Is that why you didn't want me? Have you both been laughing at how stupid I am?"

"Hiram, stop it. Nothing's ever happened between me and Esther, you know that."

"I don't know anything anymore," he replied, balling his hand into a fist and lunging towards me.

What happened next is a blur. I saw the punch coming and dodged to protect myself. Esther was screaming, and Hiram was somehow spinning and falling. Then he was on the ground, totally still, his face on the stones that surrounded the fire, the stones that were turning red. Esther's screams didn't stop.

CHAPTER THIRTY-TWO

The present

There weren't many words spoken as Alan drove them away from Glasgow. Claire sat in the back, stroking Eilidh's hair and soothing her as she cried. Walking out of Sylvia's house hadn't been easy. Sylvie had rushed after them, pleading with Eilidh to come back in and give them all another chance. It had taken all of Eilidh's strength to ignore her and put one foot in front of the other until she reached the sanctuary of Alan's car. Now all she wanted was to be back with Rich, safe in her own home, protected from revelations and surprises.

When Alan stopped at a cafe about an hour from Glasgow, Eilidh tried refusing to get out of the car, but he was insistent.

"I know you too well, Eilidh. You'll say you're fine and insist on going to work tomorrow as if nothing's happened, but you'll never actually talk it through or deal with it. You'll just tell yourself you're coping and let it eat away at you instead."

Reluctantly, she gave in, following Claire to a table in the corner. Eilidh took the seat facing away from the room so that no one could see the state her face was in. Despite having wanted to stay in the car, she somehow ended up ordering a coffee and a slice of chocolate cake. She even smiled at the young lad who took their order, putting on a good pretence that nothing was wrong.

"You know, Sylvia is right in some ways," Claire began, after their drinks and cakes had arrived. "Keith did some terrible things, but he wasn't a terrible person. There was a lot of good in him. He wanted to please people and look after them. He just couldn't handle it when things didn't go as he thought they should."

"But he cheated on you," protested Eilidh. "Sylvie is only a couple of days younger than me, and he used to hit you. You always told me there was no excuse for domestic violence."

"And there isn't. That's why I left. But Keith was a victim too. It's what he grew up seeing and experiencing. It doesn't make his behaviour right, but I can see now that he didn't know anything different, and I can sympathise with what he must have gone through growing up."

"Also, Eilidh, people didn't really talk about things like that back then," added Alan. "Keith and I were best friends for a long time, but he never said a word about how his father treated him. I wonder if he felt ashamed of it, like it was his fault, and I wonder if that's what made him so angry. It might have been different if he'd felt he could talk things through."

"But he basically sold me to you, didn't he? And it's true he cheated with Sylvie's mum, isn't it?"

Alan swallowed his last mouthful of millionaire slice before replying. His cakes always disappeared twice as fast as anyone else's.

"I'm sorry I told you about the money thing, Eilidh. It's not something you should have had to hear. I just wanted you to understand that it wasn't us that stopped him from seeing you, and I panicked. But I don't think Keith demanding that money reflects what he really thought about you. I think he was desperate by that point. Looking back, he was an alcoholic before your mum left him, and I suspect he'd picked up other addictions by the time he asked for that money."

"Yes, but it doesn't matter how desperate he might have been. It's still a very different story from him spending his life searching for me. He was violent, and he cheated on his pregnant girlfriend." Eilidh stopped and looked at her mum. "I know anyone can get tempted, but what was he planning to do if you hadn't left, or if you'd agreed to go back to him? Carry on with two families forever?"

"I don't know, Eilidh. Maybe he was relieved when I disappeared and that's why he didn't come looking for us until he needed money. I think he'd have lost his job regardless of me leaving. There had already been several occasions when he'd disappeared for a few days, and his bosses weren't happy. But I can't know that for certain. Maybe it was like Sylvia says, maybe they did only sack him because he couldn't function when I left. I don't suppose we'll ever know. But the boy I met when I was barely out of school was very different from the man I left behind."

"It's just so sad," Eilidh sighed unhappily. "Did you know he died alone in a police cell? Apparently, he'd just been rearrested, and no one checked on him."

"Aye," Alan replied. "I keep in touch with a few of the lads from down there, so I'd heard about it from them. Knowing he'd been in and out of prison was one of the reasons I thought we'd done the right thing by keeping it all secret. I thought we'd protected you from getting hurt. I never imagined things happening the way they have."

"You should have told me the truth all along. Then I'd have understood why you made the choices you did. I wouldn't have felt like my whole life was a lie."

"I know," said Claire, taking hold of Eilidh's hand. "We are both so sorry. If we could go back and do things differently, we would. We were only ever trying to look after you, but we got it totally wrong."

Eilidh reached for Alan's free hand. She knew his other would already be holding Claire's beneath the table.

"You didn't get it all wrong," she said. "You've always put me first. I shouldn't have cut you off. I should have listened."

"Well, it's easy to know the right thing to do after the event," Claire comforted. "But maybe you should listen to what Sylvie has to say as well?"

"I don't think I'm ready for that yet, and I don't think I'll ever be ready to speak to Sylvia, not after the way she spoke to you."

"That's just her way, sweetheart. I know I told you that Sylvia wasn't a nice woman, but that's not really true. She's just very protective of the people she loves, and she's a bit set in her ways."

"That's no excuse," Eilidh snapped, unwilling to let Sylvia off the hook. "Especially as everything you said about Keith was right. And I'm assuming that when she called Uncle Simon dirty, that's because she's homophobic on top of everything else. I didn't realise Grandma and Grandad had chucked him out, though."

"Well, they did and they didn't. It was all a bit tense between them when he first came out. You have to keep in mind that it was a huge deal back then. I'd never met anyone who was gay, and it hadn't occurred to any of us that your uncle wasn't straight. But they soon came round, just like they'd always have accepted me moving back in with them. I'd just convinced myself that they'd washed their hands of me, or maybe Keith had. Anyway, I suspect you're right and that Sylvia is homophobic, but she's a product of her generation. I don't think you should rule her out completely because of that, maybe you could help educate her?"

"I don't know. I don't think I need someone like that in my life, and I don't think I could really see Sylvie without Sylvia being involved."

"Well, there's no rush to decide. I'm just relieved you're talking to us again."

That night, Eilidh appreciated being back at home, cuddled up with Rich, enjoying the tranquillity of the familiar view. The resident seal was taking an evening swim round the bay, and a flock of oystercatchers lifted as one from the rocks just off the shore. It was about as far removed from Sylvia's house in Glasgow as it was possible to get. The house there was full of noise, and whether you looked out of the front or the back, all you could see was more of the same grey houses. But there had been a warmth as well, with all those people, so invested in each other's lives, crammed into the same space. Eilidh tried not to think too much about that other life in Glasgow over the next few days. Alan and Claire were trying their best to give her space to come to terms with things, but that still involved a phone call each day to check she was alright. They were so relieved they hadn't lost her forever that they were finding it hard to leave her alone. The problem was that, inevitably, their conversations always led back to Keith, and Eilidh wanted to pretend she'd never heard of him.

To avoid thinking, she threw herself into work. As the holiday village progressed, there were more and more issues for her to deal with, and she was grateful to be kept busy. Beth called up to the site one afternoon to fill Eilidh in on the latest discoveries about the previous village. The museum at Ardmhor House had a section devoted to the Clearances, and while developing it, Beth had gathered accounts of evictions from across the area—not all of which had made it into the public displays. Amongst those accounts were some dealing with the Ardmhor Clearance. Beth had made copies and brought them to read with Eilidh on site, so they could try to picture how things might have been. Construction had finished for the day, and with the machinery silent, the only sounds were the rustle of the trees and the screech of a buzzard circling overhead. Beth quietly read one account which described people being taken by surprise at first light and dragged from their homes as Lord MacAird's men set light to the thatch. Another account spoke about a woman in labour being lifted from her bed, losing her security and her dignity at the same time. Other accounts mentioned men who had resisted the eviction being bound and forcibly placed on the ship that was waiting in the harbour. All the accounts gave the same sense of chaos and panic, as smoke filled the air and families tried to keep themselves and their possessions together. It was difficult to imagine those terrible events happening in such a peaceful place. From where they were standing, Eilidh and Beth could see boats bobbing in the harbour and the ferry making its way to the pier, but it was impossible to know how it would have felt to see a ship waiting there that you knew was going to take you away forever. Beth hadn't found out any more about the factor's son and the runaway girl, but the historical association she'd been in touch with was very hopeful someone would come forward with information.

As the week went on, Eilidh felt more like

herself again. She had Rich, she had a job she loved, she had great friends, and the two people who had supported her non-stop throughout her life were still supporting her. Admittedly, she might wish they weren't being quite so intense in their support, but she had no doubt she was very much loved. When she really thought about it, nothing had to be any different from how it was before she'd met Sylvie.

Saturday saw Rich and Eilidh making their way over to Strathglen for lunch with Alan and Claire. For once, Alan hadn't been called away to deal with an emergency. Actually, there had been a minor one involving one of their neighbour's boilers, but Alan had got someone else to take a look. He said nothing was more important than spending time with his only daughter right now.

"Didn't you want more children?" Eilidh asked him, breaking both her rule that no one should question others on their childbearing or rearing choices, and her resolution not to mention anything that could lead the conversation back to Keith.

"I'd never really thought about children until you came along. kids are great, and I always enjoyed spending time with them, but I was a bit like you in that I'd never pictured myself having any. Anyway, once you arrived, that all changed.

Don't get me wrong, though, I'm not saying you should have a child just in case it turns out you like it!"

"I'm not planning on it," Eilidh laughed, while Rich looked relieved.

"What I mean is, I loved your mother, and I knew I'd love you too. Then once you were here, we both thought it'd be nice for you to have a brother or sister, so you weren't just stuck with us, but it never happened. We had some tests done after a few years and it turned out I'm a big strong bloke with very weak swimmers. The doctor said it was unlikely we'd be able to have another child without medical help, so at that point we decided you were enough."

"So you probably wouldn't have been a parent if you hadn't rescued Mum?"

"No, probably not. That's why I'd never have turned Keith away if he'd come back. I don't like how he treated your mum, but he gave me the greatest gift of my life. It doesn't matter that we don't share any DNA; you're my girl, and it's thanks to him I'm a dad."

As she brushed her teeth and washed her face that night, Eilidh thought about Alan's words. Rich was standing alongside her, laughing at the faces she pulled as she removed her mascara. As she caught his eye in the mirror, it occurred to her she'd been focusing on the wrong things. She'd always felt she belonged here because her family had belonged here, as if her DNA rooted her to the spot. Then, when it turned out her biology connected her to somewhere else, she'd felt lost. But she could see now that didn't matter. Alan was always going to be her dad, that was something that would never change. And she could belong anywhere, if she had Rich by her side.

CHAPTER
THIRTY-THREE

The past

Esther

I'd been so afraid to say out loud that I was having a baby, as if the problem might go away if I just ignored it. But I'd also hoped that if I told Hiram, he'd make everything alright. Once the words were out there, hanging in the air between us, all I could do was wait to see which way things went. My fate was in Hiram's hands. He didn't speak. He just looked around him, checking to see if anyone else had heard. Not that I imagine they'd have been interested if they had. Our little drama would usually have been enough to feed months of gossip, but it would barely have registered against the trauma the village experienced that day. Eventually, secure in the knowledge no one was paying any attention to us, he took my hand and led me into the house. Hiram's hand was cold and clammy, perhaps mine was too. I don't know whether he led me into the house gently or whether it was more urgent, like the day he'd pulled me behind him to the clearing in the woods. I honestly have no recollection. Perhaps knowing that whatever Hiram said would determine my future made it impossible for my mind to function properly.

"You're having a baby?" he said finally.

"Well, we are," I replied. "There's only ever been you."

Hiram didn't respond. He pulled the scarf away from his mouth and slowly rubbed his jaw.

"If we get married, everything will be fine," I continued. "Our baby will be born into a proper family. People might talk a bit when it comes earlier than expected, but that could happen anyway. There can't be anything sinful about a baby born in a marriage."

I was babbling by then, as if by filling the silence I could make my hopes reality.

"It's not possible, Esther," Hiram eventually replied.

"But it is," I interrupted before he tore down my dreams completely. "Everything is different now with the baby. I know our parents won't be pleased, your father especially, but surely even he'll see that us getting married is the only option."

"No, that's not what I meant. You can't be having my baby. It's not possible, we only did it once. My father says it can't happen the first time."

"Hiram, that's just what men say, so they can take advantage of young girls and tell themselves the consequences have nothing to do with them. I wish it was true, but it's definitely not."

"Or perhaps it is true, and you're just trying to pass someone else's mistake onto me. Did you think I'd be too weak, or too besotted, to question you?"

"No, that's not it at all," I shouted. "I've not been with anyone else. This is your baby, and I've never thought you were weak."

I moved closer to him, clinging to him. I could feel the tears prickling. It was all too much. I didn't know where I'd be living by the end of the day, never mind how I would cope with a child. My entire world was collapsing. But there was to be no comfort from Hiram.

"Get off me," he hissed.

He tried to prise himself free, but I was gripping on too tightly. I felt as though if I could just keep hold of him, everything would be alright. I didn't notice he'd untangled one of his arms until his hand connected hard with my cheek. The shock of pain caused me to stagger, finally releasing my grip on him. My legs caught against the edge of my parent's bed, and I fell backwards. Instinctively, I curled into a ball, protecting the child I didn't even want. I felt a hand on my shoulder, and I flinched, but this time the hand soothed instead of hurting.

"I'm so sorry," Hiram was repeating over and over.

Slowly, I pulled myself upright. He was kneeling in front of me, and I knew he meant what he was saying. It had never been in Hiram's nature to act like that, and his face was white with shock. He sat down next to me, reaching out to take hold of my hand, his face softening as he began to speak, but I'll never know what he wanted to say. As the words formed on his lips, Fergus burst through the door, and Hiram leapt to his feet.

Fergus was shouting something about our fathers being taken and us needing to hurry to the boat. He was saying that we had to leave quickly, asking Hiram what time the boat would sail. I know Hiram's voice was steady as he responded, as if nothing was amiss, but I can't remember much of what they said to each other. I was in awe of how Hiram's demeanour could change completely in just a matter of moments. Their words didn't register with me until the atmosphere between them turned. Even with everything that was happening around us, a disagreement between them was unusual enough to bring me back to the moment.

Fergus was asking Hiram why he hadn't warned us about the change in the eviction date, and Hiram replied oddly. He said they didn't need to pretend they liked each other anymore. It was around then that Fergus seemed to notice me for the first time. I mean, he'd obviously seen I was there already, but at that point, he seemed to realise I was in pain.

"What's going on?" he asked Hiram. "Did you do this to her? Have you hurt her?"

And then it was like Hiram switched again, right in front of me. The softening I'd seen before Fergus appeared was gone, and all the anger was back. Hiram laughed at the idea he could hurt me. He accused me of being with other men and trying to trick him into accepting someone else's baby. He even suggested I'd been with Fergus. Hiram was so angry, angrier than I'd ever seen. Angrier than that night in the woods, angrier than when he'd hit me. Fergus looked shocked, but I don't know whether that was because of the baby, or because of Hiram's accusations. He argued back, pointing out what Hiram should have known, that nothing had ever happened between us, but Hiram was too angry to listen. His voice had dropped to a whisper, and I couldn't make out what he was saying as he lunged at Fergus. Everything that happened next seemed to take place in the space of a second, a blur of actions that I can't bring into focus. Fergus tried to dodge out of the way. I know I screamed, and I think I flung myself forwards, somehow intending to stop them. But then Hiram was falling, he'd twisted round and was falling to the ground. I was still screaming, but Hiram wasn't moving at all. His face was on the stones that surrounded the fire, and there was blood, lots of blood. There was another sound too, a sound like that of an animal in pain. I thought it might have been from Hiram, but he was silent. Then I realised the noise was coming from Fergus.

CHAPTER THIRTY-FOUR

The past

Fergus

My life ended the day he died. Amidst the chaos of that last day, as women wailed and people fought and flames danced, his passing was the only moment when time stood still. As his body crumpled to the ground, the air was already thick with smoke and fear. At first, I thought the noises I could hear, cries like a wounded animal, were coming from him, but it was me. He would make no more sound. I fell to the ground alongside him, his blood seeping into my clothes as I turned him over and cradled him in my arms. I tried to ignore the destruction of his face as I felt for his heartbeat and willed him to live. But my will was not enough. That face, which had been more familiar to me than my own, was a mess of blood and bone. His piercing eyes, that saw so much more than I ever did, would see nothing else. It had been a day full of fear and destruction, but it was as he took his final ragged breath that everything ended. In that moment, mere seconds that felt like centuries, the future I had expected dissolved before me. Gone were the heather-clad hills rolling down to the sea. Gone were the jagged peaks of the distant mountains and the dark shelter of the woodland. The soft rain, the billowing mists, and the sounds of the village, all of them were gone. Gone, along with the person I'd thought I would walk alongside for ever. Everything I had known, and everything I had expected to know, disappeared as quickly as he did.

At some point, Esther stopped screaming. She sobbed quietly, almost as she had on the night I'd found her in the woods. I was numb, unable to comprehend the scene. I almost wished Esther would start screaming again. Her being dramatic would at least have brought a sense of normality. Instead, Hiram lay between us, dead. His face was something from a nightmare, and his blood was all over my hands. Neither of us had intended for this to happen, we both loved Hiram. But whether we'd wanted this or not, it had happened, and if we were found with him, I knew we'd pay with our lives.

"We have to hide his body," I said to Esther.

She nodded but didn't move.

"Esther, we have to hide his body and get out of here. If someone comes in now, we'll hang. No one will believe it was an accident."

I wanted to shake her, to get her to see the danger we were in, to get her to move. But my hands were covered in Hiram's blood. How would we explain her dress being covered in it as we tried to escape?

"I know what we can do," Esther said suddenly.

She jumped up and lifted the boards of her parent's bed. A pile of blankets lay underneath it, which she swiftly pushed to one side, exposing a trapdoor. The door opened easily to reveal an empty space, shorter and narrower than the bed that had covered it, but easily big enough for a person to hide in. A plan took shape in my mind.

"We need to take his clothes off him," I said.

"Why?" Esther looked at me blankly. "I don't want to touch him."

"If Hiram just disappears, his father is going to ask questions, and one of the men working for Lord MacAird is bound to say they saw him come in here with you. We need them to see Hiram walk out alive, so I need to leave pretending to be him."

"But no one will believe you're Hiram, and what will we say has happened to you?" she questioned.

"I don't think anyone saw me come in here, and no one important is going to be asking questions about the whereabouts of one village boy. We don't need to fool anyone for long, we just need some of those men to think they saw Hiram leave."

Reluctantly, Esther removed his jacket while I struggled to unlace his boots. My fingers kept fumbling over the knots, and I couldn't get into the right position to tug them from his feet. It reminded me of the nights when my father enjoyed one whisky too many, and I'd had to help my mother get him into bed. But when that happened, the worst I had to worry about was waking my father up and getting an earful. This time it was my best friend's body I was trying to undress. A wave of nausea rose in me. I had to close my eyes and breathe deeply for a minute. Even if we succeeded and escaped before anyone realised what had happened, how could I ever live with myself? Hiram's jacket had blood on it, but although I could feel it was there, the dark fabric hid the stains. The collar of his shirt was a different story. There was no way to disguise the blood on that, so we left it on him. I turned away from Esther as I swapped the rest of my clothing for Hiram's. Then I helped her put my clothes onto him. His body was still warm and pliable, but it didn't make the task any easier. We were on edge, fearing discovery any minute, too frightened to make our fingers work properly, and the horror of the situation meant it was much harder to dress an immobile Hiram than a squirming sibling.

Eventually, Hiram was dressed in my clothes. His face was beyond recognition, and with his golden hair soaked in blood, he could just about have passed for me. Between us, we lifted him into the space below the floor. I tried not to think about what I was doing as I shut the trapdoor over him and replaced the boards of the bed. Hiram's cap was still on the table. I stared at it for a moment. How long had it been there? Was it hours or minutes ago that Hiram had walked in and taken it off? It was something he'd have done without thinking, something he did every day, but knowing it was almost the last thing he did, it took on a new significance. He'd never enter another room; he'd never do anything again. I couldn't allow myself to think that way. If we didn't move, our lives would be over as well. Gently, I placed Hiram's cap on my head, carefully tucking my hair in so that no one would notice the colour. His scarf was still on the floor, and I stooped to pick it up. The colour of the material disguised the fact that the scarf was wet with Hiram's blood. Instantly I let go, as if it was on fire, burning me. However, I had to wear it. I'd need it to cover my face if we were to have any chance of persuading people that I was Hiram. Reluctantly, I reached for it again, but before I had hold of it, it was in Esther's hands. I watched her fold it carefully, turning it so the worst of the blood wouldn't be next to my face. My hands were trembling too much to tie a knot, so Esther did it for me, not that hers were much steadier.

As we looked around the room, our eyes fell on the stones surrounding the fire. Hiram's blood was already soaking into the ground, and it was all too obvious something terrible had happened. Once again, it was Esther who came up with a solution. She dashed towards the door and was back only a few seconds later with a bucket stinking of manure. It had been collected for the crops, but it was also perfect for this much grimmer purpose. We tipped the contents of the bucket over the stones and in front of the bed. It covered the blood, and we hoped the smell would deter anyone from investigating further. It wasn't enough though. Down at the lower houses, Lord MacAird's men had been destroying furniture to make sure no one returned. If we left everything intact, someone might come along and try to make use of it, and if someone moved the boards of the bed, there was a chance they'd find Hiram.

"We need to smash up the furniture, like they've been doing down the village," I said to

Esther. "We can't risk someone coming in here and being tempted to move anything. If it's just a pile of broken wood, people are more likely to leave it alone."

I picked up the fire iron and began smashing it down on the table until a split appeared in the centre.

"You have to help me," I said to Esther.

She was standing white faced by the door, watching the destruction of her home.

"We need to do this quickly," I implored. "I can't do it all on my own."

I handed her the fire iron as I began stamping on the bed, gradually fracturing it into pieces. As I ripped the heather stuffed blankets to shreds, and scattered them around the room, I saw Esther splinter the remains of the table into ever smaller pieces. Eventually, there was nothing usable left in the house. Esther crashed the fire iron down for a final time and came to a standstill alongside me. I could feel her sobs returning, and I pulled her close.

"We didn't have any choice," I said to her as I surveyed the scene of destruction in front of us. "We didn't cause Hiram's death, but no one is going to believe us. If we don't go through with this, we'll be put on trial, and they'll find us guilty. We'll die too. Do you think Hiram would want that?"

I wasn't actually that confident about what

Hiram would want right then. He'd been angry enough that he'd wanted to hit me. He'd thought I might have betrayed the biggest secret he'd ever told anyone, and that I'd been carrying on with Esther behind his back. Then I'd stolen his clothes and shoved his body into a hole under a bed. There was a chance Hiram might have wanted me to pay with my life. But I knew I didn't want to. That morning, when Lord MacAird's men had arrived in the village, I'd wondered if there was any point in carrying on, but when I saw Hiram's life disappear in an instant, I realised even if my life had to be somewhere else, I still very much wanted it. Fortunately, Esther seemed to agree.

"No," she mumbled. "I don't think he'd want that."

I checked no hair was escaping from Hiram's cap and that his scarf covered most of my face. Then I took hold of Esther's hand.

"Are you ready?" I asked.

She didn't speak, she just nodded and squeezed my hand.

"Don't panic," I said as we walked out of the door. "Just stay close and follow me."

CHAPTER THIRTY-FIVE

The past

Esther

As we walked out of the house, I held onto Fergus's hand as if my life depended on it. I suppose in a way it did. I didn't take a last look back as we walked out of the door. It had stopped being my home the moment Fergus turned over Hiram's body. I didn't want to remember it as it was now, as Hiram's grave. My home hadn't reeked of manure, and the fabric of our lives hadn't lain broken and scattered around it. The place we walked away from wasn't the place where my family had lived. Glancing down the fields and seeing the ship sailing out of the harbour, my heart contracted. We were too late, we'd missed our chance, and everyone we loved was disappearing from view.

"What will we do?" I whispered to Fergus. "The ship's already gone."

"Shh," he said urgently. "I told you, just follow me."

He led me towards the path down the fields, right past two of Lord MacAird's men.

"If my father asks, I'm just seeing to this young lady," he said, throwing in a few coughs to cover up the fact he didn't sound quite like Hiram. Or perhaps the coughs were genuine. There was a lot of smoke in the air.

"I think you've been seeing to her for long enough, given how long you've been in there with her," one of the men joked crudely.

I looked at the floor, not knowing what the appropriate reaction should be. I was sure that if I met anyone's eye, they'd know exactly what I'd just done. Maybe my refusal to look up from the ground simply confirmed their suspicions that we'd been up to no good as we said our final goodbyes to each other.

"The house is all dealt with. It just needs you to set light to the thatch," Fergus said with authority. He was still coughing slightly, making his voice throaty and unrecognisable. "I'm going to take the young lady to Inveravain on one of the horses, so she can catch up with the ship and re-join her family. We've been longer than I expected."

"You'd better hurry," MacAird's man replied. "Or you'll miss it and be stuck with her. Although I don't suppose I'd mind being stuck with this one." He looked me up and down, winking at his friend. "You take care of your lady," he continued. "Perhaps your old man's been wrong about you all along, Hiram, you have got it in you after all."

With that, he gave Fergus a hearty pat on the back, which triggered a coughing fit that was definitely genuine, and we made our way down the field to where some horses were tethered. No one tried to stop us or paid us the least bit of attention. They were too busy burning the remains of our lives.

As Ardmhor House disappeared behind us, I finally allowed myself to breathe, and as Inveravain harbour came into view below us, I dared to think that we'd actually made it. Fergus didn't guide the horse down to the harbour though. Instead, he took the higher track, leading us into the hills behind Inveravain.

"What are you doing?" I shouted into his back. "The boat will sail without us."

But he didn't reply. He just kept pushing the horse further and further up into the hills until eventually he came to a stop. We were in a narrow valley that ran down the hillside, with a small stream burbling its way through its centre.

Birch trees grew alongside the stream, taking advantage of the shelter provided by the valley sides.

"We'd better stop for a while and let the horse rest," Fergus said as he helped me down.

"What are you doing?" I shouted at him. "We're going to miss the boat. We'll never see them again."

The shape of the valley meant it was impossible to see back down to the harbour, and I could feel my heart racing, my palms growing sweaty. Perhaps we were already too late. Fergus didn't answer. He just led the horse to the stream, encouraging it to drink. Eventually, satisfied that the animal was comfortable, he turned back to me.

"We can't join them, Esther," Fergus said quietly.

"But you told those men you were bringing me to the boat," I said, unable to hide the fear in my voice.

"No, Hiram told them that."

"I don't understand what you mean," I said, my voice shrill as my panic rose.

"I'm so sorry, Esther. There wasn't time to explain properly before we left. We need people to think that Hiram ran away with you. That's why those men had to see us riding off together. But you were right earlier. We won't be able to convince people who know us properly that

I'm Hiram. If we get on that boat and join our families, everyone knows us. The passenger records will show that you got on the boat but Hiram didn't."

"But it won't matter, will it? As soon as the boat sails, we'll be safe. Even if they find Hiram and work out what's happened, they won't come to another country to find us, will they?"

"Maybe not, I don't know. But for all we know, someone could already have found his body. They might already be looking for us. Or if they realise you've got on that boat without Hiram, they might start searching for him and work out what's gone on. The ship isn't sailing straight for Nova Scotia, Hiram said it's stopping at Glasgow first. If someone works out what's happened, they could easily get us taken off the boat there. It isn't safe for us to go with everyone else."

My heart sank. I'd thought I couldn't imagine anything worse than what had happened in my house that morning, but I was wrong. Knowing that my family was on that boat, sailing away from me, was more than I could take. It was as if all my strength deserted me. My legs couldn't hold me up anymore and my knees buckled. I sank down to the ground and once again found myself sobbing in front of Fergus.

"But we'll be able to join them eventually, won't we?" I asked after a while.

"Yes, probably," Fergus replied.

I could tell from his face that he didn't believe what he was saying. It was obvious he was just trying to give me hope. I would never see my family again, and I hadn't even said goodbye. As if he was reading my thoughts, Fergus sat down next to me and put his arm around me.

"I didn't say goodbye to anyone," he said, his voice catching slightly. "I told my ma that I was getting you and I'd see them on the ship."

"Did you see my mother?" I asked him.

"Yes, I did. I'm sorry, with everything that's happened, I forgot I hadn't told you. MacAird's men knocked your father to the floor and mine was trying to help him. He'd told me to run and make sure everyone was safe. When I looked back, they were already bound and being dragged away. That's what I was shouting about when I arrived at your house. I saw your ma as I was on my way back up the fields. She asked me to find you, that's why I'd come up to yours. Your ma knew you were with Hiram, Esther. She said to tell you she loved you and that she'd understand if you decided to stay with him."

It was a long time before I could reply. We didn't talk about feelings much in my family, so to hear my mother had said that was overwhelming. But she'd think I'd chosen Hiram over them. Even though she'd given me her blessing to do so, it was still painful to think that was what they'd believe. I'd always thought I'd loved Hiram. I'd certainly wanted to marry him, even more so once I'd realised I was carrying his child. But for all the years I'd spent imagining my life with him, I'd still thought my family would be there, just around the bend in the track. I'd never contemplated choosing Hiram over them. Now they'd never know that, and I was finally realising that they never could, not if I wanted to live.

"What about Isobel?" I asked.

"She's gone too," Fergus replied. "I knew she'd be going, anyway. Her family had already decided to accept Lord MacAird's offer of paid passage, and my father had decided we'd be staying in Scotland. There was a brief moment today, as I was running up the field to get you, when I thought the one positive of the resistance failing was that I'd get to stay with her. But as it was, I didn't even say goodbye. I wonder what they'll think has happened to me?"

I put my hand over his and pulled him closer to me. There was nothing I could say to make things better. I'd thought things were bad for me, but at least my family would have an explanation of where I was, even if it wasn't the truth. I could take comfort from the fact that my mother had given her blessing for me to stay behind. Fergus had none of that. He'd told his mother he'd be back with them shortly, and all they'd ever know was that he hadn't made it.

"What are we going to do?" I asked eventually. "I mean, that's if you want to stay with me. You don't have to. Maybe I should go back and confess. If I'd stayed with my mother this morning, you wouldn't have come to look for me and none of this would have happened. So really, it's my fault, and I should take the blame. If I went back now, you might still be able to catch up with the boat in Glasgow."

"No, what happened is no more your fault than mine. I'm not letting you take the blame, and it wouldn't just be your life you'd be putting at risk," he said, looking at my stomach.

It was the first time he'd referred to the fact I was expecting a child. Hiram's child. The idea of myself as a mother seemed as unreal as everything else that had happened that day. I was relieved Fergus didn't seem tempted by my offer to turn myself in though. I might have believed it was the right thing to do, but I wasn't sure that in reality I'd be brave enough to go through with it.

"Shall we stay together, then?" I asked after a while. "As neither of us has got anyone else?"

"Let's do that," Fergus replied, smiling for the first time since he'd burst into my house earlier. "But only because I've got no one else. Not because I've known you since the day you were born, and I can't remember a day of my life without seeing you. Not because you're the only thing I've got left of my old life, and I'm not willing to let you go. Only because there's no one else."

He finished his little speech with a gentle nudge of his elbow into my ribs.

"Alright then," I said, giving his hand another squeeze. "Just because there's no one else."

CHAPTER THIRTY-SIX

The past

Fergus

We made a lot of decisions as we sat hidden on that hillside. The first, and probably the most important, was that we were going to stay together. For years, we had been nothing but a source of irritation to each other, but now, we were all each other had left of our old lives—and that changed things quickly. We were back to the days when we were little, when the three of us had been best friends, equals in our games, back before Hiram and Esther's relationship changed and we became rivals for his attention. Deciding to stay together was the easiest decision because neither of us could imagine anything else. We both wanted to cling to the one familiar thing we had left. It was much harder to decide what we should do next. We'd escaped from Ardmhor, but we didn't know if we were safe yet. It was possible that they'd found Hiram's body or that our attempt at deception had been uncovered. There could already have been people looking for us. After talking for hours, coming up with idea after idea about where we could go, we concluded that our only option was to leave Scotland altogether. It was the only way we could be certain we wouldn't be punished for Hiram's death.

The plan was to travel down to Glasgow and find a boat to take us to a distant corner of the world. Somewhere we would be unknown, where we'd be able to start again. We knew it would take us a while to make the journey. We needed to stay out of sight as far as possible and that meant using quieter, longer, less travelled routes. The one thing we didn't need to worry about was money. Hidden in Hiram's jacket pocket was a roll of banknotes, more money than I'd ever seen in my life. I tried not to think about whether using it was adding to the crimes we'd committed. It wasn't as if we could take the money back now, and Hiram certainly couldn't use it. I told myself that he'd always helped me when I was in need. He'd never have turned me down if I'd asked him for money. Surely, he'd want the two people he'd been closest to in his life to be safe and free. But I had my doubts. He might have loved us both, but when he died, he was so angry with us, and now we were covering up his death. Could he still love us at all? In the end, I had to do my best not to think about it. Hiram was dead. He could neither approve nor disapprove of our actions. It didn't matter what he would have thought.

We travelled slowly. Esther rode on the horse while I walked alongside. Each day, I'd leave her hidden somewhere out of the way while I used Hiram's money to buy us food. A lone man passing through a village didn't attract any attention, but together we were far more noticeable. When we finally reached Glasgow, we blended into the hordes of people thronging the streets, and our fear of being detected lessened a little. We'd decided as we sat by that stream on the hillside above Inveravain that we'd need new identities. We'd thought about telling people we were brother and sister, but with the baby on the way, we decided we would draw less attention if we told people we were married. I suggested the surname MacDonald. It was so common that I knew we wouldn't stand out. Esther agreed and wanted to use the name Flora, but I thought naming herself after the famous heroine was going a bit too far. In the end she settled on Betty, in honour of Betty Burke, the maid Prince Charlie disguised himself as when he made his escape. I liked Esther's thinking. The disguise had worked for Prince Charlie, and I hoped the name would work for us, too. Esther suggested I followed the theme and became Charles. So we arrived in Glasgow as Charles and Betty MacDonald, a young couple expecting their first child.

New clothes were my priority as we walked through the myriad of shops in the centre of Glasgow. I'd never been bothered about what I wore, but I was desperate to be wearing something that wasn't stained with Hiram's blood. It didn't take long to purchase a couple of changes of clothes. I'd never had clothes from a shop before. My mother had made everything I wore. For a moment, my thoughts drifted to the clothes I'd hastily discarded on the morning of the eviction. Ma had spent hours stitching each item together, fitting them to me. I was the lucky one. My little brothers only got my cast offs. But I'd wrestled the clothes that Ma had made with so much love onto Hiram's body, and I'd left them to rot beneath the floor of Esther's house. Once again, I pushed the thoughts away. They wouldn't change anything, and I couldn't afford to be distracted. I had to concentrate on making sure we were safe. I wore one set of clothes out of the shop and handed Hiram's jacket and trousers to a man begging in the street. They were good quality, and the blood wasn't noticeable if you didn't know it was there. As I waited for Esther to make her purchases, I looked around me in wonder, dodging out of the way of a horse and carriage. The scale of the buildings and the number of people was hard to comprehend. I knew Esther had always dreamt of leaving Ardmhor and seeing the big cities further south, but she'd been silent since we'd arrived. I suppose it wasn't how she'd pictured her dream coming true.

There were advertisements pasted onto the walls of buildings, many for items I hadn't even known existed, but there were also some advertising ships that would sail from the neighbouring ports. One in particular caught my eye. It was for a ship leaving Greenock for New Zealand. I knew from my school days that was about as far from Scotland as it was possible to get, and it was due to sail the next day. That was already two things in its favour, but even better, it said free passage was available to agricultural labourers. If there was one thing I knew how to do, it was work the land, and if we could travel for free, we'd be able to use Hiram's money to get a head start in our new life. The advertisement gave a deadline for applying to travel that I knew had long passed, but it also gave an address in Glasgow for enquiries, and it had to be worth a try. When Esther emerged from the shop wearing a new outfit and carrying a parcel under her arm, I had to look twice to know for certain it was her. The fashions of the city made her look so different from the girl I'd always known. After getting directions, we discovered the address on the advertisement was only a short walk away, so although we knew it would probably come to nothing, it was no hardship to go along and see.

As it happened, we were in luck. The sailing hadn't attracted the attention the company had hoped for, and they were slightly down on numbers. They were particularly keen to attract families, and as a young married couple, Esther and I were the next best thing. I described my experience as a farm hand, and they felt we were exactly what they were looking for. All we had to do was make it to the port in Greenock before the ship sailed. It was too far for us to make the journey in time with me walking and Esther riding the horse, but a railway line now ran from Glasgow to Greenock, which could get us there well before the boat's departure. We'd have no more need of the horse, so after a few enquiries, I sold it to a man who seemed delighted with his bargain. The price I got was probably far less than the horse was worth, but it was enough to buy tickets for the next train, and that was all we needed. Neither Esther nor I had ever travelled faster than a horse could move, so we were surprised to find the motion of the train carriage smoother than riding in my father's cart. But the roar of the engine and the clacking of the wheels sounded as loud as thunder, and the speed with which the scenery flew past the window seemed impossible. So I was reassuring myself as much as Esther when I held onto her hand throughout the journey.

While we waited to board the ship, we did one last thing to cover our tracks. Knowing that we'd soon be out of the country, we wrote a letter to Hiram's father. One benefit of having been taught to write by the same, very particular, teacher was that I could easily replicate Hiram's handwriting. Mr Stewart had always been concerned with appearances before anything else. He was desperate to impress his social betters and avoid scandal at all costs. That made us confident our plan would work and that Mr Stewart would ensure Hiram's body remained hidden. I wrote to him as if I was Hiram confessing to a terrible crime. In the letter, I begged Mr Stewart, as my loving father, to help me cover up what I'd done. I said that in the heat of the eviction there had been an argument over Esther, and I had accidentally killed Fergus. I explained that Esther had helped me hide the body, and we'd run away together, travelling to New Zealand under false names. We wondered if it was sensible to give the name of the actual ship we'd be travelling on, but decided we needed the story to be as convincing as possible in case Mr Stewart checked the details. Knowing there was no love lost between Hiram and his father, it seemed highly unlikely he'd come chasing after him, and Mr Stewart's fear of scandal meant we were confident he'd keep the crime concealed. I tried not to think about the lies we were telling or the fact that we were asking Mr Stewart to conceal his own son's grave. We were in too deep now, and what good would come from the truth? Hiram would still be dead. All that would change was that our lives would be over as well. Posting that letter was our last act on Scottish soil.

Neither of us spoke as the ship left the dock. I thought I'd feel relief watching the land gradually disappear, knowing that we'd made it and that we were safe. But the knowledge that we could never return, that this was our last glimpse of home, meant it was actually a harrowing ordeal, and it was an ordeal that didn't improve as the journey continued. Our free passage meant we were down in the lower levels of the ship. The ceiling barely cleared Esther's head, never mind mine, and our personal space was a cramped bunk. As we were travelling as Mr and Mrs Charles MacDonald, we were in the married section in the middle of steerage. Although sleeping so close together was awkward at first, we were grateful not to be kept apart. If we had travelled as brother and sister, as we'd first considered, I'd have been with the single men and Esther with the women. I hate to imagine how that journey would have been with nothing from my past to cling to.

As we shivered through storms in the first weeks on board, when water frequently worked its way into our section of the ship, soaking everything in its path and leaving us constantly damp, our thoughts frequently turned to our families. How were they coping on a similar ship crossing the Atlantic? We knew the weather on that route could be much worse than the conditions we were experiencing. Each time we thought of them, we would remember afresh that we'd never see them again. Then there would be anger, and tears, and harsh words from both of us. I wondered whether we would ever get used to the fact that we were alone now or whether we'd remember it afresh each time we awoke, a new horror every day for the rest of our lives. And then there were the thoughts of Hiram. All my life, I'd collected information in my head to share with him. Every new thing I saw, every funny thing that happened, I'd store up, waiting for the chance to impress him or make him laugh. Even though his death was the reason we were on this ship, my mind couldn't connect the facts. It was as if it had two sections working independently, one that constantly replayed the horror of Hiram's death, and another that stored up the sights and sounds of the voyage to share with him, only to be devastated each time it remembered why that couldn't happen. Night-time brought no relief because it ushered in dreams where I'd watch helpless as Hiram's face shattered on the floor. I'd wake shaking, relieved the nightmare was over, until I remembered where I was and that it wasn't a nightmare, it was reality. That was one of the hardest things to accept. Even if we escaped and got away with what we'd done, my best friend was dead, and it had happened because he was angry with me. I might not have understood the feelings he said he had for me, but I'd never imagined a life without him in it. Now my home was gone, my family was gone, and he was gone. Even if we kept our lives, it was a heavy price to pay.

As the storms of the early weeks gave way to heat, there were new problems on board. The monotony of our diet of salted meat and dried potatoes took its toll. There wasn't enough water to keep clean, and the stench of the animals on board mixed with the scent of unwashed people. The heat was of the kind I'd only experienced right next to a fire. It was a different hell from the damp and cold, but it was hell all the same. Another young couple on the boat became ill, and as we entered the later stages of our journey, when the ship moved back into rough seas and storms, they gave up their struggle one after the other. The crew buried their bodies at sea, and everyone on board reflected on how lucky they'd been to escape a similar fate. That gave Esther and me another idea. We could easily have been that couple. There were many times sickness had taken hold and I'd wondered if we'd survive. I resolved to write a letter once we arrived in New Zealand, if we were lucky enough to make it. I would write it from the point of view of a fellow traveller, informing Mr Stewart that his son, and his son's wife, had perished on the journey and that their bodies had been committed to the sea. As Mr Stewart didn't know the names we'd travelled under, he would never know it hadn't been us that had lost our lives on the voyage. That way, we'd be safe. Even if Hiram's body was found, we couldn't be tried for a crime if we were already dead.

Eventually, after months on board, there was the excitement of land being sighted. Leaving the boat was a strange moment. The feeling of solid ground beneath our feet was disconcerting after the rolling of the sea for so long. We disembarked to mist and soft rain, and I wondered for a moment if we'd somehow gone wrong and arrived right back where we'd started. As part of the conditions of our passage, we were to be engaged as workers on a sheep farm, the very thing that had forced many of our fellow travellers off their land back in Scotland. A wagon sent by our new employer met us from the boat, and as Charles and Betty MacDonald we set out on the final stage of our journey. The mist lifted as the wagon rumbled along the track, revealing green hills and distant jagged peaks. Esther moved closer to me and took hold of my hand. The swell of her stomach was visible beneath her clothes now. I knew she was thinking the same thing as me. The scenery was so reminiscent of home, it was almost impossible to believe we'd travelled halfway around the world. But we knew we had, and that there was no going back. Esther, Fergus, and Hiram, from Ardmhor, were no more, and Charles and Betty, along with Hiram's child, had new lives to begin.

CHAPTER THIRTY-SEVEN

The present

Two butterflies were fluttering around the flower bed next to Eilidh, but nothing else was moving. It was the rarest of days on the Scottish coast, with not even the hint of a breeze. The tide was high, the sea touching Alan and Claire's garden wall, but there were no crashing waves, not even the gentle lapping of the water over the pebbles on the shore. The sea lay flat and still as a millpond. There wasn't a cloud in the sky and even the midges were being kept back by the heat of the sun. Although it was the middle of July, warmth like this was unusual, and it seemed everything was struggling to cope. The wildlife from the shore had disappeared, perhaps conserving energy in shady spots, and the distant hills across the water shimmered in a haze of heat. Eilidh sat on a deckchair under the sunshade that usually languished in the shed. Alan was next to her, officially reading the paper, but judging from the occasional snores, snoozing. Claire was inside, fussing over their lunch.

"I've set the table in the dining room," she said, appearing at the door. "I think it'll be cooler eating inside."

Eilidh gave Alan a nudge before making her way into the house. Claire had made squat lobster salad in honour of the hot day. It was one of Eilidh's favourites, but no matter how many times Claire showed her how to make the sauce, she couldn't quite perfect it herself. No one spoke as they ate. The food was too delicious, and the air was too warm, making them all lazy. It was only later, when they were back outside and a slight sea breeze had picked up, that they finally got the energy to chat. Alan told them about a mix-up at a house he was working on. The client's supplier had sent the wrong kitchen. Fortunately, Alan had realised the mistake before they installed anything, but waiting for the correct replacement was going to delay work. Eilidh was pleased to report that nothing like that had happened at the holiday village. At the moment, everything was progressing according to plan.

"I don't suppose anything else has come up about the remains?" Alan asked.

"No, nothing," replied Eilidh. "No one had any ideas after the DNA from the missing boy's descendants didn't match, and the remains are too old for the police to be interested."

"So we'll probably never know."

"Exactly," Eilidh agreed. "Although Beth is still researching some things. She's been in touch with a historical society in New Zealand —apparently that's where your ancestor and the factor's son ran off to—and she thought someone there might have some ideas. But that was ages ago, and I don't think she's heard anything back."

"It's probably a bit of a long shot, really. It was all so long ago."

"Yeah, totally. You know Beth, though, she doesn't like to give up when it's a mystery from the past."

"Speaking of giving up," Claire interjected smoothly. "Have you still not been in touch with Sylvie?"

"That's not giving up, Mum," Eilidh protested. "I don't want to get in touch. I don't need another family."

"It's been almost three months since we brought you back from Glasgow, sweetheart, and you might not feel that you need another family, but you have one all the same. Sylvie looked heartbroken when you left, and she's done nothing wrong in all of this. Don't you think you should at least phone her?"

Eilidh bit her lip in frustration. She knew her mum was right. Regardless of anything else, Sylvie was her sister, and even if Keith hadn't been interested, Sylvie had spent years searching for her. But the whole situation had been horrible. The revelations about Keith had made her question everything. It had been bad enough finding out that Alan wasn't her biological father, but discovering her actual father had been abusive, and had essentially sold her to feed his addictions, had been devastating. She was reluctant to reopen the wounds now that things had settled down again.

"It's funny, really," Eilidh said after a bit. "When I first mentioned researching the family tree and meeting Sylvie, you were both dead against it, and now you're the ones pushing me."

"Well, we've learnt from our mistake," replied Claire. "We should have told you the truth about Keith from the start, but at the time, it seemed best to just keep quiet—what you don't know can't hurt you and all that. We should have known it would all come out eventually, and that things would be worse because of the lies. That's why I think it's important you talk to Sylvie and make sure you know the full story. I'm not suggesting that you move in with them. I'm more than glad that you're staying up here.

But it wouldn't hurt to get to know them. Sylvie sounded lovely, and I know Sylvia came off badly that day, but honestly, there's a decent side to her. She'd do anything for her family."

"Now that you're constantly persuading me to give his family a second chance, it's hard to believe I thought you and Dad were just bad-mouthing Keith so I wouldn't get involved."

"I'm not surprised you didn't know what to think, Eilidh," said Alan sadly. "After all, we lied to you for all those years. But we don't want you to miss out on anything now. You shouldn't lose the opportunity to know your sister because of mistakes we made all that time ago."

"I'll think about it," Eilidh said, helping Claire tidy up their glasses and carry them inside.

Monday saw Eilidh back at the construction site. The weather had stayed hot over the rest of the weekend, but today, although the air was still warm, the sky was heavy with clouds. The midges were out in force, thanks to the muggy weather and the nearby trees. Heat and midges made a miserable combination, and everyone on site was desperate for the working day to end. A movement lower down the fields caught Eilidh's eye. Someone was rushing up towards the site. Well, rushing was perhaps too strong a word. It was probably more accurate to say moving as fast as you can when it's warm, you're carrying a baby, and a three-year-old is running round your legs. Eilidh put down the clipboard she was using to complete a stock take and made her way down to meet them.

"Are you okay, Beth?" she shouted, as she got nearer.

"Fine," Beth puffed. "I've been trying your mobile, but there was no answer, so I thought I'd come and find you."

"Oh, it's so noisy up there I probably didn't hear, and I keep forgetting to put my phone on vibrate. Anyway, what did you want me for?"

"I've finally heard back from New Zealand, and it's amazing!"

Beth's face was red from the exertion of carrying baby Grace up the hill while wrangling Rory at the same time, but she looked as thrilled as a bride on her big day.

"Only you could be this excited about hearing from a historical society," said Eilidh, laughing.

"I know. I'm a total loser," Beth said happily. "But you're never going to believe what I've found out."

"Come on then, tell me all the details," replied Eilidh.

Beth's enthusiasm was infectious and Eilidh found she was desperate to know whatever it was Beth had discovered.

"Not yet," Beth teased. "Everyone that helped the weekend we investigated the site is going to want to hear this, so Angela said we can meet at theirs later. The apartment should be big enough to fit us all in."

"So you're not going to give me any clues now?"

"No," Beth stated firmly. "Bring Rich with you if he wants to come, and can you let your mum and dad know we'll be at Angela and Jim's at six?"

"Only if you tell me what you've found out."

"Fine, I'll ring them myself. Come on, Rory, let's get a drink at the cafe."

The promise of the cafe was enough to get Rory rushing back from where he'd been running in circles. Eilidh couldn't imagine how he had the energy. The air was somewhere between a sauna and a steam room.

"Don't worry, Beth," Eilidh called after them as they set off down the hill. "I'll phone my mum and dad. See you later."

Eilidh knew Beth hated ringing people if she could avoid it. Pulling out her phone to make the call, she noticed the time: half-past three, just two and a half hours to wait.

A strong wind had picked up by the time Eilidh and Rich made their way along the road to Ardmhor House. With the run of dry weather, dust had accumulated, and it swirled around their feet as they walked. The clouds looked ominous, and the air felt charged, as though a storm was about to break. The sitting room of Angela and Jim's apartment was busy when Eilidh and Rich walked in, which was quite an achievement. Ardmhor House was such a massive building that Angela's sitting room was bigger than Eilidh's entire house. Eilidh could see her mum and dad on one settee, and Beth's parents, Jean and David, on another. Andrew, who ran the local activity centre, and his girlfriend, Leonie, who'd done much of the heavy lifting on the day they'd explored the site, were perched on a couple of stools. Graham, the man who enjoyed mapping cleared villages, was in the corner, and a lady Eilidh didn't recognise was talking to Jim and Beth by the fireplace.

"That's Professor Blake, the DNA lady," Angela said, following Eilidh's gaze.

"Oh right, I've spoken to her before, but we haven't met. Beth's got quite a crowd here, hasn't she?"

"She has indeed," Angela replied with a smile. "And she's refused to tell me anything yet. But I think you and Rich are the last ones due to arrive."

After what seemed like an eternity of getting people settled with drinks, Beth finally clapped her hands together to get everyone's attention.

"As you all know, several months ago a body was discovered at the holiday village site, which after police investigation turned out to be very old. Professor Blake, do you want to say anything about what you found out?"

Eilidh smiled to herself. Beth was clearly channelling her work mode. She always sounded totally confident when giving presentations in the museum, but if you asked her to speak to a room full of people at any other time, she'd look for excuses to get out of it. Professor Blake sat up straighter in her chair and looked around before speaking.

"I have a special interest in trying to identify old remains through the use of DNA, which was why this case was passed on to me. The remains seem to be between 150 and 200 years old and belonged to a young male. The age of the remains would suggest they have a connection to the village, especially as it appears they were buried within the remains of one of the houses. Their age could also fit with the time that the village was cleared." She looked over and smiled at Alan at this point. "Oral histories suggest that a young man from the village disappeared on the day of the eviction, which naturally led us to think there could be a neat conclusion to this case. However, DNA samples from descendants of his family were not a match. We also tested the remains against DNA samples from descendants of other villagers, but we still found no genetic link."

"So," Beth began, taking over the story again, "it seemed as if we had no real clues to follow, but I kept getting drawn back to another of Alan's stories. He said that a girl had run off with the factor's son that day, which meant another two people had vanished from their families as well. I kept thinking that maybe they were all connected and that it must have something to do with the body. I found out the factor's son and his girlfriend had gone on a different boat to the other villagers, although as Eilidh pointed out, that was fairly obvious because if they'd gone with everyone else, no one would have been saying they'd run away."

"I didn't put it quite like that," interrupted Eilidh.

"No, you were probably less polite!" said Alan, laughing.

"Anyway," Beth said, getting them back on track. "There was a record in the old ledgers in the estate office saying that the factor had some time off after hearing his son, and his son's wife, had died on the journey to New Zealand. So, even though they hadn't actually reached New Zealand, I got in touch with a historical society over there, just in case someone had maybe written about their time on the boat with them. That was months ago, and I hadn't heard anything, but this morning I got a really interesting email from them."

"Beth, come on!" begged Eilidh. "The suspense is killing me."

"Okay, okay, I'm getting to it. So, the historical association put out an appeal for information about Hiram and Esther Stewart. I knew I'd got the factor's son's name right from the ledgers, and Alan was fairly certain the girl in his gran's stories was called Esther, but it turned out they'd been using false names, which I suppose makes sense."

"But how have you found anything out if they were using false names?" Alan interrupted.

"Well, that's the thing. They used false names, but it was the name Hiram that got the results."

"You've lost me, Beth," said Jim from his corner of the settee.

"Well, it turns out the story about their deaths was false, too. They were trying to cover their tracks. They were using the names Charles and Betty MacDonald, but they had a son shortly after they arrived in New Zealand, and they called him Hiram. Then the name continued down the family. A modern Hiram saw his name, which is pretty unusual, in an appeal from the historical society that had been shared online. The appeal reminded him of a story his granny used to tell. His gran has passed away, but he asked his mum a few questions, and she showed him this."

Beth handed everyone a set of papers, neatly stapled in the top corner. Each piece was filled on both front and back with old-fashioned writing.

"These aren't the originals. They're still in New Zealand, but Esther wrote them, and they explain everything, including who the body belongs to. Do you want to read them individually? Or shall I read them out?"

There were no interruptions as Beth read aloud. Esther's words had everyone riveted. She described the village and the people, her relationship with Hiram and her discovery she was pregnant, the day of the clearance, and the terrible events that took place in her house. She went on to explain how, along with Fergus, she had hidden Hiram's body before they made their escape, and then she'd described how the rest of their lives had unfolded in New Zealand. When Beth reached the end, everyone sat silently for a while.

"So she didn't run away with the factor's son after all," Eilidh said eventually. "And Fergus, the boy she did run off with, was the one everyone thought had gone missing, the golden boy from Dad's story."

"Yes, that's certainly how it seems," Beth agreed. "You said his name was Fergus, didn't you, Alan? And your story fits with how Esther describes him. She clearly wasn't his biggest fan to start with, even if everyone else was."

"Yet they ended up together and the factor's son ended up buried in the field," Eilidh said quietly.

"I know. It's really sad, isn't it?" Beth responded. "He was only sixteen. He must have walked out of the door of my house that morning thinking he had his whole life ahead of him, but he didn't even make it to the end of the day."

"It sounds like it was an accident, though, rather than a murder. I mean, from what Esther's written, they really cared about him, and they used his name for the baby. They didn't just forget him." Eilidh stopped for a minute as another thought hit her. "I've just thought, as Esther had Hiram's child, does that mean there will be DNA to prove that the remains are his?"

Beth smiled. "Present day Hiram has already sent a sample to Professor Blake, so we should have proper confirmation fairly soon."

"Hopefully by the end of the week, if airmail does its stuff," Professor Blake added.

Then, Graham, the man who mapped Clearance villages in his spare time, finally got his chance to speak.

"This account probably explains the lack of ruins and records as well. If Mr Stewart, the factor, believed the letter Esther and Fergus sent from Glasgow, he probably made sure the upper houses were destroyed. That would remove the temptation for anyone to go near them and find something they shouldn't. Maybe he even encouraged the spread of the woodland over them. It would also mean he thought he was covering up his son's crime, when actually he was covering up his son's body."

"Which is pretty creepy," said Eilidh.

"It is really, although Esther makes it sound as if there wasn't much love lost between Hiram and his dad," Beth added.

"True," replied Eilidh. "But they were still family."

"Which has to mean something," said Alan, catching Eilidh's eye as he spoke.

Eilidh knew he was making a point. But did it really mean anything? Did a blood connection matter if the person it connected you to wasn't interested? But then again, Sylvie had been searching for her for years, and it wasn't her fault that their father had had his difficulties. Maybe it wasn't even Keith's fault, maybe it went back further. Perhaps she ought to give Sylvie and her family another chance.

CHAPTER THIRTY-EIGHT

The past

Esther

The most surprising thing about New Zealand was its familiarity, from the mist and rain as we stepped off the boat, to the green hills and distant peaks capped with snow. It wouldn't have taken much to convince me we'd got lost and arrived back home. But we soon realised New Zealand was on a different scale from anything we'd known. Our employer had sent a wagon to meet us, and the driver said that we were lucky, as the farm was quite close to the port. After a day and a half in the wagon, and an overnight stop, I could only wonder at how far away a destination considered distant might have been.

Highland Sheep Station was the name of the farm where we would start our lives in New Zealand, and it was unlike any farm we'd seen before. The main house was more of a mansion than a farmhouse. It wasn't on the scale of Ardmhor House, but it was five times the size of the factor's house. There were shelters for the sheep, shelters for the horses, and shelters for the farmhands. It was like a village in itself. Fergus was to work as a farmhand, and I was to work in the house. I'd never imagined myself as a servant. My dream had been to marry Hiram and become a lady of leisure like his mother, but after the events of the last few months, I reminded myself to be grateful. I was alive, and my feet were back on solid ground.

As a married couple, well, as a couple pretending to be married, Fergus and I had our own accommodation. It was small, just a hut with a bed and a table, but after the confines of the boat, it felt positively luxurious. No one seemed concerned that I was expecting a baby. Several of the house staff were married to farmhands, and one of the older servants took care of the little ones whilst their parents worked. Our employers welcomed the prospect of future workers in a land with a shortage of labour.

It didn't take long to settle into our new lives.

People were as pleased with Fergus here as they had been at Ardmhor. He was a natural with every type of animal and every type of person, and soon the residents of the Highland Sheep Station were wondering how they'd ever lived without him. My life wasn't too different from before. I spent my days following instructions, just as I always had. Sometimes, I helped the cook. Mostly, I cleaned, but as I dusted around the four-poster beds and polished the sweeping staircase, I once again reminded myself to be grateful. I still had a life ahead of me, whereas Hiram lay hidden under my parent's bed. Gradually, we learnt to remember our names were Betty and Charles, and we learnt to forget how much we missed the people we'd left behind.

Then one night, about three months after we'd arrived, Hiram's child was born. I'd been dreading the event. As the oldest child in my family, I'd seen and heard enough to know that birth was painful and dangerous. As it was, I was lucky. It hurt, certainly enough for me to wonder if dying might be preferable, but it was over within a matter of hours. What I hadn't prepared myself for were the emotions. During the hours of labour, all I wanted was my mother. I wanted her to hold my hand and smooth my hair. I wanted her to whisper in my ear that everything was going to be alright, and I wanted her to see her grandson, to know he existed. Even more, I wanted Hiram. I wanted him to see what we had made, and to understand that our baby wasn't something to deny or be angry about. But as our son looked up at me with Hiram's eyes, I knew that Hiram's reaction to my pregnancy had meant nothing. It was fear talking, that was all. I knew beyond doubt that Hiram would have loved his son, and that he'd have loved him completely, in a way that his own father couldn't manage. But instead of being able to do that, Hiram was rotting under the floor of my house, and he was there because of me. I knew Fergus felt it too, and we vowed to give Hiram's son the best life possible, to love him as Hiram had needed to be loved. We knew it wasn't enough to make up for what we'd done, but that was a debt we could never pay, at least this was a start. We gave the baby Hiram's name. Our previous lives had to remain hidden, we could never talk about what had happened, or where we were really from, but this way we'd speak Hiram's name every day, and it would be as if the three of us were back together.

Unsurprisingly, Fergus was a wonderful father. He had endless patience, unlike me. It was in the months after the birth, as I watched Fergus pacing our room, rocking Hiram as he cried and soothing him back to sleep, that I realised I loved him. What we'd been through had already brought us close, and I'd long since stopped being irritated by his existence, but this was different;

pretending to be a couple was no longer enough for me. So after a while, we became husband and wife in every way apart from actually having had a wedding. We'd have liked to do that, and make everything official, but how could we without revealing our earlier lies? As far as anyone knew, we were Betty and Charles MacDonald, married long before the conception and birth of our first child. We had to be content with that.

Two years after Hiram was born, his sister joined him, and then another followed, and another, before his little brother completed our family. We had so much to be thankful for. All of our babies grew to become adults, and none of our girls were as selfish and lazy as I had been. The boys took after their fathers. Hiram's son had inherited his sensitive and inquisitive nature, but he developed a love of working the land which came entirely from Fergus. Fergus's son was a natural with animals, but elements of Hiram crept in through his older brother's influence.

Wonderful as they were, our children weren't all we had to be thankful for. The owners of the Highland Sheep Station were the best employers we could have hoped for. They valued our hard work and treated us with respect. When they wanted to expand their operations, we used Hiram's money to invest, and Fergus became a partner in the new venture. Eventually, we had a home to rival the factor's house, and I no longer had to light the fires or sweep the floors. No one looked down on us because we'd arrived in the country as a servant and a farmhand. Hard work was respected here, not the family you were born to. Our new home could have taught Lord MacAird and Mr Stewart a lot.

We'd always told our son Hiram that his name was to honour a good friend, a kind and intelligent man that we didn't want to forget. He decided it was a name that had served him well, and when his own son, our first grandchild, was born, he named him Hiram. Many more grandchildren joined that first boy, and he is now a man himself. A man with a son called Hiram. I wonder if the pattern will continue. Will Hiram's name be spoken forever in this land? A land so reminiscent of the place where he lies, but where he never himself set foot. I so hope it is.

It is now over sixty years since we walked off that ship to be met by the same rain and mist we'd left behind. Five children, seventeen grandchildren, and twenty-two great-grandchildren have joined us, and we've built a life beyond anything I'd dreamt of. Fergus might have missed the sea, but he had hills, mist, distant jagged peaks, and his own land to work, so he was happy. He left us three years ago. I'm grateful that he went peacefully in his sleep, in his own bed, but I miss him terribly.

The day after he died was the first day of my life that he hadn't formed a part of. His loss has caused those older losses to resurface. I am surrounded by family, but my thoughts turn increasingly to the family I lost on that day back in Ardmhor. I feel their loss as keenly as I did when I sat in the hills above Inveravain and Fergus explained the full consequences of our actions. My mind sometimes wanders the fields at Ardmhor, roaming down the track to the harbour, following the burn to our houses, and then walking through the woods to the fairy circle. I wonder whether any sign of our home remains, whether the fields are empty, or whether new life has replaced us. As my life nears its end, the fear of losing it diminishes, and I find myself hoping that someone discovered Hiram, that he doesn't still lie alone in the ruins of my house. That's why I am writing this down. Fergus was always against the idea, but he gave me permission shortly before he died. Perhaps he also sensed his time was near. Hiram deserves to be remembered, and it seemed important for our Hiram to know the truth. Remarkably, he showed no anger or bitterness over our lies. He had learnt from Fergus to always find positives, and the part of Hiram Stewart that questioned everything, seeing nothing as simply black or white, had always been in his blood. He had long heard stories of his namesake, our childhood friend Hiram, and is as proud to share his blood as he is proud of the father who raised him. Yet another thing I am thankful for.

In the evenings, when I sit quietly, my mind goes back to Ardmhor. Hiram has always been there, waiting for Fergus by the stream, and I see them both young again, running through the clearing together, or fishing off the rocks. I imagine Hiram has forgiven us, that he knows it was an accident, and that we were too young and afraid to handle it better. Our parents are also there, sitting outside our houses, relaxing now their work is done. I want this version of Ardmhor to be perfect for Hiram as well, so I picture Mr and Mrs Stewart back at the factor's house, but after a lifetime of missing their son, they now show him the love he always deserved. Ardmhor House doesn't feature in my imagination. I'm sure it's grown bigger and grander, but fancy buildings don't impress me like they used to. My heart is in the village, with the people who loved me. It took me a long time to appreciate what was important, perhaps a whole lifetime, but I see it now, and I imagine them waiting for me. I don't think the wait will be too long.

CHAPTER THIRTY-NINE

The present

Airmail didn't let Professor Blake down, and within a week of Beth's big reveal at Ardmhor House, there was confirmation that the remains matched with the DNA sample sent from New Zealand. The body that had lain hidden for well over one hundred and fifty years belonged to Hiram Stewart, the factor's son. He'd been just sixteen at the time of his death. Eilidh was standing where they'd discovered him. It was just to the side of one of the twelve lodges, with a clear view down to the sea. The lodges weren't complete yet, but they were well on their way. After all her worrying when work couldn't start as planned, they were right on schedule. Back then, when they'd discovered the skeleton, Eilidh could only see it as a problem, a gruesome reminder that something bad had happened at the site, and something that was going to put its bright new future at risk. She hadn't seen the remains for what they really were, all that was left of a life, but that had changed now. Reading Esther's story had made Hiram very real, and everyone was determined he shouldn't be forgotten again.

Once Hiram's identity had been confirmed, there was the question of what should happen to his remains. Beth had located Mr and Mrs Stewart's graves in the churchyard at Ardmhor, and after discussion with Hiram's descendants in New Zealand, it was decided to lay him to rest with his parents. Eilidh hadn't been convinced that was the right thing to do, as Hiram's relationship with his father had been so strained, but Esther's words had swayed her in the end. Esther had planted the idea that losing their son could have made Hiram's parents regret their treatment of him, and that led everyone to feel that burying him with them was the right thing to do. There was to be a special service the following week, and Hiram MacDonald, the descendant who had finally solved the puzzle, was arriving in a few days' time to see the place his family came from and pay his respects.

Beth collected him from Inveravain station two days before the ceremony. He was a friendly man in his early forties, married with two young children, but it wasn't his pleasant nature that made Beth so happy about his arrival: what won her over was the box full of family memorabilia he'd brought with him. There was the original copy of Esther's story, as well as photographs of Esther and Fergus, or Betty and Charles as their family in New Zealand knew them. There weren't many images of them, and they were old by then, not the young people who had known Ardmhor as their home. But seeing them, sat proudly, surrounded by their children and grandchildren, made them very real indeed. Beth was already making plans in her head to get good quality copies to incorporate into a display in the museum.

Although Hiram Stewart had been forgotten for over a century, the churchyard was full as they finally laid his remains to rest. All those who had been there at the breaking ground ceremony were present, along with those who had heard of the discovery since. The tragic death of a young boy, and the story of his lonely resting place, had touched many. The vicar read from the Bible, words that Hiram himself would have heard often enough in that very same church. Hiram's descendant spoke of his legacy in New Zealand. It was hard to comprehend that this man, well over twice the age Hiram ever reached, and his many relatives on the other side of the world, only existed because of the boy whose remains lay in the box at the front of the church. Jim offered a heartfelt apology on behalf of the MacAird family for the devastation their actions had caused and promised to keep working for the benefit of the community, to honour the memories of all those affected by the clearance of Ardmhor. Finally, at the graveside, Beth read from Esther's words. Her voice faltered as she spoke of the hope that Hiram's parents would welcome him after many lifetimes apart.

There was a lot of sniffling and reaching for tissues amongst the crowd outside Ardmhor church that September afternoon. The sky was grey, reflecting the solemnity of the occasion, but as they lowered Hiram's remains into the ground, a shaft of sunlight broke through. It reminded everyone that the day wasn't just about sadness. Hiram was no longer alone and forgotten. He could finally be at peace. After most of the group had left for their homes, or to make the most of the buffet at the Ardmhor Hotel, Eilidh remained at the graveside.

"Are you alright, sweetheart?" Claire asked. "We're heading over to the pub now."

"I won't be long," Eilidh replied. "I was just thinking, that's all."

"Do you want company while you think? Or do you want a bit of time on your own?"

"I was thinking about Keith, actually," Eilidh said, turning to look at her mum.

Claire didn't respond, sensing Eilidh would

have more to add once she'd had time to process her thoughts.

"I think they were a bit similar, Hiram and Keith. I mean, I know Keith was a grown man and Hiram was still only a child, but it sounds like they both struggled to please their fathers and that both of them found that hard to live with. And I know the circumstances were different, but they both ended up with their child being raised by their best friend instead of them."

"I hadn't really thought about it," replied Claire. "But you're right. Who knows how Hiram's story might have turned out if the eviction hadn't taken place?"

"Yes, although it might still have ended badly, if he had any other similarities to Keith. The thing is, though, I feel really sorry for Hiram, whereas I've just sort of written Keith off."

"So, what are you thinking?" prompted Claire.

"I'm thinking that I need to get in touch with Sylvie. If I can feel sympathy for Hiram, I should have some sympathy for my own father, shouldn't I? Keith made a lot more mistakes, but Hiram might have too, if he'd lived. I think I need to show Keith a bit of forgiveness and stop punishing Sylvie for his choices."

CHAPTER FORTY

The present,

six months later...

Although the sky was blue, the air was still cold as Eilidh walked between the holiday lodges making her final checks. The March sun wasn't strong enough to generate heat that early in the morning, but the signs were all pointing to a beautiful day. The sea was sparkling at the bottom of the fields that spread out below the lodges, and snow glistened on the distant mountain peaks. Eilidh crossed her fingers that the good weather would last all weekend. It was only friends and family that would arrive at the lodges over the next few hours, but she was as keen to impress them as she was any paying customers. The next few days were to be a trial run for the lodges, so they could spot any issues before members of the press arrived the following weekend. The hope was that the invited journalists would heartily recommend the Ardmhor Holiday Lodges in their publications, so Eilidh was keen to make sure everything was running smoothly. She imagined the press weekend would be quite stressful, whereas she was hoping this one might be fun. She couldn't wait to show the people she cared about what she'd helped create.

By eleven o'clock, Eilidh had finished her inspection of each lodge. She had straightened bed covers, folded towels, plumped cushions, and placed welcome baskets of local produce in each kitchen. All she needed now was people to fill the lodges. They'd told the honoured first guests, or the first victims, as Lady Angela had dubbed them, they could arrive any time after twelve. They were to go to the cafe where they'd be greeted with a drink before being escorted to their lodge. By six that evening, all the guests had arrived. The intention had been to invite a mix of people, so there were old and young, people who usually liked to camp and those who preferred luxury hotels, and everything in between. Eilidh had planned a meal for everyone on the Saturday night, and a couple of activities to make sure they fully got into the holiday spirit, but other than that she wanted to leave people to their own devices—so they could report back on anything that was wildly impractical, or that just didn't work, before the journalists arrived.

Eilidh and Rich were trialling one lodge themselves. Their home on the shore was practically a holiday house as it was, with its enormous windows and decking overhanging the sea, but that didn't mean they couldn't appreciate the excitement of staying somewhere new. They'd tried to create a classic look with the lodge interiors. Slate tiled floors, fresh white walls, and streamlined wooden furniture kept things timeless, while brightly coloured artwork and soft furnishings stopped things from being too neutral. Log burners and underfloor heating meant guests would be cosy even on the coldest of days. They wanted the lodges to feel luxurious, but they also wanted them to be easy to maintain. They didn't want trends that would date quickly, or impractical finishes that would look shabby after the comings and goings of just a few guests. Once everyone was settled into their accommodation, Eilidh wandered around her own, drifting from the bedroom to the bathroom, then through to the open plan living room, before heading out onto the deck. Given the time of year and the fact it was almost dark, the outdoor wanderings didn't last long, but it didn't stop her from completing the circuit again and again. From the deck, she could hear the sounds of the other guests doing the same, exclaiming with delight as they discovered each feature, and she didn't know if she'd ever felt prouder.

"Come over here and have a drink before the others arrive," called Rich from the kitchen.

He had a bottle of champagne in his hand and was working at the cork as he moved from the fridge to the breakfast bar. Eilidh smiled as she joined him. He'd already arranged seven glasses on the surface, along with a few bowls of snacks. Narrowly avoiding an overflow of bubbles, Rich lifted his glass to Eilidh's.

"To my fabulous wife and her fabulous creation."

"It wasn't just me," replied Eilidh, looking down at the floor, fully aware of just how smug she was feeling.

"Oh, shush, and let me be proud," said Rich, pulling her into his arms and silencing her with a kiss.

Their moment was interrupted by the arrival of Alan and Claire. Rich dutifully poured more champagne as Eilidh answered a second knock on the door. This time it was Sylvie and her partner Chris, with Sylvia just behind them. This was the other thing that Eilidh was feeling proud of: her amazing family. She'd acted on the decision she'd made the day they'd laid Hiram's remains to rest. She'd phoned Sylvie that night, and then travelled down to Glasgow the following weekend to spend time with her. They'd taken it slowly and hadn't seen any other family members that weekend, but gradually, Eilidh had made contact with Sylvia as well. Alan, Claire, and Rich had constantly encouraged her to give her grandmother a real chance, and after a while they'd met up alone and talked properly about how Keith had treated Claire and about Sylvia's reaction to her. Eilidh had made it clear they couldn't have a relationship if Sylvia was going to continue blaming her mum for everything that had gone wrong in Keith's life. Sylvia had said she didn't want to lose Eilidh again and would try her best to look at what had happened from different perspectives. Since then, they'd had a few meetings with the seven of them, Eilidh, Rich, and her parents, along with Sylvie, Chris, and Sylvia. Eilidh knew it hadn't been easy for her grandmother, and she had to admit to deliberately testing her at times, but she needed to know if they could make this relationship work. Sylvia was incredibly set in her ways, and it was hard for her to see her only son as anything other than perfect. She was trying her best, but she hadn't been able to resist a few, not particularly subtle, digs at Claire. Fortunately, Claire and Alan were determined to make things work for Eilidh's sake and reacted to each comment with the patience of saints, letting them pass without response. Gradually, Sylvia seemed to be softening, and Eilidh had high hopes they might make it through tonight without any insults. As they sat sipping champagne, Sylvia had protested that the bubbles would give her indigestion, but it didn't stop her from requesting a third glass. The conversation centred on how amazing the lodges were and the attractions of the surrounding area. Eilidh also told them the story of Hiram, Esther, and Fergus. Although Rich and her parents had heard it all before, Eilidh hadn't mentioned it to the others, and it fascinated them. Eilidh promised to take them to see the display Beth had added to the museum and to Hiram's final resting place. They had thought about adding a memorial to Hiram near where they'd discovered his remains, but eventually they'd settled on an information board commemorating the village instead. They'd concluded that while giving guests some history was interesting, focusing on where a young man had lain forgotten for well over a century wasn't really in keeping with the holiday spirit. A couple of hours later, as she kissed them all goodbye, Eilidh realised there hadn't been a cross word from Sylvia's lips. As she loaded their glasses into the dishwasher, she wondered whether swapping Sylvia's ever present tea tray for a champagne bar might be a good idea.

Eilidh had organised a boat trip from the harbour on Saturday morning, and Andrew from the activity centre was offering taster sessions, such as archery and climbing, in the afternoon. The activity centre was going to give discounts to guests at the lodges in return for featuring heavily in their promotional materials. Fortunately, the clear skies held as every guest joined in with the boat trip. There wouldn't have been room for all of them undercover if it had rained. The boat hugged the coastline for a while, as everyone admired the rock formations and wildlife along the shore, then it headed further out to sea, where the chilly breeze made them grateful for the complimentary hot drinks. After an hour or so, the boat headed back to Ardmhor harbour, giving a perfect view of the lodges nestled on the hillside. The layout of them, which seemed so haphazard on paper, made them somehow blend into their surroundings, looking as if they'd always belonged there.

Sylvia had surprised everyone by saying she fancied trying her hand at archery, although both Sylvie and Eilidh suspected it might just be an excuse to spend time with the tall and handsome Andrew. Claire said she wouldn't mind a go either, and Eilidh marvelled at her fabulous and patient mother as she watched her climb into the activity centre minibus, offering a helping hand to the woman who'd spent the last few decades berating her.

Later on, Eilidh sat on the deck of her lodge with Beth and baby Grace, enjoying the afternoon sunshine. The MacAird brothers had organised an impromptu game of rounders on the field in front of the lodges, and there were frequent excited shouts from both teams. Eilidh smiled as Rich caught out Big Jim, and Jay rushed over and hugged him for being the first person ever to get his dad out of a game. She loved that Rich and Jay got on so well now. It showed her just what an amazing man Rich was, and she was so grateful she hadn't thrown their relationship away. Sophie, Jay's partner, was lying down in their lodge. The big surprise of the previous night was that Sophie was six months pregnant. They'd wanted to keep the news quiet until they could tell people in person. Jay's excitement over becoming a father confirmed to Eilidh that they wouldn't have worked as a couple. She would never have been willing to give him that opportunity, and eventually, it would have eaten away at him. More than ever, she was certain their infatuation had simply been down to the changes going on in each of their lives. She'd always wish it hadn't happened, but now she focused on how much closer her mistake had brought her to Rich. Maybe he was right, maybe her almost affair had saved them from the black hole they'd been sleepwalking into.

The Saturday night meal was a tremendous success. In fact, it was so successful that many of the guests struggled to surface on Sunday morning. However, Eilidh took that as confirmation that the beds lived up to the manufacturers' promises. Sylvia was up, though, having a pot of tea on the deck of her lodge.

"The bairns are still asleep," she said to Eilidh, as if Sylvie and Chris were young children rather than fully grown adults.

"Do you fancy a stroll to the churchyard and Hiram's grave when you've finished that?" asked Eilidh. "It's a lovely walk, and it's not too far."

"Oh, that'd be nice, and I've just had my last sip, so your timing is perfect."

The two of them set off down the road to the church. They walked slowly, admiring the views until the white painted building came into sight. Eilidh led Sylvia over to the graves of Hiram and his parents. Together, they read the additional memorial for Hiram.

'Here lie the remains of Hiram Stewart, aged just sixteen at the time of his death. He left this world on the day of the Ardmhor Clearance and is now reunited with his parents. Through his son, Hiram MacDonald, he is remembered by many descendants in New Zealand. He was dearly loved by his friends Esther and Fergus. May they all now rest in peace.'

The words had been discussed at length and chosen along with Hiram's relatives in New Zealand. They didn't do justice to his story, but there was no way to explain that in its entirety on a gravestone.

"He was so young," Sylvia said, dabbing her eyes with her hanky. "Only a bairn himself, really. You can't help but wonder if things would have turned out differently if he'd felt able to be himself, instead of trying to please his father."

This statement quite took Eilidh aback. Sylvia had been so adamant that strong men laying down the law to their sons was the way it should be. To hear her questioning that was something very new.

"Maybe, but I suppose opening up to your parents about getting a girl pregnant wouldn't have been easy in those days, even if they were supportive."

"Well, exactly," Sylvia continued. "That's what I mean. It must have felt impossible to Hiram, when he knew his dad would probably give him the hiding from hell. No wonder he got in a panic and started lashing out."

Making excuses for violence was more like the Sylvia Eilidh was used to, but she could see it was coming from a different place than before. Sylvia was thinking about the impact violence could have on the behaviour of a scared child, rather than seeing it as the sign of a strong man.

"Do you think my dad might have done things differently if his dad had been more supportive?" Eilidh asked eventually.

"Aye, I do. I used to think my Reggie could do no wrong. We were all scared of him at times, and Keith definitely saw the worst of his temper, but I always thought it was the way it should be. I thought that Reggie was acting like that because he loved us, and because he worked hard for us. But I've been doing a lot of thinking recently. Since I've been spending time with your mum and Alan, and you and Rich, I've been thinking maybe that wasn't the best way. I always thought Sylvie and Chris not getting wed, and the fact that they decide everything together, was a sign Chris was weak, but seeing you other couples that are the same, and talking to Sylvie about her dad properly, I think I've been wrong. Maybe Reggie could have talked to us instead of settling things with his fists, and maybe it meant Keith grew up without knowing any other way to deal with things."

Eilidh was speechless. This was a total turnaround in Sylvia's views. But Sylvia still had more to say.

"The enquiry into your dad's death reached its conclusion the other week. They decided the police were at fault for not carrying out the proper checks. Anyway, there's a bit of compensation to come, and I'd been wondering what we should do with it, but we've made a decision now. I hadn't wanted to say anything to you at the moment, in case it spoilt this weekend, but it seems right to tell you now though. We're going to split the money between a men's mental health charity, an addiction charity, and a refuge for women escaping violence at home. It won't be a lot, a few thousand for each, but I think things could have been different for your dad if he'd known how to get help, and perhaps things could have been different for me if I'd realised that kind of relationship wasn't right."

"That's amazing," was all Eilidh could think of to say.

"It's too little, too late, really, but maybe it'll be enough to help them a bit. Reading about those charities has opened my eyes, Eilidh. If I'd been willing to see things differently earlier, I could have had a whole lifetime with you. There was never anything stopping me from finding your mum and you, but I didn't want to believe my boy could be at fault. I regret spending so much time defending Reggie and Keith instead of looking at what their problems were. I can't get that time back now."

"Well, you're not getting rid of me again," said Eilidh, wrapping her gran in a hug.

As they walked back to the lodges, Sylvia was back to her old self, pointing out flaws in the people they passed—usually at a volume they could hear. Eilidh smiled politely at each of them, hoping she'd have many more years of smoothing over reactions to her gran's direct manner.

Later on, Eilidh was back at the spot where Hiram had lain hidden for so long. The last of the guests had left, and it seemed the lodges were a total success, with only a few easily fixed issues being reported. She could just see her dad's car further down the coast road. He and her mum were dropping Sylvie, Chris, and Sylvia at Inveravain station on their way back to Strathglen. As she'd watched them pile into the car, with Sylvia insisting that the men had to sit in the front, and Sylvie and Claire rolling their eyes at each other over the top of her head, she'd thought how much had changed since this time last year. She'd been so certain of who she was, but those convictions had been challenged and the discoveries had shaken her to her core. They didn't mean that she wasn't still Eilidh McRae, though, it was more that she was now Eilidh McRae extra. She'd been so upset by the discovery of Hiram's body, but it turned out she had a lot to thank him for. Without his story she might never have given Keith's family a second chance, and her life would be the lesser for it. Also, without Hiram, she and Rich wouldn't have tickets booked to visit New Zealand that winter. They were going to fulfil their idea of visiting far-flung relatives, even if the connection Eilidh had to them wasn't a blood one.

As her eyes wandered across the lodges and down to the ruins of the lower houses, she hoped the previous inhabitants would be pleased with what they'd done—that they'd enjoy sounds of life returning to the place they'd called home. She wondered for a moment if what Esther had written was true. Were they all somehow still here, wandering through the woods and beside the stream? Then she laughed, it was Beth and Lady Angela that were obsessed with the dead, imagining ghosts everywhere because the divide between the living and the dead was allegedly thinner at Ardmhor, but she was Eilidh McRae, and Eilidh McRae enjoyed the living too much to get into all that nonsense. Also, she had a lot of cleaning up to do.

Somewhere in the distance, in a clearing in the woods, three children laughed and squealed. One of them was convinced she was a princess at the heart of a stone circle left by the fairies. The other two knew she was wrong: they were clearly in the ruins of a fort. But they also knew it didn't matter because they had each other, and they didn't have a care in the world.

FROM THE AUTHOR

Firstly, I'd like to thank you for reading this book. I have always wanted to write, but it took a long time to build the courage to have a go. It then took even longer to have something ready to share with others, and I am hugely grateful to every single person who takes the time to read my work. If you have enjoyed this book and are able to leave a rating or write a review, that would be fantastic! If you would like to know more about me, my books, or any new releases, you can find information in the following places;

Website - leaboothbooks.com

Facebook - Lea booth books

Instagram - leaboothbooks

Secondly, thank you to my family for putting up with me and my funny ways.

In particular, thanks to P, E, and R for letting me ignore you, trying to teach me grammar, and constantly encouraging me. I think I used up all my luck getting each one of you in my life, but you are worth never winning anything else!

Thank you to the Jeans, my amazing mum and mother-in-law, for reading my drafts and being so positive.

Thank you to my sisters, Rae and Bags, for all your feedback and ideas.

Thank you to Lindsey; I am possibly the most useless friend ever, but you've stuck with me for over a quarter of a century, and I couldn't be more grateful.

And finally, thank you Mum and Dad for giving me a love of Scotland and giving all these characters places to go!

BOOKS BY THIS AUTHOR

The Holiday At Ardmhor

Always, Ardmhor

What Was Hidden At Ardmhor

The People Who Ruined My Life

Printed in Great Britain
by Amazon